Love, Ally

BROOKS UNIVERSITY BOOK ONE

HANNAH GRAY

Copyright © 2021 by Hannah Gray
All rights reserved.

Cover Designer: Sarah Hansen, Okay Creations
Editor and Interior Designer: Jovana Shirley, Unforeseen Editing,
www.unforeseenediting.com

No part of this book may be reproduced or transmitted in any form or by
any means, electronic or mechanical, including photocopying, recording, or
by any information storage and retrieval system without the written
permission of the author, except for the use of brief quotations in a book
review.

This book is a work of fiction. Names, characters, places, and incidents
either are products of the author's imagination or are used fictitiously. Any
resemblance to actual persons, living or dead, events, or locales is entirely
coincidental.

prologue

ALLY

Staring at the tear-soaked letter in my hands, I shake my head at the words he will never read and the explanation he will never get. The only person who's ever understood me, ever *loved* me, is now hundreds of miles away and getting farther with every second I spend on this smelly, old bus. A bus filled with passengers whose shoulders are slumped and whose eyes are filled with sorrow. All of us likely headed somewhere we don't want to go.

I hope he knows I didn't abandon him. He's been abandoned his entire life; I would never leave him the way others did.

I had no choice, I tell myself those words over and over again.

I just hope, someday he can understand and forgive me. He's all I have. Or had.

I'll find my way back to him one day even if it means going through hell first. He's worth it. My storm, my love, my person. My *one* and *only* person. He has dreams, and I can't risk being the reason they don't come true. Even if it kills me because that's what losing him feels like—it feels like death. Which is unreasonable. After all, my own mother died, and yet somehow, this hurts worse. So much worse.

Our story isn't a pretty one. There's been too much tragedy for that. But I've found that the most beautiful things fought their way to be that way. And underneath the grit, there can also be a gem. Just because it isn't pretty, it doesn't mean it's any less real. Because trust me, I've lived through this fucking shitshow. It's real. *So fucking real.*

one

COLE

"It's so fucking hot out here," Knox, my teammate and one of my best friends, complains. Sounding like a little bitch. Taking his water bottle, he squirts it over his face. "I'm sweating like a hookah in church," he says. His Maine accent missing the *er* sound in *hooker*.

"At least you're sweating all the liquor from last night out of your system, you big lush," I joke, shaking my head. "That'll teach you not to drink the night before an early practice."

He's not really a lush. But he certainly hit it a little too hard last night. I think he forgot how shitty these practices can be when you show up hungover.

"For real." Weston grins at him. "You were a fucking mess."

There's a group of us "new guys" on the football team here at Brooks University. The three of us freshman—Knox Carter, Weston Wade, and myself—have already become close friends.

"What are you two, my motha?" Knox's accent drawls again. "Also, if my memory serves me right, you both were drinkin' too, dicks."

"I had two beers." Lifting my shirt up, I wipe the sweat from my face and then point to him. "*You* were shooting whiskey like it was spring fucking break in Cabo and you were about to watch a wet T-shirt contest or some shit."

"Yeah, and I had three and called it a night," Weston says, walking backward onto the field. "You were so hammered that you actually tried to fight some of the frat guys." He shakes his head before turning and jogging farther away from us.

Knox frowns, and then he turns toward me and shrugs. "Yeah, well, it's still fucking hot out." He pauses. "And those frat guys were being complete douche bags."

Throwing my helmet back on, I laugh. "We're in Georgia, dipshit. And it's the end of August. The fuck you think it's going to be, cold out?"

A stupid-ass grin spreads across his face as he points at me. "Hey, that would be fucking sweet. At least then I wouldn't have swamp ass. My fucking nuts are roasting." He chuckles. "Get it? Roasted nuts?"

"Dude, first off, I don't need to know your fucking ass is sweating or about your nuts. Ever. Second, remember when you first came here, all you talked about was how happy you were to not deal with New England winters? You really want to go back to freezing your sack off?"

Literally, all he talked about the first week we met each other was how cold Maine was in the winter and how he loved the heat in the South.

Tapping the side of his helmet, he grins. "Guess you have a point there, Storm."

"That's what I thought," I say, slapping him on the back. "Let's get the fuck back to work."

"Yo, Storm, Knox," Weston yells from the center of the field, cupping his hands around his mouth. "You two going to fuck off all day, or are we going to get this practice finished up?"

Flipping him off, I make my way onto the field.

Storm is a nickname I have had since I was younger. Not sure if you can consider it a true nickname since my last name *is* Storms. But the nickname has been with me for quite some time. Seventh grade, to be exact. I didn't know it would follow me all the way to freshman year at Brooks University, yet here I am, and all of my teammates on the football team call me it too.

For as long as I can remember, all I've ever wanted to do is play ball. It's how I got my aggression out as a kid, and even now, it still is. Only now, I have more control of my anger when I'm on the field. Everything I do is calculated and well thought out. Usually.

Football is also one of the very few things in life that I truly love. It's the one thing that has never left me, and I pray it never will. People change. This game? Well, she's one loyal bitch.

I learned at a young age that if I wanted something, I was going to have to do the work. Nobody was ever going to hand me my dreams on a silver platter—that's for damn sure. So, once I was old enough to hold a ball, that was what I did. I worked my ass off and dedicated all of my spare time to this sport. I wanted to see just how far it would take me. And honestly, I knew I'd ride with it until the damn wheels fell off.

There's only one other thing in this life that I've loved, and she went and did what everyone else had done to me. She left. And now … well, now, she's just another reason why I need this game to distract me from all the other shit in my life.

A series of unfortunate events. That's how I'd sum up these past eighteen years.

But for a while, I got to hold her, my angel. And for that short time, she was all mine, looking at me like I'd hung the moon. I got comfortable—too comfortable. I let my guard down, left myself open to being hurt. And that was what that bitch did. She fucking eviscerated me, disposed of me like I was nothing. I'm used to the feeling. I just never thought that feeling would be inflicted by her. My addictive, mouth-of-a-pirate, dark-haired Ally Lee James.

Now, she's gone, and all I have left inside of me is this rage. That rage fuels this fire for me to be faster, stronger, *better* than all of the other players. I will make it to where I want to be, and nobody will stand in my way. Not even myself.

$$XO$$

ALLY

"So, you came here from Ohio?" Sloane, my new roommate, asks in the most adorable Southern accent. Her blonde hair bouncing around as she unpacks.

I just arrived at the campus less than an hour ago, but I must say, I like it. The campus is made up with the most gorgeous brick buildings. Sidewalks and large trees line the property, making it appear like an actual neighborhood. It provides a comforting feeling, this campus.

"Sure did. You?" I answer cautiously.

I don't know enough about this chick to know if I can trust her. After all, it's the sweet and innocent ones that always get you. And she seems sweet as pie.

"I'm from Georgia. My hometown is Rangeley. About two hours south of here."

"That's cool. So, your folks aren't too far then." *What am I even saying? Does she even have folks? And why the fuck am I saying folks? Am I suddenly seventy-five years old? Do we need to break out a game of shuffleboard?*

Luckily, she doesn't seem to notice as she nods. "Yeah, they were happy I chose somewhere close by."

I inwardly sigh in relief that she didn't ask me about my "folks." *Thank fuck—*

"Your family must be sad. That's a long drive to Ohio."

Fuck my life. I thought too soon and jinxed it.

I could play it off like I have a picture-perfect family back home or some shit. But I know, eventually, when I have no visitors or I never travel home, it's going to come up. I might as well rip the Band-Aid off now.

Clearing my throat, I shrug. "I actually don't have any."

"Any what?" she says, straightening out her stack of folded clothes.

I'm not a girl who gets embarrassed. Yet here I am. Face. On. Fucking. Fire. "Err … family."

Looking up at me, she grimaces. "Oh crap, girl. I'm sorry."

Shaking my head, I chuckle and sit down on the edge of my bed. "No big deal. It's been that way for a long time. I'm all good."

It's quiet for a moment. And awkward. *Really* awkward.

"Well, do you have a boyfriend? I mean, you *have* to, as gorgeous as you are," her sweet voice drawls, breaking the silence.

"Nope. Single, not so ready to mingle."

Her mouth hangs open. "How? I mean, you are, like … dirty sexy." Her eyes widen, like she's going to piss her pants, as she waves her hands in front of her. "Sorry, I didn't mean anything bad by that, by the way. I meant it as a compliment. You are, like … the cool girl. You're, like, edgy and shit. Not like actually dirty. I'm super jealous."

I laugh once. It appears Sloane might talk when she's nervous. "It's all right. And … thanks, I guess?" *Dirty sexy? Eh, whatever. I've been called worse.*

Nodding her head in an exaggerated way, she widens her eyes. "Definitely say thanks because it's a good thing. A really good thing. Well … other than the fact that you are probably going to hog all the guys, and they won't even notice me when all of *that* is around," she says, waving her hand at me.

I smile. "You are crazy, my friend."

Has this girl looked in a mirror? She's basically a model. We're just two very different-looking creatures. I'm edgy and apparently dirty-looking, and she's a Southern belle.

Her mouth hangs open. "*And* you have a dimple? Are you freaking kidding me?! I have always been *so* jealous of bitches with dimples." She pauses. "Not that you're a bitch. You're not. You know what—"

I hold my hand up to stop her. "I know what you meant. Stop acting like I'm going to throat-punch you. I swear, I play nice." Thinking about my words, I pause. "Well, I do until someone does me wrong. Then … well, then you have a reason to be scared."

Her eyes widen as she nods. "Noted. Don't do Ally wrong, or she turns into an alley cat."

Her words catch me off guard, reminding me of my nickname. Nobody has called me Allycat in well over a year.

"Just out of curiosity, why are you single but not ready to mingle?" she says tenderly, tilting her head slightly as the words flow out of her pretty pink lips.

"I'm here to go to class, study, and get a job," I tell her with a small shrug. "No time for penises and all that comes with them."

Bobbing her head up and down, she shrugs. "All right, fair enough. No peen for Ally." She giggles lightly. "So, what are you studying?"

"Music," I answer.

"Wow, that's so cool. Do you want to be a singer?" she says with what seems like genuine curiosity.

"Maybe," I say hesitantly. "Or a songwriter. I love music and have always loved to sing. I just don't know if I want to sing in front of *that* many people." I chew my lip nervously. "I think, as human beings, it's easy to lose sight of what actually matters. Having everyone know my name—that isn't important. Helping others through tough times—that's what matters."

She nods. "That's pretty admirable that you already know that much about your future. So many people just chase the money or the fame. I applaud you for not thinking that way."

"Thanks," I say awkwardly, pushing my hands against my legs. "Anyway, what about you? What are you studying?"

"Well, uh, I haven't declared that yet. But I'm hoping to study ... criminal justice," she states sheepishly. "Right now, I'm just signed up for general classes."

"Sloane, criminal justice? That's badass!" I make a mental note to not get drunk and tell her about all the times I shoplifted. I was so hungry that I had no choice. But she might not see it that way. Plus, it's embarrassing. "Why haven't you declared? Are you just not one hundred percent sure of it yet?"

"No, I'm very certain that's what I want to do." Her cheeks grow red. "My parents wouldn't be on board with it."

"They don't know that you want to study criminal justice?" My eyebrows pull together. I can't wrap my brain around what parent wouldn't be proud of their child for chasing a degree like that.

She shakes her head. "Not really."

"Do you think they wouldn't want you going into that type of career? Too dangerous or something?"

"Yeah, something like that," she mutters, looking down at her hands.

She seems nice enough. She's got that *Cover Girl model* look going on with her beautifully curled blonde hair; flawless, creamy skin tone; light-green eyes; and pink lips. She's like ... an American Girl doll. Absolutely manicured and in a damn sundress while unpacking her things on a Tuesday. She's gorgeous. And extremely put together. But something about her seems ... masked. The sundress, the hair—I'm not buying it. Not one bit. Those who try to be perceived as perfect, more times than not, are just as flawed as the rest of us. We're all fucked up. Some of us just hide it better than others.

I look down at my own attire—a faded black Guns N' Roses T-shirt, showing a few tattoos on my arms, and secondhand cutoff jean shorts that are fraying at the bottom. I'm a far cry from being put together. Then again, that isn't my style anyway. I'm somewhere between edgy and punky.

I run my hands through my own long dark-brown hair. "I suppose I should finish unpacking." I shrug and offer her a small smile.

Suddenly shooting up, she grabs her small crossbody bag before turning toward me. "Orrrr, we could go to the cafeteria and get food? That sounds much better. Besides, they have an ice cream machine."

I ponder it for a second. Sure, this girl isn't who I'd typically run with. But that isn't a bad thing. I could use some … normal friends. Not like anybody is actually normal, but she seems nice enough. And it has been since … well, forever since I've hung out with normal people.

Sitting up, I grab my cell phone from the bed. "Yeah, screw unpacking. Ice cream sounds much better," I say honestly.

COLE

Making my way off the field behind the rest of my team, I hear Coach call from behind us, "Storm, my office after you've showered and changed and no longer smell like ass."

"Yes, sir," I answer, though I have no fucking idea why Coach wants to talk to me.

"Somebody's in trooooouble," Knox mocks from behind me.

"Uh-ohhh," Weston chimes.

Holding my finger up, I flick them both off.

Showering fast, I throw my clothes on. Every passing second of not knowing what he could possibly need to talk to me about makes me incredibly anxious. *He's probably kicking me off the team.* I have no idea why he would, but ever since I got to college, I've been waiting for the other shoe to drop. *Life is far too good right now.*

Poking my head inside his open door, I tip my chin up. "You wanted to see me, Coach?"

Looking up from his playbook, he waves me in. "Close the door behind you, son."

Fuck. This is bad. Really bad.

I do as he said and have a seat. "Everything all right, sir?"

He pulls his glasses off. "I've got to ask you something, and you need to tell me the truth."

I nod. "Okay."

"If I make you QB1 and team captain, can you handle the pressure? Because I'll be honest with you, Storm. I've seen a lot of promising players come in here, guns blazing, and burn themselves out—fast. You're only a freshman after all."

Clearing my throat, I lean forward. "I am one hundred percent confident that I can do it, Coach. And not to sound cocky, but I'll do a damn good job." My eyebrows pull together. "But what about Ricky?"

Ricky is QB1 right now. He's a senior, and he was just promoted to the position last year. I know I'm a better quarterback, but one problem is, he possesses the leadership over the team. Most of these guys have played with him since their freshman year. Their allegiance lies with him. Not me.

Messing with the visor of his hat, he leans back in his chair, looking discouraged. "This will be Ricky's fourth season with me. Boy's like family now. But this season, we're going after that championship. And you, boy, well, you're the one who will take us there. I know it."

So far, I like Ricky. He's been good to me. But I'm only in college long enough until I'm eligible to enter the draft. So, I'm not really here to make friends. It's a cutthroat sport, and seeing as my team is called the Wolves, I might as well act like one.

"You can count on me, Coach," I promise him. "I'll take this team as far as I can."

The corner of his lips turns up in the smallest smile. "I believe you. I've watched you since you were a freshman in high school. You have the ability to read other players. That's as good as a damn superpower on that field."

"Thanks, sir," I answer, averting my eyes from his.

Reading people is something you pick up when you constantly have to watch your back, growing up. People come into your life, and many might have ill intent. The type of lowlifes my father brought into our home when I was just a boy is a prime example of that. Some of them would be his best friends when he had drugs. But once the drugs got low, greed reared its ugly head.

"Well then, all right," he says. "Now, get the hell out of here and get some rest. We've got double practice tomorrow. First one is at five a.m."

"Yes, sir," I answer, heading toward the door.

Double practice. Fuck my life.

$$\mathcal{XO}$$

"Yo, what did Coach need you for?" Knox asks, head half stuck in the fridge.

I swear, we can't keep shit here to eat with him around.

When I set my duffel bag down, Weston walks out of his room.

"What, did you get kicked off the team? They find out you actually have a vagina, so you aren't eligible to play now?" Weston says, cracking himself up.

We might be in a dorm. But compared to the typical shitty dorms here, this one is a lot nicer. We each have our own small bedroom, and in the middle is the living room/kitchen area. So, even though three big dudes in a dorm sounds awful, it's actually not too bad.

That's not to say we wouldn't all rather rent a house off-campus. But Brooks University has this rule: every student, even athletes, must stay in a dorm their freshman year.

"He, uh … he wants me to be starting quarterback," I answer, ignoring Weston's smart-ass remark. "And team captain."

Pulling his head out of the fridge, Knox jerks his chin up. "You fuckin' serious?" He grins. "Not that I'm surprised. Seeing as every D1 college wanted you." Suddenly, he frowns. "Even though I'd probably make a better team captain." He waves his hands around. "But it's all good."

I can tell he's just kidding around. I don't think Knox would want the responsibility of team captain. Weston, on the other hand, could probably handle it. He takes this shit as seriously as I do.

Knox is a funny dude. But he's more prone to fucking off than we are. And Weston … well, I haven't figured him out yet. We have a good time together, the three of us. But Weston sometimes takes off for a few hours, and he never tells us where he goes. It's fucking weird. Then again, I'm sure I do shit that they find weird too.

Like this letter I carry around everywhere I go.

"Well, Storm, that there is badass." Weston grins.

I look between them and shake my head. "I came here for this position. But, shit, guys, it sucks for Ricky. It's his senior year. I'm not trying to come in and take his spot, you know? But I guess it's just how it is."

This sport is all I've ever had in life. I've never had family—well, besides *her*, but she left. Football has had me in the lowest parts of my life.

I was offered a full scholarship to a lot of other colleges, one being my longtime dream school in Texas. But ultimately, after doing some soul-searching and really thinking about it, I decided I wanted to come to Georgia and attend Brooks University and be a Wolf. They have one of the best football programs in the country, and they've had tons of players go into the NFL. That's the goal, the dream, the fact. I will play in the NFL. And the world will know my fucking name. And I'll make it there because I worked hard. Not because I was handed it on a silver platter, like so many of the guys I've played with.

And when I do make it there, I'll thank nobody besides the coaches I've had. Because they are the only ones besides myself who have helped me get to where I want to be. On the other hand, I also know all of the people who left me are reasons why I've always been so motivated. I want more than what I've always known.

"Bro, I get it." Taking a bite of a sandwich he concocted, Knox smirks and shakes his head. "But Ricky is going to fucking hate you."

"True that," Weston mumbles.

I shrug. "Ricky isn't handing out tickets to the NFL, is he?" I narrow my eyes at them. "No, I didn't think so. So, if he's mad, well then, fuck him."

Inside, I do feel like a dick for taking his spot. I hope he understands. Then again, when he was a freshman, if he'd been offered the starting quarterback position, would he have said, *Well, let me ask around with my friends, make sure they don't mind?* Fuck no, he wouldn't have. He would have taken it in a heartbeat. Anyone in their right mind would.

Ricky isn't going to the NFL. I'm not being a prick; it's just the truth. You either have it or you don't, and Ricky doesn't have it. He's good—no doubt about that. But the natural ability isn't there.

"Geesh. Don't get your tampon twisted in wrong, fucker. I wasn't saying you shouldn't take it; I was just stating the obvious—that Ricky, along with his pals, will be pissed." Finishing his sandwich, he wipes his hands off.

The three of us met a few months ago when we moved in early for football training. Most other students have only just started filtering in this past week. But athletes get special privileges to move in early. I couldn't wait to get the fuck out of my adoptive family's house, so I jumped all over that shit.

Weston punches my arm lightly. "I was just busting your balls, man." He looks down and shrugs. "I get it. I understand why you're worried about it. But fuck it, man. Nobody is going to get you playing pro ball besides you. Like you said, Ricky isn't punching your ticket to the NFL." He laughs. "If I had the chance to take your spot as team captain, you bet your sweet ass I'd steal it." He widens his eyes. "You're my boy. But football is football."

"Fuck off. You're just lucky that the Wolves' tight end graduated last year. You can play your position without feeling like a fucking snake." I nod my chin at him and then at Knox. "Same with you, dick."

"Whatevs," Knox says. "Now that you're team captain, you'll basically be able to get any chick you want in your bed." He wiggles his eyebrows. "Probably still not as many as me though. Because I'm the real MVP."

"Keep telling yourself that, brother." Weston shakes his head. "Whatever helps you sleep at night."

Knox has already been named starting receiver, and Weston is starting tight end. Both are crazy talented. I have no doubt the pair of them could make it to the NFL too. Though I'm not sure Knox's family approves on that for his future. Me? I *need* that for my future. I need to know I'll never be hungry for days again. I need to prove to myself that I am enough. And that

I am talented. It sounds dumb—I know it does—but I just want to feel like I'm worth something.

Making my way into my room, I collapse on my bed. And just like they always do whenever I stop moving for five seconds, in come the memories of her. Memories I can't outrun.

I can't help but wonder where she is or who she's with. And then, just like always, my mind travels back to the times when she was around. To a time when I had someone who looked at me like I'd hung the moon.

Her blue eyes glimmered as she smiled, biting her lip nervously. "Tell me honestly, what did you think?"

"I think you have the most beautiful voice," I told her truthfully before pulling her onto my lap. "And I hope to fuck you don't forget me when you're the next Taylor Swift, out touring the country and dropping number one hits."

"I feel like I'm more of a Halsey," she said, arching an eyebrow.

"No ... you aren't."

She looked embarrassed before finally shrugging. "I know that, dick. I was kidding."

"You aren't Halsey, baby. You're Ally Lee James. So much better."

Sighing, she laid her head against my shoulder, peeking up. "Do you really think I'm good? I mean, if I wasn't, it isn't like you'd be like, Ally, you suck dick. Stop singing.*"*

I couldn't help the chuckle that escaped me. "Well, you actually do that well too."

"Storm! I'm being serious!" she hollered before smacking me on the chest.

"I mean it, Ally. You're good. In fact, there's no other sound I want to listen to." I thought about it for a second before winking. "Well, unless it's you screaming my name."

In usual Ally form, she rolled her eyes. "You're an idiot."

Standing and lifting her with me, I walked us toward the pond. "No doubt. But I'm your idiot."

"Don't you dare do it!" she shrieked as we got closer to the water.

"Sorry. I'm awfully hot. I think I need a little swim to cool me off."

She flailed around as I walked us in slowly before finally going under.

"You peckerhead!" she yelled but laughed when we came back up. "I'm going to get you back for this!"

"We'll see about that, won't we?"

As I held her, as always, it became unbearable to not need more. Especially as her soaking wet white tank top clung to her skin and her wet hair fell down her back.

"Pain in my ass as you might be, I'm still going to miss you while you're at football camp for two weeks," she said, resting her head on my shoulder.

I could tell that she was dreading the day that I had to leave.

So was I. I'd been sick to my fucking stomach about leaving her. I hated the thought of her being alone in that house. With those people.

"Me too, baby. I don't have to go. I feel like I should ditch." I smiled. "I'd rather stay here and force you to go swimming with me every day anyway."

Her breasts pressed against my chest, stirring something inside of me awake. Making me want more.

She gave me a small nod. "*I know. But I want you to go. This could help you so much. It could get you noticed by college scouts.*"

"*I don't need any help. I'm already fucking great,*" I joked.

"*Hmm ... I'm not so sure about that.*"

Lifting her up, I raised an eyebrow. "I think somebody wants to be thrown."

"*You wouldn't.*"

"*Oh, sweetheart, I would. Unless ... you take that back.*"

She bit her lip and tilted her head to the side. "Never," she whispered.

"*Okay then." I shrugged. "You leave me no choice.*"

I started to bring her down like I was going to throw her, but instead, I threw her up and caught her, her legs landing perfectly around my waist again.

"*You jerk! I really thought you were going to throw me.*"

"*I thought about it," I told her honestly. "But I was afraid you'd cut my nuts off.*"

"*No." She widened her eyes. "Just your dick.*"

Laughing, I reached over and tuck her long, dark hair back behind her ear. She watched me, her chest rising and falling. I could feel myself growing hard as her legs tightened around my waist.

"*Storm," she said softly, "I love you.*"

The way her eyes were looking into mine, I knew what she wanted—no, what she needed. I had to leave in the morning for camp, so I didn't want to waste another minute, not giving her exactly that.

"*I love you," I told her before my mouth devoured hers. Swallowing up her soft, sexy moans.*

Needing more, I walked us out of the water and laid her down on the grass. Pulling her shorts off, I leaned over her, kissing her again as my fingers sank inside of her, making her cry out.

Snaking her hand around, she pulled my zipper down. Reaching inside, she took my painfully hard length into her hand.

In reality, we were just two kids who had nothing and nobody besides each other.

But in that moment, we were two kids who finally knew what it was like to love someone so damn much that it almost made you crazy. We loved each other fiercely, teetering on the edge of insanity.

I despised the thought of being without her for two weeks. Actually, the thought made me sick. So, the rest of that afternoon, I planned to spend it as close to her as I could. Fucking her in any and every way possible.

"*I need you," she whispered.*

"*Right now?" I rasped before burying myself deep inside of her before she could respond.*

She cried out, her nails digging into my back but never in the spot where I didn't like to be touched.

Hooking her legs around my waist, she brought our bodies closer. Gazing up at me, her blue eyes were filled with so much love. And I knew it was all for me. Every last ounce of it.

Finally, someone looked at me that way. And it was the only person who mattered in this whole fucked up world. Ally.

This, right here, was my favorite place to be. With her and nobody else.

And I knew in that moment, if this was all I ever had the rest of my life, if I never made it into the NFL, if I never had more than a few dollars to rub together, I'd still be a happy motherfucker for the simple fact that I got to love this girl as fiercely as I could. And that she loved me as furiously as she could.

It was a damn good feeling.

Coming back to reality, I have the urge to go for a run. Even fresh from practice, I can't stand to sit still. I know I won't outrun the memory of her, but I can sure as hell try.

The thing is, I'm not just running from her; I'm running from everything. I'm not ready to feel anything. My whole life, I've done my best to keep my mind so busy that it doesn't have a second to feel anything from the past.

Until her, I didn't allow myself to feel anything. And when I let her in, when I looked into her eyes, I finally felt something. I finally felt *home*.

This hollow feeling in my body sometimes feels like it might be the death of me. She filled all of the empty places in my soul and made me finally feel like I was a whole human and not just an empty shell who was just existing. Now, she's gone, and all I feel is empty. Empty and bitter. Football helps numb the ache slightly, but even that can't take it all away.

I know that despite her leaving, she loved me too. I think I was the only person in the world she had ever let inside of her heart. The only one who ever knew the real her.

I would have kept her safe. I would have continued to make her laugh. And I never would have left her. Ever. Still, she left me without saying a word. Like I was nobody and meant nothing. *Just like everyone else.*

three

ALLY

Walking toward my dorm with my earbuds in, I can't help feeling like I'm wandering. Wandering through this campus, wandering through the days, wandering through my life.

As "The Freshmen" by The Verve Pipe filters out of the tiny speakers and into my ears, images of Cole Storms flash into my brain, and they don't stop. Creating the most heartbreaking yet beautiful slide show in my mind.

That grin with the single dimple in his left cheek that always made it so damn hard for me to stay mad at him for long. Those eyes that were forever changing between blue and green, depending on the weather … or his mood.

I was never that girl who wanted to bask in the misery of painful memories. In fact, I would have made fun of other girls a few years back for doing this type of shit. In my own head, of course, not out loud. Yet here I am, throwing myself into this deep pit of despair, rolling around in it like it's a fucking field of flowers.

It's pathetic—I know that it is. But torturing myself with the memories of what I'm missing is the only way that I feel close to him. The only way I feel close to anybody.

I long for his touch, and I yearn for his kiss. Sometimes, when I close my eyes, I can almost feel him here with me. But when I open them up, I'm brought back to the harsh reality that I'll likely never see him again.

I just want my heart to feel something, anything, besides the aching feeling that it does. And he's the only one who can do that. He's the only one who can make me whole again.

But I will admit, now that I'm at Brooks University, I do see a glimmer of hope. It's small, but it's there.

The second week of classes is nearly over. And aside from my schoolwork, I've also started a job. It's at a restaurant right off campus, called Lenny's. So far, I'm enjoying it. It's usually just me and one other waitress, Carla. I absolutely love her. She's a mom of three teenage boys, and she enjoys smoking cigarettes, coffee, and cussing. I feel like we're a friendship made in heaven.

A part of me feels like she's the mother I wish I'd had. She's far from perfect, but she loves her boys more than life. I pray that, one day, they understand how lucky they are to be loved like that. To be loved in such an unconditional, selfless way. What a gift that would be.

When I first met her and Lenny, the owner, I knew that they were good people. I knew that they had been put in my path for some sort of purpose. I don't trust easy, but with them, I just knew they weren't going to do anything to hurt me.

Because of the fact that I'm sort of an orphan who has pretty kick-ass writing skills, which helped me write sob stories to colleges on why they should give me a scholarship, my schooling is free. And despite me being a proud person, I don't feel bad about the handout. Life has kicked me in the vagina so many times that I'll set my pride aside for a free college degree.

While I might be tuition-less when it comes to college, for things like clothing, food, and other essential items, I'll need cash. So, getting a job was my only option. And besides, I like to keep myself occupied at all times. If I sit in idle mode, that's when the weight of everything bears down. And that's when I think about him.

And that damn dimple.

Turning the key, I push open the door to our dorm to find Sloane sitting on her bed, holding her Kindle.

Looking up, she pulls her reading glasses off. "Hi." She smiles.

"What's up?" I answer back while setting my bag down.

"Not much. But I'm glad you're home. I have, like … a huge favor to ask." Standing up, she paces around nervously. "Huge."

I frown and walk over to the refrigerator. Pulling out a can of Diet Coke, I pop it open and take a sip, sighing. *Diet Coke … the crack of my life.*

Turning my attention back to my weirdly anxious roommate, I raise a brow. "Do you have scabies?"

Her eyes widen. "What? No!"

"Fungus?"

"Wha—"

"Oh." I widen my eyes. "I see, you've got the syph …"

"Syph?" she says, scrunching her nose up.

"You know, syphilis. A rash, fever, perhaps a headache." I shrug when her eyes grow to the size of saucers. "I paid attention in wellness class."

"Well, no! I do not have any of that … that … disgusting stuff!" she practically squeals. "What is wrong with you?!"

I love that everything makes her blush. She is the opposite of me. It takes a lot to embarrass me.

I grin. "I'm just kidding. I was just giving you shit for being nervous."

"Har-har. Sooo funny, smart-ass."

Plopping myself on the bed, I give her a tight-lipped smile. "All right, girlfriend, why the hell are you moving around so much, like you've got ants in your pants?" I ask, leaning back on my elbows. I can tell she's nervous, which also makes me nervous because I don't know what the hell she's going to ask me as a favor. "Why are you so nervous to ask me whatever it is?"

"I … need you to go on a date with me," she murmurs, biting her nails—something I've noticed she does a lot.

A cough escapes my throat even though I try to hold it in. I did not think I gave her the vibe that I was into her. And I sure as shit didn't pick up on her being into me. Maybe I'm misunderstanding her. Either way, it's totally cool. I'm just into the D, not the V. Making this awkward.

"Like … *with* you? As in a date with … just you and me? Or …" I ask, needing clarification. "Because, well, I'm flattered and all, but—"

Her mouth hangs open as she realizes what I'm saying. "Oh, no, not like that!" She waves her arms around. "God, no! I'm not asking *you* out, Ally."

Holding my free hand up, I almost choke on my Diet Coke. "Sorry, we don't know each other that well. I wasn't sure what you meant by that. Wanted to double-check, you know? Just to be extra sure we were on the same page." Circling my hand around, I give her an apologetic smile. "Please, carry on."

Shifting back and forth on her feet nervously, she sighs. "There's this guy, Knox. He's in one of my classes, and … he asked me to go to a movie with him. I wasn't really comfortable with meeting up with some guy I barely know." She pauses, giving me a pointed look. "You know, Lifetime movie shit can really happen. Kidnappings and stuff."

I nod slowly, keeping my eyes trained on her. "Yeah … not really seeing where I come into this …"

"I told him I wanted to bring a friend, so then he said he wanted to bring a friend, and now, well … I guess we're both bringing friends," she says, covering her face with her hands, baby-pink polish on her perfectly manicured nails.

Me? I'm rocking dark blue, and they are most likely already chipped. Fifty-cent nail polish doesn't typically last very long. But I still think I should get an A for effort because in my opinion, painting nails is a pain in the balls.

Pushing myself up, I tilt my head to the side. "So, let me get this straight. One dude could kidnap you and lock you in his basement. *But* because you bring a friend ... and he brings a friend, that shit won't happen? Like, no skinsuits or creepy basements? You know, the ones with the door that lifts up on the outside of the house." *I watch too much* Dateline.

"Well, I mean, if he's a psychopath, he's less likely to act like one in front of three other people. I doubt his friend would know if he was a mass murderer. In the Lifetime movies, the friends never know."

"Or"—I point my finger at her—"hear me out. Maybe the friend is also a skinsuit, *lock you in the basement* freak too? Maybe together, they are just a team of Craigslist killers? Maybe *that* is what's going on here."

She shakes her head and laughs. "Don't be absurd, Ally. Wow, how much Lifetime do *you* watch?"

My mouth hangs open, and I literally have to push it shut. The nerve this chick has. She's the one who brought up Lifetime and dragged me into her awkward first date. Now, I'm absurd?

But so far, she's been giving me really good vibes, and she seems like she's going to be a great friend. Besides, I could use some over-buttered popcorn and sugary candy right now.

Let's not forget about delicious, bubbly fountain Diet Coke either.

"When?" I ask wryly. Thinking she likely means tomorrow or this weekend. Maybe I'll be working and have an excuse not to go. That will be a sure sign from above that I should not have to go on this double date.

Looking at her watch, she suddenly rushes to her dresser. "We need to leave in ten minutes!"

There I sit, mouth hanging open yet again. "Tonight, Sloane? To-fucking-night?"

"Sorry!" she yells over her shoulder before turning back toward me. "By the way, you have the worst potty mouth. Like ... ever."

"Sorry. I'll try to work on that," I quip back.

"Really?" She sounds surprised.

"Fuck no," I say dryly.

She giggles. "It's okay. I sort of like it anyway. You keep things interesting, for sure, Allycat."

XO

COLE

"Jesus Christ, Carter. I don't even like movies," I growl at Knox. "Why couldn't you have asked Weston? That fucker probably loves movies and shit."

I'm not lying to him either. I really don't like movies. Actually, I loathe them.

I hate sitting still for any period of time. Life's too short to do crap like sit through a shitty fucking movie. I've always been too restless for that.

"Oh, quit your bitchin', would ya? He went somewhere tonight. Go figure. And besides, this movie looks funny as shit."

"Is shit funny?" I deadpan.

"Oh, go fuck yaself," he drawls in that Maine accent that sounds like a Southerner and a Canadian had a baby. "Anything with Vince Vaughn is good. You should know this."

That sends a pain right into my core. Vince Vaughn was always Ally's favorite actor. I swear she watched the movie *Wedding Crashers* one hundred times. She could recite the entire thing. And *Old School* too.

"I just don't understand why in the fuck you couldn't come alone. Were you scared she'd take advantage of you, ol' boy?" I smack his back. "Need me to protect you?"

Wiggling his eyebrows, he smirks. "I'd love for her to take advantage of me. This girl is a solid ten." His smirk turns to a frown. "Except … she dresses like she's stuck-up. Cardigans, sundresses, sweaters—that type of shit." Grinning, he punches my arm. "Then again, it's always those ones that are the wildest ride, if you know what I mean."

I actually don't have a fucking clue what he means. Ally, well, she certainly didn't dress stuck-up. And she also definitely didn't put off the vibe that she was.

She was edgy, badass, mysterious, sexy, beautiful, and often intimidating to other chicks.

"So, why the fuck am I here then? Why not just come alone with her?"

He cringes. "She wanted to bring a friend."

I start laughing. "Ohhh shit. So, what you're saying is, she thought you were a fucking serial killer and didn't want to come alone?" Stepping back, I look him up and down, rubbing my chin. "You sort of do have that creepy-as-fuck look about you," I say, tormenting him. He doesn't, but I like getting him wound up. It doesn't take much with Knox.

"Fuck off," he grunts. "Do not."

"Tell you what." I shrug. "You can buy me popcorn and a soda for dragging my ass here. Deal?"

He rolls his eyes. "Dude, you drive the most expensive truck Chevrolet makes, and you need me to buy you popcorn?"

"Fucking right I do." I give him a cocky smirk.

He thinks I have money. He thinks I come from money. I don't. Even with this limitless credit card in my wallet, I know I'm a fraud. One of my best friends thinks I'm something that I'm not. And I'm too much of a coward to tell him.

"Oh shit, there they are." His entire face lights up as his eyes spot someone I have yet to.

Shaking my head, I continue to laugh, trying to come up with something else I can say to get under his skin. He might be a good friend of mine, but it's funny as hell to annoy him.

My eyes follow to where he's looking. Fuck if the laughter doesn't die right in my throat. And the blood running through my veins? Well, it turns to fucking ice. And there's a second where I feel like I might pass out.

Am I seeing a fucking ghost?

If I am seeing a ghost, it's the most beautiful thing I've seen in my entire life.

XO

Once I snap out of it and realize that I'm not seeing a spirit but a real fucking person, I can't believe my eyes. And for a split second, I'm certain my damn heart fails me and stops beating, stalling like the fucking five-speed truck I used to own, the one with a shitty clutch and rusted-out floorboards.

I fight to catch my breath as I take in the most beautiful creature that has ever walked this earth. Then, I remember that this girl—this stunning, sexy girl standing before me—is nothing but a traitor. And I snap the fuck out of it.

Realization that she might be the girl that Knox is meeting hits me, and suddenly, I'm seconds away from punching one of my best friends in the face.

My hand forms a fist at my side as he gets closer to them. The thought of him even talking to Ally has me in a blind rage. A rage that I know for certain could tear this entire movie theater to pieces. Brick by brick.

I huff a breath of relief when he approaches the blonde in the sundress and not the brunette beauty who is dressed in mostly black clothing. It would have been awkward as fuck to lay him out in the middle of this lobby. But unfortunately, that's what it would have come to. I can't have another man looking at what rightfully belongs to me.

Fuck no.

The two girls, beautiful as they both are, are polar opposites. The blonde is all shiny, bright, and perfect. Not that Ally isn't perfect—she's perfect for me—but she isn't perfect in the same way the squeaky-clean blonde is. Ally's mysterious, dark, and intimidating.

The blonde might be good-looking, but she doesn't hold a candle to the girl standing next to her.

She spots me, and her eyes widen as she takes me in. And for a moment, it's like the entire world stops. The other moviegoers walking by no longer exist. It's just us. Two best friends and lovers who haven't seen each other in well over a year.

Her brown hair is even longer now, reaching down to nearly the bottom of her back in thick waves. Her lips are painted that shade of red she always liked. Pale pink just never cut it. After all, she was never one to blend into the shadows. Fuck no. She stood out everywhere she went. I don't even think she cared to be noticed; it was just unavoidable. She'd have fuckers stopped in their tracks, just at the sight of her.

Same style. Ripped jeans and a black top that shows the bottom of her stomach. Along with baby-blue Converse on her feet. She always looked like a badass bitch. That's why nobody fucked with her. Well, that, and because she was with me. Back in Charlotte's Falls, nobody dared to fuck with me. I was a foster kid with anger problems. And I was damn protective of what was mine, and Ally belonged to me.

I might have been thrilled to see her for a moment, but the remembrance that she left me without so much as a measly scribbled note hits me. And suddenly, I hate her all over again. Just like I did that day I came home and they told me she'd taken off. Leaving me like I was nothing. Like *we* were nothing.

No text message or phone call. Nothing. All I have left of her is a note from years ago. A note I carry around in my pocket like a little bitch.

My entire life, everyone has left me. But her? I thought she was loyal. Thought she'd never leave.

She played me for a fool. And now? Now, I want to make her feel like one too.

Stepping up to her, I let my eyes roam over her. "Wow"—I attempt a cocky smirk—"they really will let anyone into this theater, won't they?" I shake my head and circle her like a shark circling its prey. "Must be hard up for business." I turn toward Knox. "What the fuck is *she* doing here anyway? I sure as shit would have stayed home had I known she'd be here."

Knox is too busy giggling like a sixteen-year-old girl with his date to even acknowledge me. He links his hand in hers and spares me a glance. "We're going to get some food."

Motherfucker didn't even hear me.

Gone are her nerves, replaced with feistiness as she steps in front of me, eyes narrowed slightly. "What the fuck are *you* doing here?" She tries to come off as unaffected, but her voice shakes the smallest bit. Something only I'd pick up on. "Was this a setup or some shit?" she snarls, putting a hand on her deliciously sexy hip.

Ah, yes. Her filthy mouth is still intact too.

Ally swears like a damn pirate. And though I have no idea why, it turns me on. So. Fucking. Much.

"I could ask you the same thing, Allycat."

I try to act like a cocky bastard, but it isn't an easy task since I haven't seen her in fifteen months and don't have the slightest idea where the hell she's been. Not to mention, the slight amount of her cleavage showing causes my dick to strain in my jeans. As I'm sure is happening with every other fucker in this place.

Unable to stop myself, I gaze around the lobby in the movie theater to see if any asshole's eyes are lingering on my girl. There are a few checking her ass out as they pass by, and I can't blame them. That ass is legendary. The majority just seem to be watching our interaction as we stand off like a bunch of wild animals who were born and trained to attack.

Because we were.

Nobody taught us though. We had to teach ourselves.

"Yo, Storm, movie is startin' soon. Hurry your ass up," Knox calls from the food line, a huge-ass popcorn in one arm, his date in the other.

When I turn my attention back to the villain in front of me, she arches a sexy, dark eyebrow, and an amused smirk plays lazily on her lips. "Storm, huh? How original. Wherever did you come up with such a clever name?" she coos, tilting her head to the side.

The sight of her pisses me off. She and her traitorous soul don't deserve my fucking time. She lost that right a long time ago.

"Some meaningless chick I fucked gave it to me." I shrug. "It sort of stuck." Stepping up to her, I lean toward her ear, feeling her heat radiating off of her body, responding to mine. "I guess that's the one good thing that hateful bitch did for me."

She flinches, and I have to fight off feeling like a dick. I'm hurting, and I want to hurt her. But that doesn't mean that it's an easy thing to do.

"That was nice of her to give you such a sweet nickname," she says once she's recovered. Her eyes widen. "From what I've heard, your dick never did fully satisfy her."

As I keep my eyes trained on her, my lip turns up slightly. "Her screams beg to differ."

And, oh, did they differ.

She was fully satisfied. Always.

We became best friends in seventh grade when we both landed at the same foster home. That day, I knew she was mine. Almost like my body and soul recognized her immediately. Like I had been waiting for her to show up.

But when she left, I was like a fiend, having withdrawals from her. I'm not so sure those withdrawals have ever subsided.

Our tie toward each other is one that I could never put into words even if I tried. It was unbreakable. At least, I thought it was.

I stuff my hands into my pockets, and my fingertips feel the small folded-up paper that I shoved into one this morning. Like I do every day. I'm pathetic, but hey, I don't really give a fuck.

I'm glad she doesn't know I carry this around with me. She doesn't deserve to know that even though I hate her, I still need this piece of paper like it's my fucking lifeline.

Not missing a beat, she quips back, "Did she ever mention she was considering going to college for theater? Turns out, she's an excellent actress."

I forgot how it is with her. The banter. The comments. She can be sweet too. Sometimes. But she has a rough side to her, a side that could eviscerate her prey. I only saw her use it when someone did it to her first. Almost like she was ready and waiting for the world to hurt her again, like it had so many times before.

She'd always had her heart locked up tighter than Alcatraz, always afraid anyone who tried to get close had ill intentions. But she finally let me in, and I never would have broken her trust.

Until now.

Now, I want vengeance.

Knox and his chick suddenly appear next to me. "Dude, what the fuck? The movie is starting soon. We've probably missed all of the previews."

The same moment I start to ask who cares about the previews, Ally snorts.

"Who actually likes previews?" she says, reminding me that we are almost the same person. Too alike at times.

Frowning at Ally, Knox looks at me. "You know I love previews, man. I've told you," he whines. When I give him a blank look, he scowls. "Do you not listen when I talk?"

It would be hard to hear everything he says. Because honestly, that motherfucker talks a lot. But I can't say that to Knox. He's become my best guy friend. He might talk as much as a fucking thirteen-year-old girl, but he's a good guy. And he'll always have my back. I know it. What we have on the field is something I've never experienced. I hope we ride this thing right to the NFL. I hope we get drafted to the same team too. That would be a dream.

"Of course I know you like watching the previews," I lie. I can't imagine anyone enjoying fucking previews. But he's a different breed. Putting my arm around his shoulders, I shake him lightly. "Let's go watch this shitty movie, yeah?" Glancing back at Ally, I narrow my eyes. "There's nothing to talk about here anyway. Waste of my time."

She flips me off and walks in front of us toward the theater. Her ass moving perfectly as she does. She's always had one of those asses that makes people stop and stare at it. It's thick. On a petite girl? That's fucking perfect.

"You know her?" Knox whispers. "You must because you seem a little … hostile toward her."

Shaking my head, I pat his shoulder and follow Ally. "Story for another day, brother."

"More like story for the ride home, dickface." He whistles under his breath.

"Nah, man. Not worth our breath," I say loud enough for her to hear.

four

ALLY

I can't wrap my mind around the insanity that the double date I got dragged on ended up with none other than Cole fucking Storms.

Well played, universe. Well played.

I had hoped and prayed every single day these past fifteen months to see him again. But I wanted it to be somewhere private. Somewhere I could explain why I'd left. Not in a damn movie theater, surrounded by our friends and where he could wave his dick around and show everyone how big it was by treating me like dirt.

Asshole.

I'm absolutely dumbfounded that he's here, in Georgia, right now. I mean, hell, last I knew, he was jacking off to the thought of going to college in Texas. He wanted to play football there, thought he could go and be some *big shit on turd mountain* star. I should know after all. *I* was going to go there with him and enroll in the music program. That was the plan anyway—until life went to hell in a handbasket. But all the time I knew him, he never once mentioned Brooks University. Then again, neither did I.

I haven't seen him in well over a year. Fifteen months, to be exact.

I haven't spent this time apart making friends or finding myself. How do you find yourself when you feel so broken?

I spent the first six months surviving in the hell I had been sent to while also healing from the horrible events I had faced the day I left. The rest of it was spent in a homeless shelter, where I used the computers at the library next door to earn my high school diploma. Wrote a *poor me* letter to a bunch of colleges. Much to my surprise, they ate that shit up and accepted me, and some even gave me scholarships.

Lucky for me, the online classes were a breeze, and I ended up passing most classes with straight As. So, I had that on my side too.

I wasn't surprised to see that Cole still looked good. At the expense of sounding like a gigantic pansy, my knees felt weak when we walked into the movie theater. There was a moment when I first saw him, and all I wanted to do was jump into his arms. Like old times. I wanted to feel his arms around me as I smelled his sexy, masculine scent and have his heart beating against my own chest. Having him that close without being able to touch him was torture. My heart has ached for so damn long. Seeing him was what I'd imagine coming home felt like. To a home where you were loved and it was all warm and familiar. For a second, it felt like that anyway.

Then, he opened his beautiful mouth and had to be a complete dick. And as always, my walls went up. And that fight-or-flight response kicked in, turning me into a bitch.

I can't blame him for being mad at me. I know he's placed me in that box with everyone else who has hurt him. But I am also not the type of girl who just takes insults. Especially when they are coming from the one person who, before we were ripped apart, would have knocked another man out for speaking to me that way. Even if they only called me a bitch, he would have lit them up.

It boils my blood that he thinks that little of me, that he thinks I chose to up and leave. How could he ever believe there was a world where I would do that to him?

He'd never treated me like that in all the years I'd known him. It was like he wasn't even him anymore, which broke my heart to think that I was to blame for turning such a gentle giant into a cruel man.

Cruel as he might be, I keep going back to how damn good-looking he is.

It's only been fifteen months, yet somehow, he looks even bigger. His entire body is made up of pure, hard, deliciously lickable muscle. His brown hair is shorter than it was back then too. And now, he has more facial hair.

I won't lie; I dig it. And knowing underneath his shirt, on his back, there is a tattoo of me, well … unless it's gone, that is. He probably covered that shit up with a damn four-leaf clover—or worse, a giant football.

We both started getting inked at age sixteen. We were underage, but Cole had connections because he worked in the tattoo parlor, helping out.

His arms are still bare. By now, I'm sure his back is nearly covered. He had scars on his back—scars he thought the ink could somehow not only hide, but also mask the everlasting pain.

Those tattoos though. On his muscly back …

Tattoos and muscles. Every bitch's weakness.

Well, this bitch's weakness at least. But Lord, there's nothing hotter than big, strong arms, covered in dangerous-looking ink. My heart speeds up, and parts of me ache, just thinking about clawing his back tattoo as he has me pressed up against a wall. Just like old times—only now, it's been so long since I've been with him, since I've been with *anyone*. I'm sure I could have picked some random dude to hook up with, but I didn't want to. The thought of being with anybody but him made me cringe.

There's no hiding the reasons why the girls back home wet their panties over him. He's hot as fuck. He knows it too. That smirk? Yeah, no one smirks like that and doesn't know how sexy they are. And to anyone on this campus, I'm sure that's exactly what they think. Star football player, hotter than hell, a cocky motherfucker who doesn't have a care in the world. Even I'll admit, he paints a pretty picture.

I know Cole better than anyone on the face of this earth. He might be cocky in his football skills—as he should be because he's an incredible athlete—but nobody knows that deep down, he has more insecurities than a teenage girl. And I don't think anyone can blame him for that.

Like me, he's a foster kid. His mom has never been in the picture. She left when he was just a baby. He doesn't even know what she looks like. He has no pictures, no name, nothing of her. He tries to play it off like he doesn't care, but I know from experience, there's a void you feel when you don't get that unconditional love parents are supposed to give. I filled that void for him, just like he filled mine. But when I left, I was just another person who hadn't stuck around.

His dad didn't leave by choice though. According to Cole, his father always made him feel unwanted. He died when Cole was ten. Overdose. Just like my mother did. And then he was bounced around to different foster homes until he landed at Dave and Marion's, the same one where I would soon end up.

His whole life, he's been pushed aside. Take it from a girl whose parents didn't want her, it leaves a mark. And not a pretty one either. More like the kind that you get from a rusty, old fence. It grabs the skin, ripping it on contact, jagged and uneven. Leaving you almost never the same as before. Flawed.

That's what he and I are—flawed.

But in each other, we were able to find a safe haven. And even though the universe ripped it from us, just like it had done every single thing we'd ever had, for that period of time, he was the best thing that had ever happened to me. Still is to this day.

He would have given me the world if he thought it would make me happy. He would have figured out a way to even if he killed himself trying. He was the epitome of the perfect first love. But more important than that, he was my very best friend. My only friend.

He doesn't look at me the way he did before though. He thinks I left him because I simply wanted to. As if I woke up one day and decided I was bored. If only he knew it was so much deeper than that. But I can't tell him about it—not yet anyway. I'm not ready, and neither is he.

Instead, I'll do what I do best. Play the coldhearted bitch that everyone thinks I am—blame it on my resting bitch face. But it'll come in handy now that I need to keep him at arm's length.

Maybe I do come off as frosty to the outside world. But since I came out of my mother's womb, I've been taught to keep my guard up. Trust absolutely nobody—ever. That is the only way I keep myself protected. Not from him though. He's not one of them. He's one of the good ones. Few and far between.

I find a place to sit, and Sloane follows me, sitting in the chair next to mine. Knox takes the seat next to hers so that we're all together.

Not Cole though. He goes a few rows in front of us, plopping his ass down next to some floozies who giggle and twirl their hair like a bunch of morons.

Dumb bitches.

Sloane leans into me and says, "What was that?"

Fuck, I must have been thinking out loud.

"Nothing. Thanks for inviting me." I force a smile. "This is fun."

This is not fun. *At all.*

I'm using every ounce of self-control I have not to run up to their row and smash those girls' faces against the seats in front of them. It isn't their fault that he's sitting with them. They just happen to be at the wrong place, at the wrong time. If it were anybody else, I'd say, *You go, girl,* because I think we are all free to do whatever we damn well please. But unfortunately for them, it *is* Cole. And when it comes to him, I can be a monster. I'm not a violent person, but that man brings out feelings inside of me that normally stay dormant.

It doesn't help these girls' cases that I've never seen him with a girl who wasn't me. My heart can't handle it. And this feeling that is flowing through every vein in my body is unrecognizable. Almost as if someone stuck a needle into my arm, pushing toxins in.

My eyes drift back to Cole, causing my fists to involuntarily curl, and I have to all but chew my cheek off to keep my cool and not lose my shit.

Don't give him the satisfaction. He's hurt. He's acting out like a five-year-old. It isn't your problem. I can tell myself those words over and over again, but it doesn't dull the sting my heart is feeling.

The fury rolling inside of me only grows every passing second as I sit, subjected to watching him flirt shamelessly with these girls. These girls that I know don't even give a fuck about him.

It was one thing to assume he had moved on this past year and was likely banging other chicks. It's another thing to physically see him flirt right in front of my face.

Some nerve he has.

I consider finding myself some random dude to go cuddle up next to. That would give him a taste of his own medicine and piss in his Cheerios for the day. *Double win.* But I don't want to stoop to his level. Besides, I know he's just upset. I hope that's all it is anyway. I have a hard time believing that he's actually over us. We were inseparable.

"Oh, okay. Well, I got you popcorn." Sloane smiles, passing it onto my lap and then handing me a cup. "And a Diet Coke."

Gratefully taking both, I smack my cup against hers. "I'm one lucky bitch to have you as my roommate."

"And friend," she says wryly. Almost reminding me that we are indeed friends.

I pause and glance at her. "Definitely that too," I agree.

Having girlfriends isn't something I was accustomed to, growing up. What normal girl wanted to befriend the nervous kid in the class who had tangly, unbrushed hair and dirty clothes? Not to mention, I was constantly either late or missing classes. That left me as a loner—or if I was lucky, one of the guys. And once Cole and I met, we were sort of a dynamic duo, attached at the hip.

I think it's true what they say. The ones who act the most confident are the ones who can barely stand to look at themselves in the mirror. They might carry themselves like a badass, but on the inside, they cringe, walking into a room. Afraid everyone is laughing at them. I say *they* and *them*, but really, what I mean is me.

I wear tight leather jackets and black crop tops that show my stomach, and my body has a variety of ink on it. If you saw me walking into a place, you'd probably think I was some sort of badass. I carry myself to be perceived that way. But inside, I'm struggling, like anybody else. Inside, I'm still a scared, little twelve-year-old girl who just wants to have a damn birthday cake like the rest of the kids my age. Instead, I was gifted with finding my mother dead on the couch with a needle in her arm.

I'm not alone now though. And that's something I need to focus on. I have Sloane, and I have the people at my new job at Lenny's. And they are all kind, welcoming people. They've already made me feel like we're a family there.

I glance at Knox. He's cute—no doubt about that—with his messy brown hair, goofy smirk, and laid-back demeanor. I might not know Sloane that well, but I know he seems to be just her type. He's sweet and charming.

Moving my stare to Cole for the thousandth time, I wonder how he stands it. The people surrounding him, invading his space. He's never been that type of person. He's never needed or wanted people in his bubble that didn't actually care about him. He didn't want people just there to fill a void. He wanted them to have a purpose, and if they didn't have a purpose, he wanted them gone. That left him less open to getting hurt. Now, it looks like he'll let anyone into his circle.

It seems I'm not the only one who's changed.

I shake my head to myself. They are only next to him because he's now a hotshot football player at an impressive college. Sure, he's cool and all, but a lot of the students at this school are a bunch of rich pricks. They probably have no idea where he came from or who he really is.

Pulling my jacket tighter, I feel an ache in the pit of my stomach as I continue to watch him. Maybe I don't know Cole Storms anymore.

XO

The movie's nearly halfway over when I see the blonde sitting next to him stand up. I think my heart stops beating when I see her reach out and pull Cole up by the hand.

As they make their way past my aisle and toward the exit, I don't miss the smirk the douche bag shoots me.

"Attaboy. Get some!" Knox yells to him as they pass, laughing once they're gone. Completely and utterly oblivious to the fact that he just made himself look like a total douche canoe.

That catches both Sloane and me off guard.

"That's disgusting," she snaps, flinging her head to face him. Her entire mess of blonde hair flying in every direction. "And incredibly rude. Have you never been on a first date before? Because news flash: you just failed the test."

"Wha—fuck, I'm sorry. I didn't mean to be disrespectful," Knox says.

I have to give it to him. He looks genuinely sorry. I don't think his goofy brain really even comprehended it was rude when he yelled it. But it *was* a dickwad move. I don't blame homegirl for being pissed. I likely would have punched my date in the balls if he'd pulled something like that. Then again, I've been told I'm a little cray-cray.

Standing, she looks down at me. "Can we go? I'm over this."

This movie is funny as shit, and Vince Vaughn, my favorite actor, is in it. But if my one and only friend wants to leave, then that's what we are going to do.

Standing, I nod. "Sure thing."

"Seriously, don't go. I was being fucking stupid. I'm sorry," Knox pleads.

She keeps walking, flicking him off. "Fuck off, douche bag," she whispers aggressively.

I have to hand it to her. I'm proud as a peacock. I didn't know she had it in her to put a man in his place. She always seems so sweet and PG. Maybe I read her wrong, and I didn't realize it.

Once outside, we head to her car, and she throws her hands on her face. "Shit! My phone is in there!" She sighs. "I really don't want to go back in there."

Patting her shoulder, I give her a small smile. "I'll get it. Be right back," I say.

Walking into the theater, I'm shocked to see Knox in the same spot, all alone. He even appears to be sulking.

His face lights up when he sees me. "Is she—"

"Not coming back," I cut him off, snatching the phone from the seat. "I'm just grabbing this," I try to whisper, not wanting to disturb the other moviegoers any more than we already have. Although, when I gaze around, I see the majority of them have their tongues so far down each other's throats that I'm surprised they're not coming out of the other's asshole.

Running his hand through his hair, he cringes. "Damn it. I knew I shouldn't have said that to Storm." He sighs. "It's just how us guys are with each other. I didn't mean anything by it. It was fucking stupid though."

"It was." I nod. "Try harder next time." I don't wait for a response before I walk away.

It was his first strike. The poor guy deserves one more chance at least. But I think she should make him work for it.

I'm almost out the door when the family restroom door swings open, and Cole and the blonde stumble out. Her hair is a mess, and he smirks. A callous smirk.

I try not to let my gaze linger too long, but it's hard. This man that I have loved since I was in seventh grade is doing everything in his power to hurt me. I know that's what his plan is. It isn't hard to see.

"Classy," I mutter just loud enough for him to hear before I head outside.

He wants to get a reaction, and I refuse to give it to him. He can hate me all he wants. He can even try to punish me for things I had absolutely no control over. But I won't give him the satisfaction of acting affected. The way he's acting, he doesn't deserve it. And besides, if he ever finds out the real reason why I left, he'll be the one looking like a complete tool.

Pulling the car door open, I hand Sloane her phone.

"Was Knox still there? Or was he with all those slutty girls?" she blurts out instantly, proving that she does care for this guy.

"He was there. He was alone," I answer as we pull out.

"He was?" she says, surprised, turning her head toward me.

"Yep. I'm all for you making him sweat it out, but look, I have a gift at reading people. I think he's a good one."

"Y-you do?" Her voice sounds unsure.

I nod. "I do."

"Good to know because, Ally?"

"Yeah?"

"My judgment usually sucks." She laughs.

"So, what you're saying is, I could be a serial killer and want to chop you up and feed you to my cat, and you wouldn't pick up on any creeper vibes?" I deadpan.

Her eyes widen as she glances over at me. "Shit. Are you going to do that?"

"Nah. You're too skinny." I pause for a moment. "Besides, I don't even have a cat. Allergic."

We both laugh, and admittedly, it feels good. I like Sloane. I can tell this just might be the start to a beautiful friendship. And I'm well aware that I sound corny as fuck, saying that. Honestly, I don't even care.

She might look like she's perfectly put together. Her edges seem smoothed out while mine are so damn sharp that they could cut you. But I know she's not as innocent as she might appear. I know there's a side to Sloane that I'm betting not many people have seen.

I hope, one day, she trusts me enough that she can show me that and tell me all of her secrets.

And I hope to one day trust her to tell her mine.

five

COLE

Finishing my last rep, I push the bar up. My muscles are screaming with pain. But truthfully, I don't mind. The pain distracts me from my thoughts constantly going back to Ally.

Walking over to my water bottle, I squirt some into my mouth.

The image of Ally's face flashes across my mind as she saw me and whoever the fuck that girl was I took into the restroom. I guarantee she thinks I fucked her. She's wrong. I didn't.

That was the point—for her to see us. I wanted her to hurt because she'd hurt me. But when I saw her face, shit, it made me sick to my stomach. I'd never intentionally hurt that girl in my life. Well, until then.

She tried to hide it, play it off with some snide remark, per usual. But I know that girl better than the back of my hand. She was hurt. And if I'm being honest with myself, no matter how pissed I am at her, I still have a lot of love for Ally. She's my fucking family. I'm man enough to admit when I fucked up.

And fuck up I did.

"You never did tell me what the fuck was up with you and that sexy, dark-haired beauty from the movies," Knox says next to me, wiping the sweat from his face with a towel and then throwing it over his shoulder.

"Dude, you call her sexy again, and I'll rearrange your teeth," I threaten him without thinking twice.

"Oh, simmer the fuck down, would ya? Geesh, someone's panties are in a bunch." He chugs down his Gatorade. "Anyway, I want to know, what the fuck is up with you two?"

Shrugging, I say, "Nothing to tell, man."

"Oh, fuck off. A blind person could see that you two had history." He shakes his head. "Come on. Tell Knoxy boy. Don't leave a brotha hanging."

I sigh. "We grew up together—that's all."

"As in Florida?" he asks, completely oblivious.

"No." I shake my head. "Ohio."

I've never told him that I grew up in Ohio, bouncing between shitty foster homes.

His eyebrows pinch together. "Ohio? I thought you were from Florida."

I blow out a breath. *Fuck, I did not want to get into this with him.* "I moved to Florida a year ago with my adoptive family. I had grown up in Ohio with my dad but moved to a different part of the state when I was twelve to live with a foster family," I explain, having to all but force the words out.

Luckily, Knox and I came earlier than the rest of the team to work out, so it's just us here. I hate opening up to anybody about this shit, but Knox and Weston are quickly becoming like brothers to me. So, eventually, I'm sure I'll have to tell Weston too. Though I have to admit, I'm sort of glad he's not here right now. I don't think I could handle spilling my guts to both him and Knox at the same time.

His eyes grow wide. "Fuck, man. I had no idea. Sorry."

"How could you? I keep that shit to myself." I play it off with a grin and smack him on the side. "It's no big deal. Don't go turning into a pussy on me. I can't be changing a litter box and buying you cat food," I joke.

From what I've heard, Knox grew up in a traditional mom-and-dad household. He's the oldest of four kids. I'm sure they probably traveled to Disney World and shit as kids. Likely ate pancakes for breakfast. I bet the Easter Bunny and Santa always found his house. Shit, he probably even had a lunch box with a matching thermos. So, I'm sure my situation sounds traumatic to him. And trust me, it was. But it's also all I've ever known.

Weston doesn't talk about his family much, leading me to believe that, like me, he has some skeletons dancing in his closet. Then again, I think everybody does.

"So, you knew each other from Ohio?"

"Yeah. We met when we were twelve." I don't tell him she was a foster kid as well. That isn't my story to tell; it's Ally's. "Anyway," I say, needing to change the subject, "did you make it right with the blonde chick?"

I guess she didn't take to him cheering me on to get laid last night. That was a knucklehead move on his part. You don't take a chick to the movies and do something like that. Chicks are too sensitive for that.

"Nope. She thinks I'm a slimeball." He grimaces. "Not that I can blame her. What the fuck was I thinking, yelling that dumb shit out?"

Rubbing the back of my neck, I eye him over curiously. "Why do you care so much? You met her once."

"She's hot—that's why. And she seems cool," he answers quickly, but I can tell it's more than what he's letting on.

Knox seems like the type of dude who could sleep with any girl he wanted, but in the end, he just wants a girl to cuddle with and take home to his mom. He wants someone sweet and nice. The safe choice.

Not me. I want someone who can stand beside me. Not behind or in front of me. She needs to be bold and strong. That's why I know Ally is it for me. She is the strongest damn person that I know.

"Well, I'm sorry to break it to you, but if you pissed Blondie off, then you likely pissed Ally off too. And that girl doesn't play," I tell him honestly.

If you're in Ally's circle, she'll do anything and everything in her power to keep you safe. And if she trusts that blonde chick, she'll be loyal to her. Which I'm guessing she does, or she wouldn't have gone to the movies with her. She would have told her no.

Good news for Sloane, bad news for Knox. Ally is fierce. And sometimes, she scares the piss out of me. Though I'll admit, I enjoy provoking her. At the movies, I knew she was likely losing her shit, watching me flirt with those annoying-as-fuck girls. I expected her to jump up and tell them to get the fuck away from her man. Only she didn't. That's when Operation Restroom came into play.

Looking back now, I see that it was all immature as shit to do. But there was the devil on my shoulder, telling me to punish her for her sins. And leaving me was a big fucking sin.

"Great. Now, I have to make it right with not only Sloane, but Ally too?" He groans.

"Afraid so, brother. Afraid so."

"Oh well. Let's go to Lenny's. I'm fucking starving."

"Sounds good, big dawg. Let's roll."

Lenny's is a restaurant right off campus. It's a bit of a hole in the wall, but they make a mean burger. Over the summer, we ate there basically every day. But now, with double practices and classes, we've had no time. It beats the hell out of cafeteria food.

It's killing me that I don't have Ally's new number. She changed it way back when she left Charlotte's Falls. I tried to get information out of my foster parents, Dave and Marion, but they were mute. They are both shady fuckers anyway. Hell, I've even entertained the idea that they ran her out of town. Only problem is, I can't think of a motive.

I wasn't mad that she went and found herself a family. Because if they were decent to her, then great. I mean, it still sucked for me and went against our pact, but if it gave her the life she wanted, even better. All I ever wanted was a good life for that girl. And even though I wanted to be the one to give it to her, I would have been happy if someone else did it first.

What's unforgivable for me is the way she went about it. In the couple weeks that I was gone at football camp—which I had been lucky enough to get chosen to not only attend, but to also go for free—she left. She changed her cell phone number and never reached out. Gone like a fucking ghost. Quit her job, disappeared from the foster home, never so much as glancing back. Not even for the person she'd said was her soul mate. To me, that's bullshit.

But now, she's back. That girl who fixed me after everyone else in my life broke me down, well, she left too. Leaving me once again shattered, incomplete, empty, and even more fucked up than before. Oh, and spiteful.

So fucking spiteful.

Now that she's within arm's reach, so close that I could hold my hand out and touch her smooth, creamy skin, I can't trust her anymore. Not after she took off so callously.

That's the fuel behind the part of me that wants to hurt her the way she hurt me. Only more.

The only problem is, the other part of me—the bigger part—wants to pull her in and never let her go. I want to make her realize how much she missed me while she was away. I want to make her cry out my name like she used to and make her laugh until the tears are rolling down her cheeks again. I've missed that so much. I've missed *her* so much.

Now the question is, which part of me is going to win? That's the fucked up part. I already know the answer. She's my kryptonite, my drug of choice, and the only one who can bring me straight down to my knees. I can't push her away, no matter how badly I want to.

six

ALLY

"Can I get you anything else tonight?" I ask the sweet couple seated in my section.

"No, thank you. Everything was great." The mom smiles as she bounces the baby on her knee.

"That's what I like to hear. I'll be right back with your bill."

I'm still new here at Lenny's, but I've waitressed before, so I caught on quick. I can be bitchy in real life, sure. But as a waitress, I have impeccable customer service skills. I need the money. Bitchy waitresses don't make good tips—that's a fact.

I hear the door open and shut but don't look up as I circle the total on the couple's bill. "Sit anywhere you'd like," I call out.

"Fuck, where's your section? So I can avoid it," a voice drawls.

I'd know that voice anywhere. And even though I hate to admit it, that voice makes my heart damn near skip a beat.

When I look up, Cole's cocky smirk greets me.

Blowing a loose strand of hair out of my face, I put my hand on my hip. "I'm the only waitress tonight, dipshit. So, you can either deal with it or go somewhere else." *Shit, there goes those impeccable customer service skills.*

He probably isn't going to tip me anyway. Well, unless he tells me to dress warm when I go to hell. That would probably be it for tips from him when it comes to me.

"What do you think, fellas? Should we mosey on down to King's Pub instead? Say fuck this place?" he says to his friends, though his eyes never leave mine.

"King's burgers suck, man. I want a fucking Lenny's burger." Knox pouts.

The fact that he's dissing our competition makes me already like him more. King's is down the street, and Lenny can't stand the owner. Apparently, they go way back.

"What he said," the other one chimes in.

He wasn't with them at the movies. Or if he was, I didn't see him. He's cute. Dirty-blond hair and a completely jacked body. The three of them together are sure to give every bitch they pass whiplash. Though neither Knox nor this other dude hold a candle to Cole.

Excuse me while I clench my thighs at the sight of him.

"Fine," Cole answers and struts over to the corner booth, taking a seat.

"Do you need menus?" I call over to them before I deliver my other table their check.

"Nope. Three Lenny's burgers, three fries, three Cokes," Knox yells back.

I glance at Cole to check that is what he wants, and he gives me a single nod.

Such a cocky fucker these days.

When I make my way to the couple's table, the baby babbles and smiles at me. As he holds his chubby little hand up, drool runs out of his mouth. It melts my heart of stone.

"How old?" I ask.

"Nine months," the dad answers, smiling proudly while handing me cash to cover the check. "Keep the change."

Tucking it in my apron pocket, I nod. "Thank you. He's precious. I hope you three have a wonderful evening."

While I wait for their food to be finished, other than delivering their drinks, I avoid the guys' table altogether. Weeknights are slow, and they are the only table here right now.

The picture of him and that slutty bitch walking out of the restroom is etched into my brain, unfortunately. Making me more hostile to Cole than I typically would be.

Trying to make my facial expression somewhat welcoming, I deliver their food.

"Fucking right. I've been dreaming about this burger all day," Knox basically pants.

Licking my lips at the sight of Cole, *not* the food, I look between them. "Is there anything else I can get you?"

"Nope," he says curtly. "There's nothing *you* can help me with."

"I'm sure you got plenty of *help* in the movie theater restroom," I coo. I shouldn't give him the satisfaction that I care. But goddamn it, I couldn't help but say it.

He chuckles. "And there it is. Allycat here is jealous," he says in a satisfied tone.

I'm already regretting opening my big mouth. Now, he knows it bothered me.

I scratch my cheek with my middle finger. Leaning closer to him, I drop my voice lower. "Don't flatter yourself, asshole. I have no interest in catching whatever diseases you're lugging around with you these days."

Both his sidekicks burst out laughing. Cole says nothing, just glares at me.

"Hey, is Sloane still mad at me?" Knox asks in between bites. An apparent frown on his face.

I shrug. "I have no idea. Do I look like her keeper?"

"Well, no. I just … I just thought—"

Putting my hand up, I stop him. "You thought you'd just yell some stupid shit at dipshit here"—I jerk my thumb toward Cole—"and you pissed her off. Now, you need to make it right. Understood?"

With his eyes wide, he nods frantically. "Y-yeah, yeah. I got it."

I set their check down in the center of their table. "I'll take that whenever you're ready," I say and walk off.

We closed five minutes ago, which means I can get my side work started and get the hell out of here.

XO

I'm on the other side of the restaurant, wiping down the tables, when I feel him behind me. Without turning around, I sigh. "What do you need, Cole? Change?"

"Nah, it's all set on the table," Cole answers surprisingly softly.

"Okay. What do you want?" I retort back at him. "Because I'm trying to get my shit done so that I can get out of here. So, if you have any smart-ass remarks, save it." *There goes that A+ customer service again. Right down the shitter.*

His last name is Storms, and when we first met, with the way he went through life and the way he played football, I couldn't help but begin calling him Storm because he *was* a storm—a force, a weapon. He took his shitty life, and he used the bad parts to make himself better and stronger. Like Mother Nature, there has never been any stopping that boy when he wants something. It's inevitable.

The funny thing is, since I was a kid, I've always loved storms. Much more than sunny days.

I can remember when my mom was all fucked up on whatever drugs she'd snorted or shot into her veins, and she and her friends would be partying in the living room. I'd lock the door to my bedroom, scared someone would get in and try something. I would look out my window, and I would pray for a big ol' storm to come and drown out the noise. That way, for a few short hours, everyone would be feeling the chaos of the same storm that I was. It made me somehow feel less alone. Even as I got older and after my mother overdosed and died, I'd still find the nearest window and just watch, listening to the rain pelt off of the roof and against the windows. It calmed me. Maybe other kids my age would have been scared and climbed in their parents' bed. I didn't have that option, so I learned to embrace it.

That's what made Cole's nickname so special and something only we had. He knew what I meant when I called him "my storm." Because he calmed me, and he turned the loudness into white noise. He took away all of my pain. But now that he's some big football star, everyone and their grandmother calls him by that name. And it somehow seems far less genuine now. What used to be something special between us now makes me feel like I'm just like everyone else. And it reminds me that I now share him with an entire campus.

"I owe you nothing. You left me, remember?" he says out of the blue. Anger seeping from his voice.

"I'm aware of that." *I didn't have a choice but to leave you, asshole.*

"But for your nosy-ass information, I'm not carrying around diseases with me. I'm clean."

Spinning around slowly, I lean against the table, folding my arms over my chest. "Congratulations." I cock my head to the side. "You use condoms. It doesn't make who you've turned into any less disgusting." I say it with venom because that's how it makes me feel when I think about him with another person that isn't me.

Stepping toward me, he invades my space. His delicious scent instantly filling my nose and crippling my brain, turning me stupid.

Looking down at me, his eyes are filled with pain and not anger. "How would you know what I've turned into, Ally? You haven't been around me in fifteen months." In an instant, the anger returns as a vein bulges in the side of his neck. "Fifteen. Fucking. Months," he says through gritted teeth. "Like a fucking ghost, *poof,* you were gone." His fingers grip my chin roughly, and he looks like he might erupt. "You left me alone. You joined that fucking club of disappointments in Cole Storms's life. You. Get. No. Fucking. Say. Anymore."

My chest heaves from him being so close. My breaths become so shallow that it actually hurts. "You're right. I guess I don't." I narrow my eyes. "But you fucked a girl in a restroom, Cole. That's pathetic. So, yeah, excuse me for thinking your dick probably isn't the cleanest these days."

I cannot hold his gaze any longer, and I avert my eyes to the floor. I feel my hard exterior crack the smallest bit. That's what I'm afraid of—that he'll break me down. He has the power to do it.

His lips move closer to mine, lingering over them and making my knees weak. I remember exactly what he tastes like—sweet mint. And now, that's what I'm craving.

"And if you hadn't cut me off, I would have been fucking you instead," he says callously. "This is on you, Ally. Not me."

I can feel his breath against my mouth, making my entire body feel numb and my legs turn to Jell-O.

What a pathetic bitch I'm being.

His words shouldn't do this, but they cause an ache in places that should not be aching for him. A longing deep within me that only he can fulfill. He's being a dick, but damn, I've missed him.

All of him.

"Everything all right, Al?" the owner, Lenny, says, coming out of nowhere.

Giving him a tight-lipped smile, I nod. "All good, Len. Mr. QB here was just on his way out," I say before turning my head back toward Cole. "Isn't that right, *Storm?*"

He eyes me over for a moment before backing away. "Sure is." Turning, he struts out. "Yo, Knox, Weston. Let's roll."

And then he's gone.

While I can breathe again, my body feels completely empty and cold.

"What was that about?" Lenny asks, a broom in his hand.

Lenny and his wife have owned this place for thirty-five years. She passed away a few years ago, but he refuses to stop working. At the age of seventy-three, he shows absolutely no signs of slowing down.

Rushing over to Cole's table, I begin to clean it off. I don't like Lenny working any later than he has to, so I always try to get my tables cleaned and everything put away for the next day in a timely fashion. Even though he lives above the restaurant anyway. So, luckily, he doesn't have to travel home late at night.

"Nobody," I mutter.

"Didn't seem like a nobody," he answers.

"Well, maybe he was somebody to me at one time, but now, he isn't."

Putting his hand on my shoulder, he looks me in the eyes. "That boy's eyes never left you. Not the whole time he was here. I might be old, but I'm not blind."

My heart softens for a split second before I ice up again. "You're right; you are old. You are probably getting senile and seeing shit. Or maybe you've got cataracts," I joke before patting his hand.

Even though we haven't known each other long, we already banter nonstop. I've never had too many people in my life I can count on. Yet I somehow know Lenny will be in the extremely exclusive group that I have.

Taking the bill from my apron, I can't believe what I'm seeing. They left me three one-hundred-dollar bills as a tip.

"Jesus Christ," Lenny huffs under his breath, spotting the cash. "Nobody, my ass."

"Hey," I say, holding the money up. "At least that pain in my ass is good for something, right?" Taking two of the bills, I try to pass them to him. "Here, all I did was take their order and bring it out. You cooked it."

He backs away, shaking his head and raising his hands up. "That's all yours, Al. You earned it. You get on out of here. It's a school night."

"Yes, sir." I know better than to argue with him. He won't change his mind. "I don't work tomorrow, but I'll see you Thursday."

"Yeah, yeah," he mutters before heading back into the kitchen.

XO

Locking the front door, I hear Cole's voice come from behind me in the darkness, and I turn around.

"Tell me you weren't planning to walk home alone," he growls, pushing off of a jacked-up black truck. "Because that would be really fucking dumb."

It should have startled me, made me jump … *something*. But I think my mind already knew he'd be outside, waiting for me.

When we'd first met, he'd instantly become my guardian, always making sure I was all right and that I was taken care of, even before himself. One thing I can say about Cole Storms: if he considers you his family, he'll protect you at all costs.

"Well, I have no other way to get home, so yes, I'm walking home," I huff out. "Besides, campus is not even a mile up the road."

"It's nighttime, Ally." His voice comes from the darkness.

I throw my hand up. "The entire way is lit sidewalks! Jesus, did you forget how I—no, how *we* grew up? Walking at night isn't a big deal. At least, it never was."

In reality, I am a little spooked to be walking home alone at night. The day I left the Falls, I learned just how horrible people could be. But forcing myself to suck it up and push my fears aside—in this case, while walking home—is something I need to do. For me.

"Yeah, well, once you came to Charlotte's Falls, you were no longer alone. You became my problem after that."

"Well, I'm not your problem anymore, Cole."

Before I even realize it, he has me pushed up against the side of the building. He smells like mint and pine, just like he used to. Even in the darkness, I can see his eyes glaring down at me.

"You will always be *my* problem," his deep voice barks, his delicious, minty breath hitting my face, numbing me like Novocain. "You really ought to know that by now."

His hand cups my cheek, moving down to my neck. He grazes my skin with his fingertips, causing my entire body to melt into him.

His eyes move to my lips for a moment, and there I stand, wanting him. Needing him. He makes me feel like myself again. *Finally.* I've craved him since the day I left. And I can say without a shadow of a doubt, if he tries to take this further, I'll let him take it as far as he wants.

"And what if I don't want to be your problem anymore?" I manage to say through my breathlessness.

"We both know that isn't true. So, take it the fuck back," he snarls like a dog protecting its bone.

"I don't know anything anymore," I breathe out. "Everything I thought I knew is different now."

He flicks his gaze from my eyes to my lips and back again. Slowly, he blinks, snapping himself back to reality.

Stepping back, he stuffs his hands in his pockets. Almost like if he doesn't restrain them, they'll roam my body. Deep down, I know that's what I want though. I want them on me.

"Get in the truck, Ally." He doesn't ask. He demands.

"You can't tell me what to do, Storm." Stepping up to him, toe to toe, I put a hand on my hip. "Maybe back in the Falls, I let you." A bitter laugh escapes my mouth. "Hell, I probably even followed you around like a pathetic fucking puppy dog. But that was then." Stepping up even closer to him, I glare up into his eyes, gritting my teeth. "But this is now," I hiss.

I turn to walk away, but before I even make it a full step, I'm snatched up and slung over his shoulder—his deliciously muscular shoulder.

"Motherfucker!" I yell, kicking my feet and flinging my arms.

Gripping my ass cheek with his hand, he squeezes. "We could have done it the easy way, Ally. But no, like always, you have to be a pain in my fucking ass," he roars.

"Put me down, asswipe! Or so help me God, I will cut your balls off."

Feeling him chuckle beneath me only infuriates me more.

Cocky motherfucker.

COLE

Opening the door to my truck with my free hand, I slam her ass down in the seat. Not gently either. But after trying to tell me no and attempting to walk off, she doesn't deserve gentle.

Getting an inch from her face, I nod my head toward hers. "I swear, if you run, I'll just keep doing this. And I have an early fucking practice tomorrow, Allycat, so don't pull any more shit tonight."

Her chest heaves as she glares at me. Her cleavage glistening in the moonlight. Causing me to second-guess not fucking her against the building. She's pissed—that's obvious.

You see, Ally has never had anything of her own that someone hasn't tried to take. Me taking her independence to walk home, well, that makes her fucking livid. The thing is though, she's sexy when she's angry. My dick twitches in my pants as I watch the rage radiate from her body.

Shutting the door behind me, I'm shocked when she actually keeps her ass in the truck.

Good girl, Ally.

Maybe she's learning to listen to me.

I climb in next to her and turn the key. The loud purr of the Duramax engine roars to life.

A perk of being part of a fake-as-fuck family who doesn't really want you but wants your talent? A sweet fucking ride.

I drooled over having a truck like this for years. I knew I'd have one someday—when I was in the NFL. But I never imagined I would have one now. Then again, I never imagined Ally would leave, giving me no choice but to go live with some random rich people.

I still didn't want them though. Even tried to push them away. But my shady foster parents told me if I didn't go, they'd spread some shit about me to college recruiters, and I'd likely never see the day to play college ball, let alone the NFL. The dream of playing football at the NFL level was bigger than my pride, so I said fuck it, and I have been with them for a little over a year.

I'm eighteen now, so technically, I could say fuck them anyway. But they are nice enough to me, so I haven't cut ties yet. And besides, they gifted me this truck. So, I suppose I can't hate on them too much.

He was some hotshot in the NFL years back but blew his knee his second year in and never made it back. Talk about a shitty fucking situation. That's every athlete's worst nightmare—to get injured and not play anymore.

The mom is a schoolteacher, who makes a mean chicken potpie.

But I'm not stupid. I know they are using me for my talent.

One thing I've learned though is, you need to take advantage of the breaks life hands you. And people like Ally and me? We don't usually catch too many breaks. So, I had to take this one.

The ride to her dorm only takes a few minutes. I can basically feel the steam rolling off of her as the anger flows through her veins.

When I pull up in front of her dorm, she turns. "How did you know which dorm hall I'm living in?" Her voice is laced with skepticism.

Staring straight ahead, I rest my wrist on the steering wheel. "I know people, Al. I find out everything I need to. You'd do good to get that through your head sooner rather than later."

It's the truth. I'm a pretty big deal on campus, and people basically bow at my feet. It's nice, but I also remember that they wouldn't be there if I wasn't the captain of the football team. They might all seem like my friends, but they aren't. They are opportunists. Every one of them.

"Oh, right." I can basically hear the eye roll in her voice. "You're some big dick on campus now, so suddenly, you have connections and have turned into a fucking stalker."

"Not a stalker. But big dick?" I smirk. "Hell yes." Turning toward her, I reach out and graze my fingers on her chin, causing her to quiver. "But you already knew that, didn't you?"

She ignores me and pulls away from my touch. "Well, thank you for the ride," she mutters.

And I have to practically pick my fucking chin off the ground. Ally saying thank you after I basically kidnapped her? Did hell freeze over? Can pigs fly? Especially after that dickhead move I pulled last weekend at the movies, trying to rub it in her face that I hooked up with someone. The fuck was I even thinking?

"I don't want you to walk at night. Ever," I tell her, preparing for the backlash.

"I don't have a car, Storm. I hate to break it to you," she says and waves around at the truck, "this lifestyle didn't happen for me."

"Where did you go then? I want to know where the fuck you've been."

She looks down at her hands that are resting on her lap. "One day, I'll tell you all about it. But not tonight. I'm dead-ass tired, and I have an early class tomorrow."

Climbing out of the truck, she turns to me. "Thanks for the ride. But I'm not a child. You don't need to worry about me walking home."

I always fucking worry. And I always will.

I run my hand down my face and look over at her. "It's just how I am with you. Can't be any other way than this."

I can't even apologize for it either. If anything ever happened to Ally, it would be my fault. I truly believe that the universe gave her to me. I don't pray or attend church or believe in a whole helluva lot. But I know one thing for sure: that girl was put here for me to love her. And I wish more than anything that that's what I was still doing. That's all I want to do.

She nods and looks up at me with those big, heartbreaking eyes. "I know," she whispers before closing the door.

And I know without a shadow of a doubt that she believes me. She knows I can't help how I am with her.

As much as I want to hurt her for leaving me, I can't. I need her close to me. I need her like I need my next fucking breath. And even though I should let her take care of herself, like she's asking, I can't do that either. There's too much bad shit that could happen to her. I can't risk it. Not when it comes to her.

My brain travels to just how far back it began—when I started losing my mind to protect this girl.

"You seem pissy," I said to Ally. "What happened?"

I was worried she might not fit in right away. Those kids could be assholes. It was only her fourth day of school, but I had been here for three months. I had gotten here before Ally, and unlike my last high school, I was respected. The football program here was kick-ass, and I was the best player in my age group. Shit, I was better than the older kids too.

"Rebecca and Melissa were making fun of me in English. And then in PE, Trevor Stanhope and Brett Lewis were being dicks. It hasn't even been a week, and I already hate this place."

Hearing girls had been mean to her pissed me off. But hearing that dudes had been, too, made me fucking livid.

"I'll take care of them. Don't worry your pretty little brain."

She frowned. "I'm a big girl, Storm. I've been on my own a long time. I can handle a few spoiled rich kids."

"You don't have to though. I can do it for you."

"I don't want you to do that." She slammed her locker shut. "I said, I can handle it! Stop acting like you're my protector or some shit."

I had no doubt she could handle anything herself. But I also didn't care either. From day one, I had known she had been put here for me to watch out for her, and that was what I was going to do.

"Ally, look, you are one bad bitch. Hell, you scare me sometimes. But you are my family. And one day, you'll be my wife. If you need a friend who won't defend you, well, that ain't me." I took her hand in mine. "Unfortunately, even if you need that type of man, you can't have him. Because you're already mine."

LOVE, ALLY

She tried to act irritated, but I knew better. She already loved me too much for that. She just didn't know it yet.

She's always wanted to take care of herself, but I just can't let her do that. I've never had anything or anyone of my own to love, and once she became mine, I guess I sort of smothered her.

I won't make apologies for keeping what's mine safe.

seven

ALLY

A yawn rips through my throat without me being able to stop it.

I hate math.

I hate math.

I fucking ... hate ... math.

This is the only class I dread coming to. It's boring as hell, and I have to fight not to fall asleep. It's equivalent or worse to watching paint dry.

Thank God it's over any second.

"Class dismissed," the professor says, as if reading my mind.

Gathering my things up, I start to head toward the door. My stomach has been growling for forty-five minutes. I need food.

"Ally?" a smooth, unfamiliar voice comes from behind me.

When I turn, my eyes find a tall, muscular dude with blond hair. He's attractive—there's no denying that. But comparing him to Cole would be like comparing a beat-to-shit Jetta with the exhaust falling off to a brand-new Mercedes. Cole being the Mercedes, of course.

"Um, yeah?" I answer, tossing my hair over my shoulder to get it out of my face.

"I'm Kent. I've seen you around a little." He grins. "You're not exactly easy to miss. I wanted to introduce myself." He smiles, revealing obnoxiously white teeth.

I need my sunglasses. Those bad boys are damn near blinding.

"Oh." I give him an awkward smile. "Well, hello, Kent. Nice to meet you."

"Do you want to go out some—"

"The answer is no, Woodworth. Back the fuck up," Cole's deep voice growls from the doorway.

"Storm, what the fuck is it to you?" Kent tosses back at him before a douchey smile creeps onto his annoying-as-fuck face. "She was into it."

That makes me want to punch him in the balls. I was certainly not into anything to do with this cocky, overly groomed dickwad.

"She's off-limits. Walk. The. Fuck. Away." He steps forward, his muscles rippling underneath his white T-shirt. The vein in his neck making a dangerous appearance.

"Or what, Storm?"

"I don't know. Try it, and I guess you'll find out."

"Yeah, okay." Kent laughs. "You pissin' on her to mark your territory?"

Cole smirks. "She doesn't need me to piss on her. She's already mine."

Rolling my eyes, I walk between them and toward the door. "Save yourselves the time and energy, boys. I'm sure both of your dicks are tiny, so I wouldn't bother whipping them out and getting the measuring tape to see whose is bigger."

Leaving them both standing there, looking like complete morons, I head to the food court to meet Sloane. I can't help but think of how annoying it is that Cole shows up here and treats me like trash, yet he still tries to control my every move. That's bullshit. And even though I wanted nothing to do with Kent or whatever the hell his name was, I don't appreciate being cockblocked by Cole Storms. I don't appreciate it one bit.

Payback is a bitch. And I like to serve mine ice-cold.

eight

ALLY

"I'm so excited to go to this football game," Sloane squeals. "Football is a huge deal back where I'm from. This is like having a little slice of home here at college."

I smile and shake my head. "Your accent is the cutest shit I have ever heard. Kinda pissed that I wasn't born in the South."

She's like a little Southern belle. Though I can't wait until she feels comfortable enough with me to tell me her real story. After all, everybody has one.

She smiles. "Me and Ally go together like peas and carrots," her Southern accent drawls slowly, sounding like Forrest Gump.

"This is why we're friends." I smile so hard that it actually hurts my cheeks.

"Ahem, bitch … we're best friends."

"Fo' life." I wink at her. "For real though, Sloane, thank you for being my friend. It means a lot—to have a friend and be able to trust them. I haven't exactly had a ton of friends in my eighteen years."

"I mean, I tried to switch roommates, but they said no. So, I suppose I'm stuck with you now, aren't I?" she says, completely indifferent.

My mouth hangs open as I whip my head toward her. "Wh—"

"I'm kidding! I'm kidding! Lousy joke. Sorry," she says, throwing her arm around me. "Thank you for being my friend, Ally. I'm really happy that we were paired as roommates."

Even when she's mean as a joke, she can't stand the thought of hurting someone's feelings. I could learn a lot from Sloane—that's for damn sure. Nonetheless, I'm so happy to have her as not just a roommate, but also as a friend.

Aside from Cole, this is the closest thing I've ever had to a best friend. It's weird, talking girl talk. I've never been one of *those* girls. I was respected back in Charlotte's Falls but only because of Cole. Girls saw me as a pariah. I had stolen the hottest guy on campus. And even though he was still a poor foster kid, it wasn't hard to see with the football skills he possessed that he was headed places. *Big* places. So, naturally, they all loved and adored him. Me? I was tolerated.

"So," Sloane says sweetly, "if you don't mind me asking, what is up with you and that Cole or Storm or Storms or whatever the heck his name is?" Turning toward me again, she scrunches her face up. "Seriously, what even is his real name?"

I laugh. "His name is Cole Storms. I started calling him Storm when we were twelve. It's sort of his second name now." I roll my eyes. "Well, now, he's called it by everyone and their damn grandmother. But before, it was my thing. I called him Storm."

"Okay, well, that doesn't answer my question. What is up with the two of you?"

I sigh at her persistency. It's not that I don't want to share; it's just that things between Cole and me have always felt so sacred. "We're old friends, you could say."

"As in … old friends who used to get naked and roll around? Or just plain old friends?" she asks, arching an eyebrow.

My mouth hangs open. "Sloane Leighton! So much for you being the innocent girl I pegged you for." I shake my head. "I'm almost never wrong about people either. You slipped right under my radar."

"Eh, guess it's true what they say. Looks can be deceiving." She shrugs. "Anyway, did you know he was coming here? To Brooks?"

I shake my head. "I had no freaking clue, I swear. I thought he was going to Texas. Then, I came to Georgia, and bam, he's here." Pulling my hair up, I tie it in a ponytail. "And that makes my life more complicated."

She nods. "Understandably so. But I have to ask, did you wish for him to be here?"

I think before I answer. "Not here specifically. Only because I never gave it a thought that he'd ever in a million years attend Brooks," I explain. "His dream school was always in Texas. And I wanted to attend there too." I blush. "But when I applied there, I got rejected. So, here I am."

Looking forward, she continues walking. A smile suddenly touches her lips.

"Why are you smiling?" I grunt. I can only imagine what thoughts are going on in her *everything is flowers and candy* mind. She's all light and colorful. I'm more dark and dreary.

"Well, it sounds like …" She pauses, her finger tapping her lips.

"Like what?" I ask. My curiosity killing me.

"Like destiny," she says softly. "You both ended up here for a reason."

"Oh my flying fuck." I elbow her. "Destiny? Are you kidding me?" I joke it off, but I've thought about it myself. I don't typically believe in that type of shit. But I can't deny the fact that the universe has delivered me to that man not once, but twice.

"What?" she shrieks. "What's wrong with the word *destiny*?"

"Well … to be blunt, I think it's a bunch of horseshit."

"Maybe you should start believing in it," she says before leading the way to our seats. "Because I'm not sure what other sign you need from the world to tell you that you were meant to be in each other's lives. It's pretty dang obvious to me."

Destiny couldn't have brought us back together. Could it?

I shake that thought off. So far, destiny hasn't been that kind to me. I seriously doubt it had anything to do with the man my heart beats for being at the same college.

nine

COLE

"Storm," Coach calls to me, waving for me to come over to him. "Get your ass over here."

Jogging over, I nod to him. "Yeah, Coach?"

He furiously chews on the gum in his mouth. "We both know Ricky took it hard when he learned the news that he'd been replaced." Messing with the bill on his hat, he frowns. "I hope you can get the boys to fall in line behind you. They need leadership. They need someone they can depend on."

Putting my hands on my sides, I nod. "Yes, sir. I just hope they'll accept me. If not, we've got no shot at the championship."

He leans in closer to my ear and pats me on the shoulder. "Then, make them fall in line. Earn their respect, son. You get one, and you'll get them all."

With that tidbit of advice, he turns and walks to the sidelines. Leaving me hoping and praying I will earn these guys' respect as their new captain.

This is far from my first rodeo in the game of football. They aren't going to just welcome me with open arms after I replaced their main man. I might be seen as the big man on campus these days to the students, but to this team, I'm just the new kid who came in hot and was instantly handed the keys to the kingdom. All I can hope is that they understand that if they work with me, I'll lead them right to a championship.

Coach calls us in, and we form into a huddle. I don't miss the douchey looks coming my way.

"Look here, boys," he says, looking around at all of us. "This season is ours for the taking. We have the team, we have the talent, we have the ability. So, what do you say? Let's start this game off right."

No one says anything besides Knox and Weston, who yell, "Let's go!"

I glance around at the snarls coming my way. I can't help but feel awkward as fuck. Suddenly, I'm transported back to a time when I was a kid, living with my dad. Dirty clothes and hair that was too fucking long for a boy. I was labeled the weird kid in class. Thank fuck when I got to Charlotte's Falls, the guys cared more about my football skills, and the girls cared more about the way I looked. Finally, I was respected.

Coach's lips form into a line, and he shakes his head. "Well, if that's how it's going to be, you can all warm my damn bench. How's that sound, whiny asses?"

They all glance around at each other before finally realizing that this is Coach Beal. And Coach *don't* play.

Collectively, they eventually nod. Other than Ricky, who just stands there, scowling. Likely planning my death.

Coach gives us a pep talk. Runs through what plays we'll start with and what to look out for with this team. The offensive coach then steps in, talking to me and Knox mainly. And then, just like that, it's fucking game time.

Before heading out onto the field, I jog over to Ricky. "I'm sorry, man, for how it all played out. I hope you know that."

He looks away from me, his jaw noticeably tensing. "They'll never listen to you, Storm. Most of those guys have been with me since freshman year," he answers bitterly before looking me up and down. "They aren't going to play with a stranger who showed up here, acting like some big shit. You're still a kid. You've got a lot to learn to catch up to me."

Pulling my helmet on, I shrug. "Like I said, I'm sorry. But they'll either learn to work with me or they can lose this season for me, themselves, you, and Coach. That's on them," I answer sharply before making my way to the center of the field.

Normally, I don't get nervous before a game. Actually, I never do. But that's because I've always had teammates who were like brothers. Now, I only have Knox and Weston. The others see me more like an enemy. Yeah, we're all really good. But a team is just that—a *team*. It isn't a single person or a pair or even three. It's a group coming together to execute a win. Or to try their damnedest and lose with grace. Either way, it's done together.

I pray to fucking God they can set aside personal shit and just show up and play. But something tells me it won't be that easy.

XO

We're only a few seconds from halftime, and as I predicted, they are choosing to work against me and not with me. I don't get it either. Issue with me or not, they should have enough respect for this game to fucking play. To just show up. It's a damn disgrace and an embarrassment to football.

The defense is letting me get sacked. *Over* and *over*. The only one on the field who has blocked me from getting hit is Weston. He hasn't even been able to try to run one into the end zone because besides him, I have no protection. And I've had to depend solely on Knox to throw the ball to because everyone else is purposely making me look bad by missing the pass.

By the time we file into the locker room, my body is in immense pain, and my heart is racing because I'm so fucking pissed off that I can hardly see straight. I cannot for the life of me understand a universe where you don't at least try your best in a game.

I should be focused on giving a speech, amping them up. But I can't. I can hardly look at their pathetic faces.

If they can't show up for me, why should I come in here and waste my breath on a speech?

Back in Charlotte's Falls, if someone pissed me off, I'd straighten them out without thinking twice. But I'm in college now, and everything is scrutinized under a microscope. I can't afford to fuck up and ruin my chances at being drafted. Even if that means keeping this anger inside until I explode. I might not be able to beat the piss out of these fuckers, but I can at least let them know what's up.

I see a few of them snickering among each other, looking in my direction.

"Laugh it up, fucksticks. Hopefully, you have no dreams to play at a higher level." Taking a drink of my Gatorade, I shake my head at them. "Because after tonight, nobody will want you. I promise you that much."

"What the fuck did you say to me?" Dex, a defenseman, growls as he comes charging toward me.

I can't get in trouble if it's self-defense. Right?

My fist curls, and that feeling of adrenaline rushes through my body. My sore-as-fuck body, thanks to these assholes.

"You heard me." I smile arrogantly. "I thought, *No way would these pussies throw away a fucking game tonight over a position.*" Shaking my head, I laugh bitterly. "Turns out, I was wrong. You all should take those jerseys off; you're a fucking disgrace to this team."

Reaching back, he curls his fist before starting to come toward me.

Before he does it though, Knox pushes him backward. "Cut the fucking shit, Dex."

"What do we have here?" Now, Ricky steps up to Knox. "You riding Storm's dick like the Coach is?"

"What the fuck did you just say, son?" Coach Beal's voice booms.

Turning toward him, Knox grins. "Coach? Allow me?"

He rolls his eyes but doesn't stop him.

Knox turns his attention back to Dex before he laughs once and shakes his head. "Well, you see, Dex, I like to do this thing called winning." Looking back at me, he pretends to act confused. "How many games did they win last year, Storm?"

I didn't want to do this shit to Ricky, but he's left me no choice. He's not fucking up my future just because he has a vagina. Fuck no.

"Six," I answer smugly. "Lost six."

Looking around the room, Knox shakes his head. "Six out of twelve fucking games. I mean, I'm not good at math or anything, but that means you lost half of your games." He claps his hands. "What a bunch of go-getters you all are." Moving his eyes to Ricky, he jerks his thumb toward Weston. "Weston here, his team won state. My team, we lost state, but at least we'd made it there. And, obviously, Cole fucking Storms led his team to a state championship and won it." He pauses. "How many of you fuckers made it to state in high school?"

A few mumble, and a few raise their hands though not many.

"That's about what I—"

"Get to the point, Carter," Coach grunts.

Knox nods. "The three of us are out there, busting our asses. And for what? For the rest of you to sabotage this game." He stops and looks over at me. "With this guy right here, we *will* win games. But Jesus fucking Christ, you have to do your jobs. We all get it—you have loyalty to Ricky. That's sweet and shit. You can suck his dick once this game is over. But goddamn, I want to win games. I don't give a fuck about your hair-braiding, nail-painting relationships. Tuck your pussies in and play ball. I'm good. I'm real fucking good. So is our new quarterback and tight end." He waves his hand around at us. "We can either be a three-man team. *Or* we can all work together. It's your call, boys."

It's a good speech. A speech I should be giving. But my anger over how this team is playing makes me unable to do that. Unable to act like a true captain in this moment. And that's a damn shame.

If I'm being honest, I don't have a helluva lot of faith that Knox's words will work. But I'm hoping to fuck it does. I'm not sure how many more hits I can take tonight. And more than that, I really, *really* hate losing. Especially when I know Ally is watching. I can feel her eyes on me the whole time. I just wish I could hear her sweet voice cheering me on.

XO

ALLY

"That was some game," Sloane says next to me as we walk back toward our dorm.

We stayed at the stadium for a while, walking around and getting more junk food. I forgot how much I had missed football games. There's just something so nostalgic about them.

Of course, there's also that small part inside of me that misses being there specifically to cheer for Cole. He always swore he could hear my voice in the crowd, yelling for him. I was never sure if I should cringe or smile at that.

She isn't kidding.

Watching the first half, I could have sworn that Cole's team hated his guts. It was like they purposely left him open to get sacked. It was painful to watch. Along with infuriating. Honest to God, if it had been back when we were hot and heavy, I would have probably run out on that field and kicked those fuckers in the nutsacks for allowing him to get hit so many times. There were only two teammates out there who seemed like they were with him and not against him.

In all of his football career since I've known him, I've never seen his teammates do that. I'm sure it wasn't easy for him—being treated like an outsider.

But thank fucking Jesus himself, by the second half, they all played together like an actual team. He called out plays, and they actually listened. His teammates started to protect him. And yard by yard, they were back in the game. In the end, they won by thirteen points.

I've always been one who loves a good comeback game. Though I do hate that it started so rough for him.

"Sure was. I saw you over there, checking out the wide receiver's ass," I tease her.

I'm not sure if she was looking at his ass, but she was certainly looking down in the direction of Knox Carter. To my knowledge, they haven't talked since that time a few weeks ago at the movies. He's tried to call a bunch though. I can tell she's liking the chase.

Not that I can blame her. Who doesn't enjoy being hunted?

"Was not." She blushes. "Okay, maybe a little. What can I say? It's a nice ass."

I burst out laughing. Something about a seemingly sweet and innocent girl talking about a guy's ass is hilarious.

"I got a glimpse of it, girlfriend. It's a nice ass," I agree.

"Hey, Sloane! Sloane's friend!" an extremely chipper voice chirps.

Turning, I see a tall, leggy redhead. Her boobs are pushed clear up to her chin. Which is easy for her to do because they are ginormous. And fake.

"Hi, Rachelle." Sloane smiles, but it doesn't seem that sincere. "Some game, huh?"

"I wouldn't know. I was too busy ogling the man meat to pay attention." She pretends to fan herself. "So, will you two be going to the party at the football house off-campus?"

"Oh, I'm not sure. Probably not." Sloane shakes her head softly.

"More men for me." Redhead chomps on her gum obnoxiously. "Storm, Knox, or Weston … one of those boys will be slamming me into the headboard before midnight."

"We'll be there," Sloane and I squeal at the same time.

Unfazed, she pulls a tube of lip gloss from her back pocket and smears some on before rubbing her lips together aggressively. "Guess I'll see you there."

Watching her sashay away, I turn to Sloane, raising an eyebrow. "I know my reasons for the change of heart, but what are yours?"

She groans. "Because she sleeps with everybody. She's the campus bicycle—everyone rides her."

"And?" I tilt my head.

"And I don't want her to sleep with Knox." She puts a hand over her eyes. "I don't know why."

"Eh, don't feel bad." I shrug. "I sure as shit am not going to let her fuck Cole either. Especially not after the shit he pulled in math class. I'll show him I can be a pretty good cockblocker too." An evil grin covers my face. "Let's do the damn thing."

ten

COLE

"**H**ere, brother," Knox says, handing me a beer. "You need it after the fucking bashing you took tonight."

"Thanks." I take it and grin. "This and about ten ibuprofens ought to do the trick. Thank fuck the guys finally cut the shit. Not sure how many more hits I could have taken on that field."

I'm sore. My muscles ache, and my skin is bruised. But we won. And at the end, we were a team. I call that worth it.

"You boys looked good out there." A redhead rubs my arm before doing the same to Knox's. "Reeeally good," she says slowly, biting her lip.

Shrugging her off of me, I take a step back. "Thanks."

Knox takes that opportunity to leave.

Asshole.

She has me cornered. And while I can be a dick, I don't want to hurt this chick's feelings.

"Are you—"

"Not interested," I grunt. "Sorry."

Her lip pokes out, but she recovers quickly. "I'm just interested in one night …"

Now, I'm all for this chick wanting to get hers. This is college, and it's time for fun. But there are not enough drinks in here to make me sleep with her. Or anybody for that matter. The guys would laugh if they knew that I'd only been with one chick, but honestly, I don't give a fuck. I guarantee with that one girl—Ally—I've experienced more sex than they ever will.

I see Ally walking toward us, her eyes burning into the back of this red-haired chick's head like fire pokers.

She looks vicious as hell for someone who claims she doesn't want to be my problem anymore.

I'm not surprised when she struts right up. I just have no fucking clue what she's going to say. That's the thing with her—at times, she's unpredictable.

Stopping in front of me, she turns her body toward the horny chick.

"Girl to girl, be careful." She leans closer to the girl. "Word around campus is, he has untreated crabs." Moving her eyes to me, she smirks. "Those can be nasty little critters to deal with."

This girl just told someone I have an STD. What in the actual fuck?

The chick glances at me and then back to Ally.

She snarls at Ally, "Why didn't you say that earlier then? I told you I was planning to be fucked against his headboard." Turning toward me, she licks her lips. "Hard."

"Among two others," Ally deadpans. "And sorry, *sweetheart*, I would have told you, but I kinda thought you were kidding. I didn't think you actually came to parties, hoping to jump on a dick."

Red's mouth hangs open at Ally's harsh words.

"Well, how do you know what he has? Have you two been together?"

"No way, girlfriend." Ally shakes her head nonchalantly. "But a girl in my science class was with him, and … well, long story short, she ended up at the free clinic not long after."

Ally isn't even taking a fucking science class right now. I would know. I had her entire schedule printed off.

Glancing between Ally and me, the redhead slowly backs away before stalking off.

Eyeing Ally closely, I smirk. "If I had crabs, that would sure suck for you, doll." I move my entire body into hers, invading her space, and her eyes shut as I do. "Because then, I'm guessing, you wouldn't want me to fuck you, right?"

Her body shudders at my words.

"You wouldn't want my dick inside of you right now if that were the case. Would you, baby girl?"

"You want to play cockblocker, dickwad?" She steps up to me, fearless, as she always is. "Let's. Fucking. Play."

"You didn't want ol' Kent's dick anyway, Allycat. We both know that. And I sure as fuck didn't want the redhead with the fake tits." Moving my mouth to her ear, I drop my voice lower. "You know I like mine real," I say before stepping back.

Rolling her eyes, she huffs before marching off. No doubt irritated that she didn't get under my skin.

Everybody loves a good game of cat and mouse. Ally has proven that she certainly does. But I'm not playing for much longer. She needs to be reminded who she belongs to. And that's me.

ALLY

Gazing up at the stars, I want to kick myself in the ass for letting my feelings for Cole get the best of me. He fucked the girl at the movie theater. *In a goddamn restroom.* So, why did I show up here, acting like me stopping him from screwing this one chick is going to make one damn bit of difference in who he takes home at the next party?

I might pretend I want to get in the way of him sleeping with someone else strictly because of the shit he pulled with that Kent dude. But really, I just can't stand the thought of him being with anyone but me. I thought we'd be each other's first, last, and only. Now that that's gone, it seems like everything else is out of reach.

"You out here, thinking about if fucking me is worth the crabs?"

I turn to see Cole standing under the porch light.

"Some shit you pulled in there, sweetheart."

"Some shit you pulled in my math class. Showing up like a stalker and sending Kent away."

He grins, and that damn dimple pops out. I have to avert my gaze so that my heart doesn't do that annoying fluttery thing.

"Kent's muscles might be big, but that doesn't make up for the fact that the dude's got no brain. He's a few French fries short of a Happy Meal. You didn't want any, Al. I saved ya."

"Oh, gee, thanks," I say sarcastically. "How thoughtful of you."

Lifting his drink, he throws it back with ease.

"That's a deadly habit," I joke.

"So are you." He shrugs. "Yet here I am, coming right back for more."

"I didn't ask for you to crop up in random places and try to stake claim in my doings," I say, holding my arms out at my sides. "I'm doing just fine without you, dick."

His eyes burn into mine for a moment. Intense anger radiates from them and into me. I can feel everything he is right now.

I think he hates me. I really think he hates me.

"Good," he mumbles before turning toward the door. "Glad to fucking hear it."

As he walks in the door, he lets it slam behind him.

How did we get here? How did two people who had each other's backs the way we did end up burning each other down the way that we are?

I lied. I'm not fine. Not without him. And I fear I never will be. No. I *know* I never will be.

eleven

COLE

"**S**hit, man. That tattoo of the hot angel is fucking huge," Knox says, leaning over me. "Your back is damn near covered, and yet you have none on your abdomen or arms?" Scratching his chin, he eyes it over again. "Wait, is this huge-ass angel Ally?"

"Holy shit, it is!" Weston laughs. "Fuck, man, you got it bad!"

"Piss off," I grunt.

"All right, all right. Anyway, why no tats on your stomach, chest, legs, arms, face? Do you have any on your pecker?" Knox laughs. "That would be painful as fuck."

"No, asshole, I don't have my dick tatted, Jesus. And I don't know why I don't have any anywhere else. But I am getting one today, right here." I point to the inside of my upper arm.

The ones on my back cover shit that I don't want to see. That's their purpose—to hide the past. The rest of my body doesn't have any scars on them. So, the way I see it, it's fine to be left alone.

I hand the piece of paper to the tattoo artist, and he looks at it and glances at me. "You want *Love, Ally* with the letters X-O under it?"

I nod. "Yep. In that writing. *Exactly* that writing."

The letter that I had from Ally was what got me through the days while she was gone. Reading her words, knowing they were for me, carried me through. Making life a little less painful.

"He's so fucking whipped," Knox whispers to Weston. "So. Fucking. Whipped."

"You're just jealous because Sloane won't touch your wiener," Weston answers, watching me carefully, giving me a knowing look.

He's never talked about a girl, but something tells me he's got some scars from one, just like me.

"What's your future wife going to say"—Knox laughs—"when she sees you've got a chick's name on your arm?"

"Well, considering she'll be my wife, I think she'll be fine with it," I state matter-of-factly.

"Ohh shiiiit," he says under his breath before pretending to whip the air.

"Laugh it up, fellas. One day, you'll be doing this same fucking shit." I give them a pointed look. "Then, you'll understand."

twelve

ALLY

Most Sundays, I work a double, but today, I only worked the morning shift, leaving the rest of my day free for schoolwork and exploring the campus with Sloane.

After getting our iced coffees, we walk the sidewalk toward the quad. Feeling like completely normal college kids, living the life. And I have to say, if Cole wasn't here, at this campus, I don't know if it would feel so much like home.

Knowing he walks the same sidewalks as I do, goes to the same library, and eats at the same shitty food court, it somehow brings me comfort. I don't feel as much like a stranger in this place.

"I love this place." Sloane smiles. "This campus just feels so free."

"Free?" I raise an eyebrow. "Interesting word choice."

"Yes, *free*. No parents, no curfews, no prior engagements—aside from class, of course. Free."

"Free," I singsong. Realizing that the word *free* could mean different things to her and me. Yet I have to agree with her. Here, I do feel free.

A truck I instantly recognize as Cole's comes roaring up beside us with Knox hanging out the window, his hat on backward.

"Hellooo, ladies." Knox whistles.

Sloane gives him a small wave and giggles.

Cole tips his chin up at the iced coffee in my hand. "What? Giving up the Diet Coke for the harder stuff?"

Up until a few months ago, I had never even tried iced coffee. Or any coffee at all. I was Diet Coke all day, every day. But now that I've indulged in this sweet goodness, I don't think I'll ever give it up.

"Oh, please," I scoff. "Diet Coke is the crack of my life. I'll never give that shit up. But this"—I hold my cup up—"I've discovered is pretty damn good too."

"I see," he drawls. He leans forward on his steering wheel, his muscles rippling against his shirt, making my mouth water.

"You beautiful ladies need a ride?" Knox asks, his eyes never leaving Sloane. "Maybe hang out a bit?"

I don't miss the glare he receives from Cole. He never did like anyone else calling me beautiful. Seems as though not much has changed when it comes to that.

"We're good," I call back before looking at Sloane. "Shit, I'm so sorry. I didn't even ask you if you wanted to go. Do you, uh, want to go with them?" I ask her in a hushed voice.

Tucking her blonde hair behind her ear, she glances over at the stopped truck. "Sort of, but if you don't want to, we totally don't have to. It's okay either way. We can just go home. I'm fi—"

"Stop rambling," I tease her. "You always act like I'm going to bite your head off." I regret the words as soon as they come out. I pat her arm. "If you want to go, we'll go. It's cool."

"Really?" she hush-squeals.

"Really, really," I answer, trying to sound more enthused than I am. I fail miserably. Luckily, she doesn't seem to notice.

The truth is, I'd love to hang out with Cole again. But there's one part of me that feels pain just by being around him. The floodgates open, and bam, in come the memories. Memories that I can't talk about with him, and I suck at keeping secrets.

Then, there's the other part of me that knows how easy it would be to fall back into the same old thing with him.

It's a lose-lose situation.

"So, what's it going to be, ladies?" Knox says, his eyes fixed on Sloane.

Sloane shrugs shyly before walking toward the truck. "Guess we're going to take you up on that."

Following her to the truck, we climb into the backseat.

Even though I rode in his truck the other night, it was dark, and I didn't get to see how fancy it really is. With stitched black leather and TVs in the headrests of the truck, this thing is insane. We never could have even dreamed up this type of shit, growing up the way that we did. And here he is, living it.

I feel a twang of jealousy in my gut. But not because I'm jealous of him having nice things—that isn't it at all. It actually makes me happy that he does because I know how much he deserves it for all he's been through. I'm jealous because it's no longer him and me against the world. He has a family. And I don't. Cole was my family. Key word: *was*.

But he deserves all the luxuries life has to offer. What I didn't realize was how much it would hurt, recognizing that just because life stopped for me didn't mean it stopped for him. Actually, quite the opposite, it seems. I was clawing my way out of hell while he's been living the high life. I can't help but wonder if he even noticed I was gone. I know that's me being crazy though. Because I know he loved me. Yet seeing his new life leaves an ache deep inside my gut.

"You're awfully quiet back there, *Allycat*," Cole says while flicking his eyes to mine in the mirror.

"Just taking in your new lifestyle—that's all," I murmur. "This truck is ridiculous."

"You be a good girl, and I'll even let you drive it." He winks.

"Gee, thanks," I mutter before staring out the window as we pass by the campus's large brick buildings.

I don't know when I'll ever stop having this feeling of resentment when I look at him. I wish I could stop it. Sure, the other feelings and attraction are all still there too. But when it comes down to it all, I'm pissed at him. I thought he'd find a way to get to me. I *needed* him. I still do.

These thoughts didn't start all at once. The day I was forced to leave Charlotte's Falls, he wasn't around. And all I wanted to do was get to him. When I was packed up on that bus at the age of seventeen, I wanted more than anything to tell him I wasn't leaving by choice. And beg him to save me.

But the longer I sat with the reality of what had happened to me, the more the anger slowly sprouted, growing with each day that passed that he didn't come find me. I'd sworn he would. He was the only one who could help me. But he was apparently at his new family's house in Florida.

"You two want to come over and watch a movie?" Knox asks, directing his words mainly to Sloane.

She glances at me, so I mouth, *Up to you.*

It's funny. Cole's never been a big movie watcher. He'd watch some comedies I forced him to see, but he'd bitch the entire time. He's always had a hard time with just staying still for very long. He always needs to be on the go. We'd go on jogs or to the gym, where he'd work out and I'd ogle his body, and sometimes, we'd just have sex to fill the quiet. He just wasn't comfortable with being still. Me? The still is where I find serenity. I need that quietness sometimes.

"Sure. That sounds nice," she tells him.

We're going to watch a movie with Cole and Knox.

What could possibly go wrong?

XO

Not long after getting to the guys' dorm, Knox and Sloane go to his room. Because he has one ... you know, a room. Of his own.

Dick.

The dorms athletes get are much nicer and a helluva lot bigger than the dinky ones us normal college kids get.

Following Cole into his own room, I gaze around at the way-larger-than-mine room he has—again, to himself!

I can't help but notice the new clothes and new items that he never had before. If my heart wasn't beating the way it does only for him, I'd swear we were perfect strangers who had never met.

"So"—I clear my throat awkwardly—"is it just you and chatterbox Knox who live here? Because I'll be honest—this is bullshit. Our dorm room is a fraction of this size."

He watches me, his eyes awakening every inch of my skin, making me somehow feel self-conscious at his gaze. "No, Weston lives here too."

"The third guy from Lenny's the night you came in and were a dick?"

"That's the one," he says back curtly.

"Where is he now?" I ask curiously.

He wasn't at the movies either.

"Fuck if I know. He takes off sometimes and doesn't say where he goes." He walks over to the window, his voice low. "You want to go for a walk instead?" Cole says, leaning against the doorframe.

"You still can't sit still for five minutes?" I tease him to lighten the mood before sitting down on his black leather couch.

"I mean, I guess I could. Or you could let me fuck you. Just for old times' sake. Then, I wouldn't *have* to sit still." he bites back, the words holding some sort of anger and pain in them.

His words bring something inside of me to life that's been dead since the day I had to leave. The ache for him grows inside of me. I think of how nice it would be to just feel close to him again. But I can't just let him have sex with me. That would be pathetic. Wouldn't it? Then again, it's been a *long* time. I could use it too.

Jesus, I'm an idiot. A horny idiot. I need to get my shit together.

Reading my thoughts, he sits next to me. "Fine," he says. "We can watch a movie. But first, we're talking."

At those words, I jump up and head toward the door. "A walk sounds good. Let's walk."

I know, eventually, we're going to have to talk. But not yet. I'm not ready yet.

He gives me a satisfied grin and pushes himself to stand, following me out the door.

Once we're outside, we start walking down the sidewalk. I don't miss the other students walking by, all trying to get his attention. Guys nodding their chins up, fist bumps. Bitches pushing their titties up so far that I'm surprised they don't strangle themselves. I roll my eyes. I miss when it was just him and me. I miss when he was my Storm and not everyone else's. Now, he's not mine at all. He belongs to this new world, where everyone wants to be his friend.

"You keep rolling your eyes, and they are going to get stuck like that," he drawls. "Didn't anyone ever tell you that?"

I sigh, nervously running my fingers through my hair. "You're a big star now, *Storm*." I put emphasis on his nickname. "Why are you wasting your time, hanging out with a nobody like me?"

"Why did you leave? Or are we going to just keep avoiding that?" he says, completely ignoring my question.

I look down at my feet. I can't tell him the truth. Something about saying it out loud seems so impossible.

"I wanted more for you. I knew without me around, tying you down, you'd get your happily ever after. And a good family," I lie through my teeth. Knowing each time that I don't tell the truth, I'm only digging myself further into a grave. I hate lying to him. Up until now, we were always so honest with each other. "I didn't want you to have to worry about me anymore. You deserve to live your own life. I know I'm dead weight," I explain, glancing back up at his stormy-blue eyes. They swirl with so many emotions; it's hard to even dissect what he's really feeling right now, looking at me.

Getting an inch from my face, he narrows his eyes. "That wasn't the fucking plan, Ally. The plan was to stay together as long as we could and then go to college in Texas. Together."

"So, why not Texas? It's still there. Why are you here? Did you know I'd be here?" Part of me hopes he'll say yes. That he came here for me and only me.

A blanket of frustration covers his face. "I just decided to come here. Besides, it was you who went and fucked up everything. Tell me, for what, Ally? What was so important that you had to cut me off the way that you did?"

I shrug. Trying to play it off as nothing. "I told you, I … I wanted more for you."

The home we were in wasn't with the sweet foster parents that you might dream about. Though I'm sure they do exist, but I just wasn't graced with them. We were in a home where they were at their max capacity for children allowed. Not because they loved children, but because each child they housed meant a bigger monthly check from the state coming to their mailbox. That's how the system is though—broken. Technically, the court could have ruled that it was in Cole's best interest to go with one of the many adoptive families that showed interest, but once he was a dick to the couples, they almost never came back.

Until the family he has now, apparently.

Then again, they are as slimy as our foster parents. After all, I know they offered cash just to be chosen to adopt Cole. I learned that the day I left Charlotte's Falls. And I'm sure his athletic abilities played a huge role in their interest in him.

I can sing, and I can write lyrics, but my talent wasn't broadcasted. So, to families looking to adopt, I was just a rebellious teenage girl, who already had a handful of angry tattoos. And that screams trouble to anybody. They could look at my file and read all about how fucked up my entire life had been. All of the times social workers came into my home and took me away from my mom, only to give me back a month later. That's what happened though. She'd lose me, and she wouldn't really care. But then she'd fight for me back, perhaps attend a few therapy sessions, proving she was doing well, and bam, I'd be back to living with the devil before sundown.

They'd also see notes from the school, showing how many absences I'd had. Absences from when I was just a kid, alone in my mom's shitty, run-down trailer. She was either passed out from dope or on a bender for days at a time, forgetting completely that she had a young child at home. It was all there for them to see in that manila folder.

Once, when I was seven, I dared to walk to school alone one day. My mom hadn't been home for a few days, and all I wanted was a hot meal at school. The hot meals that the other kids called gross.

My mom had been too fucked up to get groceries, much less make dinner. But as I headed to school, a walk I swore wouldn't take me more than an hour, I got lost. Very fucking lost.

I remember wondering, *If I don't find the school, will I be lost forever?*

I now understand how ludicrous that is. After all, the school would have eventually noticed I wasn't there. But when you're seven, you don't think about things like that.

Eight hours later, I was found, passed out on a sidewalk. I had become so hungry and dehydrated that my body literally shut itself down.

Yeah, they got the chance to read all of those lovely notes. Who would read about how damaged a child was and say, *Hey! Sign me up for that one?* Nobody.

Cole's file was just as sad and thick as mine was. But unlike me, he had football skills that college recruiters were traveling across the country to witness. It was easy to see that boy was going places. Me? I sang the national anthem at all the high school games, and that was about it. Who would want me?

As he eyes me cautiously, his jaw tenses. "Was your family worth it? The one you left me for?" He steps away from me and begins walking.

I swallow the lump in my throat. "It was. They were great," I squeak.

Yeah, right. What family? There was never one. But I can't tell him that. If he knew the truth, he would never look at me the same. *We* would never be the same. The shame I hold inside about the truth, it's unbearable at times. I can't burden Cole with that. He carries so much of his own shit.

He stops walking yet again and steps closer to me, grabbing my hand. He tilts my chin up with his thumb, his eyes burning into mine. "I know you're hiding something. And I promise you, I will find out what it is. I always do."

I know he will. He has a way of finding everything.

Shaking my head softly, I keep my stoic face intact. "There's nothing to find, Storm. Give it up."

"To the rest of the world, you might have a poker face. A damn good one at that. But not to me, Ally. I can read you like a fucking book," he says dryly, releasing my hand and pushing me away in the same movement.

"So, what about you?" I say, changing the subject, looking down at my feet. "How's your new family? What are they like?"

He's quiet for a few seconds before he starts to walk again. "They are fine. Better than Marion and Dave," he answers honestly, referring to our foster parents.

"Wouldn't take much." I snort.

"I know they only adopted me because of football. But I figured, what the hell? I had nothing left anyway."

That stings. I know he's referring to how I walked out, leaving him with nothing. The truth is, without me doing that, he wouldn't be in college, wouldn't be driving that fancy truck, and he sure as shit wouldn't have ever had a future in football. Everything I did, I did because I loved him. Correction: *love* him.

"Tell me more about them. What are their names? What do they do?"

"Jenn and Matt Hansom." Stuffing his hands in his pockets, he glances at me before continuing, "She's a schoolteacher. He's a coach. Wanted to play pro ball, but an injury took him out."

"Football?" I ask.

He nods. "Yep. Now, I suppose he needs me to get him into the NFL world so that he can live vicariously through me or some shit."

"You don't know that," I say, giving him a pointed look. "They could have wanted you for a lot of other reasons besides that arm of yours," I tell him to make him feel better. Though I know it isn't the truth.

"You're different, Ally. I don't know what the fuck happened, but something did. You barely look me in the eyes anymore when we talk."

"You're an idiot. I'm the same," I say, shaking my head. I walk faster in front of him.

His large hands grip my waist, and he holds me in place. Fingertips digging into my skin, making me come alive at his touch.

"Cut the shit," I hiss, attempting to get away from him. Though it would be so easy to melt at his feet in a damn puddle.

In this moment, I thank the dear Lord that the sun is going down and that hardly anyone is around campus.

Pulling my back against his chest, his mouth near my ear, he growls, causing my whole body to shiver, "Baby, you should know by now that pushing me away only makes me want you that much more." I feel his hard erection press against my ass. "Feel that?" he says roughly. "That's what you do to me when you act up. I've been patient with you, but my patience is wearing thin. Fast."

Having him this close again—his scent in my nose, intoxicating my brain, and his hardness reminding me of all that I've missed—it would be so easy to just give it up to him right now and to fall back into our old ways. This man, he was my safe place, my best friend, and the one who helped me through my shit for such a long time. But I have secrets now, and I'm not the same girl I was when I left the Falls.

"Fuck off," I hiss like a rabid cat.

Picking my feet up off of the pavement, he walks us between two buildings before setting me down.

Spinning around, I step into his space. "You cannot just fucking manhandle me anytime you damn well please! Goddamn it, Cole!"

With hooded eyes, he sneers with amusement. "Oh, I can, baby girl, and I will. I'd fuck you right against this building if I needed to."

I control the shiver that runs up my spine. "I don't give a shit if being campus royalty has gone to your head. You need to get out of here with this ... this ... big-dick energy," I bark, jabbing him in the chest with my finger.

This only causes him to chuckle, which I find absolutely infuriating. "Allycat, you and I both know if I have big-dick energy, it is in fact because I have a big dick." He tsks me. "And I'm certain that you remember just how big my di—"

Holding my hand up, I stop him before he can say any more filthy words that make my heart race. I swear if I hear him use dirty words anymore, I'll end up having sex with him against this building.

A smirk creeps onto my face. I can't help myself but to have a little fun with this. "Well, *babe*, I've seen bigger," I lie.

He's the only guy I've ever been with, but I'm still annoyed with the events at the movie theater, so I'm being childish.

His face instantly turns to stone, and his eyes darken to almost black. "Glad we parted when we did then. Since you clearly became nothing but a whore. Just like the rest of them."

My palm connects with his cheek before I can stop myself. "Fuck you, asshole," I say through gritted teeth, and my nostrils flare. "Don't you dare speak to me like that. You might have forgotten that I don't put up with that shit, so let me remind you real quick." The anger flows through my veins. "I don't give a fuck who you are on this campus. At the end of the day, under that uniform, you're no better than I am. So, you can go ahead and fuck yourself."

His grip tightens on my wrist for a few moments, and his fingertips dig into my skin. His chest heaves with anger, and his eyes are now damn near black.

Finally, he releases it, and I turn and walk—no, run back to my dorm. Only stopping long enough to text Sloane to let her know I left.

Things will never be the same between Cole Storms and me. We both hold on to vile things that go by the names of resentment, anger, and distrust.

He looks at me as the one person he had until he didn't. He thinks I dropped him like an old, worn pair of shoes I no longer wanted. And I look at him as a painful reminder that nobody has ever protected me from the monsters that lurk. Even he couldn't protect me, and for that, I'm fucking mad.

I don't see how we could ever get over those feelings. Then again, I don't know how we could ever get over the other feelings either. The ones that go by the names of love, passion, and desire. Because honestly, I just don't see a universe existing where I don't feel all of those things for Cole Storms.

And to be real, I don't think I want to.

thirteen

COLE

"My man." Weston slaps me on the back. "Nice fucking work out there."

"You too, brother." I grin.

Three games down, three games won. The season is looking promising, and our team is finally working like a well-oiled machine.

The first game started rough. The guys didn't exactly welcome me with open arms. But I think Knox helped them see the bigger picture—our football careers. Once he reminded them of that, they finally got their fingers out of their asses and started working with me, not against me.

Ricky quit after the first game. And for that, I do feel bad. But he chose to walk out on his team, and that's on him. If I ever got injured, he would have been the one to come in for me, and he deserted us. I lost a lot of respect for him because of that.

Sure, I can be a cocky motherfucker, no doubt. But I know without the team, I'd be nothing. The first game when the defensemen didn't protect me was a prime example of that. We all need each other. It's corny to say, but there really is no *I* in *team*.

The one good thing about Ricky quitting is, the rest of the team now treats me as one of them on and off the field. We need to bond in order to be the best. Whether it's running together, eating meals together, or working out together, it all strengthens the crucial bond we need to have. And now that he's out of the picture, they can kick it with me, guilt-free.

I turn the shower on as hot as it will go, and my aching muscles appreciate the scorching water as it pelts off of my skin. I love this game, but fuck, is it hard on the body.

I noticed Ally and her friend weren't in their usual seats. Knox and the blonde chick, Sloane, haven't been spending much time together since a few weeks ago. The same night they came over for a movie and it ended with Ally running away from me. Good times.

And I haven't seen or heard from Ally since then either.

Not that I can blame her. I called her a whore. The fuck was I thinking? I'm actually shocked she only slapped me. I fully expected a punch, possibly a knee to the nuts. I would have taken it too. I'm not the type to disrespect a woman by calling her names. But that's what losing her has turned me into. A complete dick, apparently.

The old Ally, the one I knew before, she would have decked me without hesitation. But now, she's timid. She doesn't look at me the way she did back then either. Hell, she barely looks at me at all. I don't understand it.

I know we will end up together. There is no other person on this earth that I want. And there is no other man in the world that I would ever allow her to get close to. Fuck that. She belongs with me. She'll come back to me. I know she will.

I remember the day she showed up in Charlotte's Falls. Long, dark hair with blue eyes—that, at the time, were almost too big for her face—scrawny-ass chicken legs, and a damn grungy AC/DC shirt. Oh, and bright blue Chucks that were definitely thrift-shop shoes. Yet she was the coolest twelve-year-old girl around town.

I had gone through my life completely numb. Until her. Once she came into my life, I laughed again, smiled again. Hell, even felt again. She was—and still is—the only person I ever spoke to about finding my dad, overdosed. She had found her mom the same way. Only worse for her, she'd found her mother on her birthday. In some tragic, fucked up way, it united us. No matter how poisonous and awful this world was, we had each other. Until she upped and left.

That's what made it so much worse than your typical high school breakup. The other kids splitting up, they had family; they had friends. We had nobody outside of each other. Sure, kids at Charlotte's Falls kissed my ass because I could throw a damn ball. But those kids were *not* my friends.

My arm is my lifeline to making it to the NFL. Yet, the night she left, if someone had said I could lose my arm and never play ball again just to keep her, I would have told them to cut the fucking thing off right then and there. I might need my arm to throw, but I needed her to feel.

The leaving for another family—I could have forgiven her for that. After all, it is ultimately up to a judge whether we go or stay. But to change her cell phone number, delete all social media, and literally disappear is unforgivable.

Or it would be to anybody else, that is. I know I forgave her the second I laid eyes on her at the movie theater. The second I pushed her up against a building and felt her body come alive, well, that was when I knew I needed her back.

But first, I need to find out where in the fuck she's been all this time.

Turning the shower off, I reach out and grab my towel. Wrapping it around my waist, I step out and gaze around the locker room, realizing over half of the team has already left.

How long of a shower did I take?

I must have gotten lost in my thoughts. It isn't hard to do.

Throwing my clothes on, I see Knox is sitting on the bench, looking at his phone, grinning.

"The fuck you so happy about?" I toss at him.

Glancing up at me, he leans back and smirks. "We've got us a party tonight—that's what."

"Where?" I ask, pulling on my sneakers.

"The baseball house. Nolan just texted."

"Dude, I swear you have the numbers of everyone on the entire campus," Weston gripes.

Standing up, Knox swings his arm around Weston's neck and messes his hair up. "Don't be jealous, big boy. You and Stormy are my BFFs fo' liiife."

"Get off of me, you fucking weirdo," Weston grumbles, but he can't stop himself from laughing.

Knox is just one of those guys. You can't help but love him. He's a funny motherfucker, even at his own expense.

He comes over and tries to pull the same shit on me, but I shove him off of me and shake my head and laugh.

"You're an idiot."

Looking at his phone again, he nods. "Yep, I'll agree with you there. But this idiot is headed to a party and to find some tail."

Slinging the strap of my duffel bag over my shoulder, I cock my head up. "What, no more Blondie?"

"Sloane? Nah, I'm all good there. Too much fucking work," he says, but it sounds forced.

I think Knox had some real interest in that chick. I hope I didn't fuck it up for him with my disagreement with Ally. That would make me feel like a dick.

"Knox, be straight with me. Did I fuck it up for you?"

His eyebrows pull together slightly. "Fuck what up for me?"

"Things with you and Blondie. Did my shit with Ally get in the way of you and her?"

He smiles and shakes his head. "Nah, man. Nothing like that. It's just too hard to keep up with a chick. Besides, we've got football to focus on. As freshmen, we all have a lot to prove. I'm not trying to show up here and tie myself down to dinner dates and Lifetime movie marathons with some girl. I'm here to play ball."

I don't need a distraction either. But honestly, Ally's never been that to me. She's always helped to keep me focused. The time we were apart, football lost some of its shine to me. I missed knowing she was in the stands. I missed her watching me work out or seeing her doing her homework on the bleachers while I had practice. I missed all of that. I'd never had family in the stands under the Friday night lights. But after I met Ally, she was the one who always showed up and cheered me on. She was the one in high school who drew my last name and jersey number on her T-shirt.

I fight back a grin at the memory of her voice screaming for me during the games. No matter how loud the stadium got, I always heard her above everyone else.

As much as I want to see Ally, I probably should at least attempt to give her some space. So, even though I'm not in the mood to go to this party and be around a bunch of annoying-as-fuck college kids, who are no doubt going to invade my space and pop my bubble, I could use the distraction.

Besides, I'm here at Brooks University. I might as well play the part. Even if the part isn't who I really am. Because I'm a fucking fraud.

fourteen

ALLY

"Sweetie, you can head home. I've got it here. It's Saturday night, and you're a college kid, so get your ass out of here and act like it," Carla tells me as she starts a new pot of coffee.

"Nah, it's okay. If anyone should leave, it should be you. You can go home and hang out with your boys." Wrinkling my nose up, I frown. "Besides, I don't have much interest in the college night life."

I'm not lying; I really don't. Making money sounds much more appealing. The secondhand laptop I bought is on its last leg, so I'm saving to buy a new one, and that shit isn't cheap.

She laughs and shakes her head. "Look, love, I'm aware you don't have teenage boys, much less three of them, but let me tell you, they are fucking exhausting. And sometimes plain ol' gross." She presses a hand to her forehead. "I'm good to stay here. *This* is my break. I can go out back and smoke a cigarette if I want to and drink coffee in between working. All is good." When I don't say anything back, she widens her eyes. "For real, weekend nights here have been slow. We all know everyone's over at the pub down the road."

"I can hear you!" Lenny calls from the kitchen. "My food is way better than the crap they serve at that shithole!"

Looking at me, she rolls her eyes. "I agree with you, sweet thing," she calls back to him. "But that doesn't change the fact that I'm still right. Miss Ally here needs to go be young and free. She's been working five shifts a week *and* attending college." She puts her hand on my shoulder. "I just don't know how you do it, sweetheart. You're going to burn yourself out." She widens her eyes. "Or worse, give that pretty face of yours wrinkles," her Southern accent drawls.

Pushing through the swinging door, Lenny wipes his hands on his apron. "She's right. Maybe you are working too much, Al. We can hire another waitress. That way, you'd have more da—"

"Fuck no," I cut him off mid-sentence. "I don't need any more days off. I like to work. I *need* to work."

Eyeing me cautiously, he finally nods. "All right, you'll keep your shifts. But not tonight. Tonight, you're headed home for the evening. Or to party or whatever the hell you kids do these days. I'll see you bright and early tomorrow for the breakfast shift."

"I can stay," I say, glancing between the pair of them. "I really don't mind."

"Go have fun. Go to a party. Wear a tight dress and show off that sexy body." She frowns. "I know I wish I could," she whispers the last part under her breath.

"Fiiine," I huff out. "If you insist. But if it gets busy and—"

"It won't get busy. We'll be lucky to have another customer the rest of the night. Everyone is at King's Pub," Carla says, examining her painted nails. "It's the new place to be these days."

Lenny puffs out a breath and stalks back into the kitchen, pushing the swinging door rather aggressively.

"Too much?" Carla says, looking up at me.

Stifling a laugh, I nod. "Yes. Way too much. Lenny hates King's Pub. You know this."

She does know this, but that's just how she is. She's like Becky in *Waitress*—aside from the fact that she is not sleeping with the cook. Because the cook is Lenny, and that would be gross.

"Well, he can hate it all he wants, but they are still the ones who get every ounce of business on weekend nights," she answers in a hushed tone.

Gathering my things up, I nod. "Yeah, well, that might be true, but we still get the most for breakfast and lunch."

My apron pocket was full before eleven a.m. this morning. We were packed.

"Yeah, yeah. Have a good night, girlie. See you tomorrow," she says before blowing me a kiss.

Once outside, I pull my phone out, opening multiple texts from Sloane.

Sloane: I think I might go to a party at the baseball house with some girls from one of my classes.

Sloane: These girls are acting crazy. I need my BFF!

Sloane: They are also sort of bitchy and petty. Seriously, where is Allycat when I need her?

That makes me smile. I have only known her a month, yet she's calling me her best friend.

Sloane: So, don't kill me ... Cole Storms asked where you were, and I said work. He freaked out, saying something about walking home in the dark. Now, he's headed your way. Like I said, don't kill me.

Sloane: Are you mad?

Sloane: OMG, you're so mad, aren't you? ☹

Great. Just great.
The last message was sent ten minutes ago, so if I'm lucky, I have five minutes to make it back to my dorm.

Me: I'm not mad. Did he already leave?

Sloane: Yep. Don't hate me.

Sliding my phone into my pocket, I start to haul ass toward campus.

This isn't a sketchy town. It's clean, and everything is lit up at night. I know I'll be fine, making it back to my dorm safely. Now if only I could convince Cole of that.

I'm not even a quarter of the way home when I hear the roaring engine of a truck approaching. I already know it's likely Cole. Once its headlights come into view and it begins to slow, I see that I'm right—it is him.

Thank you, Sloane and your big fucking mouth.

I don't mean that. I know she didn't intentionally throw me under the bus. How could she have known he'd go all caveman and shit? She doesn't know how he is when it comes to me.

"Get in the truck, Ally," Cole's voice booms as his truck comes to a stop.

As always, he isn't asking me; he's telling me. Like I'm a goddamn child.

"Why are you here?" I call back to him. "Isn't there some big party tonight to celebrate your win?"

Sloane texted earlier, letting me know they'd won.

"Shouldn't the campus king be there, entertaining all of his admirers? Not here, stalking me, the poor peasant."

"No interest in that, Cinderella," his smooth voice purrs. "I told you I didn't want you walking home alone, but once again, you have to be a pain in my fucking ass."

"I don't have a car, dumbass!" I shout at him.

"Quit being a bitch for five seconds of your life. You know you can always fucking call me. My number has never changed. Unlike some people's."

I don't answer, just continue to watch him. Weighing my options to take off running or bow out gracefully.

"You going to get in or what?" He jerks his chin up.

The more I consider running, the more I realize that it would suck.

I'm tired, and I don't have it in me. Besides, he'll just act like a complete barbarian and chase after me. And he's much faster than I could ever dream of being.

Pulling my hood up, I cross the road and climb in the truck. Never sparing him a glance.

On the short ride home, he doesn't speak or even look at me. And I don't say a peep either. He's the one who wants to play Superman, always coming to my rescue, so he can do the talking.

I don't have a damn clue what he wants from me or if he wants anything at all. All I know is, it's hard to live my life as me when he's trying to control me and take away every ounce of independence that I have.

I know he's only doing it because he cares. Like he said, he doesn't know any other way to be with me. I believe him when he says that. I don't think he means to smother me. It's just who he is.

Amy Lee's voice flows through the speakers, singing the words to "Broken" by Seether. Somehow, I don't think it's playing just by coincidence. The words, the way their voices are so tortured and shattered—it's exactly how I know he and I both felt every single day that we spent apart.

Without him is sort of like walking around in a world full of colors and only seeing black and white. Losing him numbed me to anything and everything good in this world.

Unable to help myself, the lyrics pour out of my mouth, under my breath. I try to keep my voice as quiet as possible. Singing is my outlet. The same goes for songwriting. Getting the words out, good or bad, it's healing in a way.

Pulling in front of the dorm, he slams the truck in park.

"Thanks for the ride." I jump out before he can respond.

I'm tired. And when I'm tired, I'm bitchy. I need to get to my room and be alone, by myself, where I can't lash out and say rude things to anybody. Well, other than myself.

It's only crazy if you answer yourself too. Right?

Cole doesn't follow me, surprisingly enough. Maybe he's learning about this thing called boundaries. Though I seriously doubt it. He probably just wants to get back to the party. Bitches to see, crowds to please.

Gross.

As I push the door open and step into my dorm, all I'm thinking about is how nice a can of cold Diet Coke and a huge-ass bag of Cheetos sound. *Wild Saturday night.* First things first though. I need to change into comfy pajamas.

I smile at the thought of what Carla would say. She'd tell me I was wasting a perfectly good Saturday night. But I'm tired. Working and classes are starting to wear on me. I need a night to regroup.

I've just changed into my pajamas when there's a knock at the door. Knowing that Sloane is at a party and that Cole just dropped me off, I wonder who in the actual fuck is outside my door, my heartbeat speeding up slightly.

"Open up, Ally," Cole's deep voice says, answering my thoughts for me.

I contemplate not going to the door. Why should I let him in? He'll probably get all up in my personal space, and I'll momentarily want to dry-hump his leg like a dog in heat, all because he smells and looks so damn good. Then, I'll be left feeling like an idiot, and he'll probably still be wearing that cocky-ass grin on his hot-as-fuck face.

"Ally! Open the fucking door!" he growls. No doubt causing a scene in the hallway.

Such a prick.

Walking over, I swing it open. "What do you want, Storm? I'm tired."

His eyes rake over my body, and suddenly, I remember, I'm wearing a white shirt and no bra. A tight white shirt.

Perfect.

Folding my arms over my chest, I scowl at him. "Seriously, why are you here? Did I walk from my mini fridge to my bed alone and you needed to come save the day?" I snort. "Save me from the big, bad wolf?"

Intense eyes burn into mine. "I am the wolf, sweetheart," his rough voice says slowly. "Who will save you from me?"

His words make me shudder. Embarrassingly so too. Because he notices, and a devil-like smirk creeps onto his face.

I gulp. "Okay, wolf. A-wooooooo." I pretend to howl. "Why the fuck are you here? At my dorm. Right now, interrupting Netflix and Cheetos."

"And Diet Coke?" he says, amused.

"Well, duh."

Ignoring my previous question, he steps around me and comes inside. Uninvited.

"Excuse me! What in the hell are you doing, dipshit?" I curse at him. "This is my dorm! Not yours!"

Gazing around, he spins his ball cap backward, making himself even more annoyingly hot. "I've been thinking, and I've decided something."

"You … thinking?" I widen my eyes. "Sounds dangerous. How did your brain not explode?"

"I've decided, I'm done playing games, Ally," he says, ignoring my banter.

"Well, you're a football player, so games are sort of part of the job."

"Okay, smart-ass, let me clarify. I'm done playing *your* games."

"Ooh, I'm so scared. I'm just shaking over here, 'bout to piss my pants."

Finally, he's reached his limit for my need to beat around the bush. I can't help it; that bush has monsters living in it, and it's untamable. Once you start to pick it apart, everything comes out. Leaving you wishing you'd left it the hell alone.

Trust me, you don't want to fuck with that bush.

"Enough deflecting," he growls. "I want to know why the fuck you left Charlotte's Falls. I'm not leaving till I know the answer."

I know better than to think he's bluffing. If Cole wants to know something, he'll stop short of nothing to find his answer.

"I'm tired of going round and round about this. The universe played some sick fucking trick by landing us both here, in Georgia. But this campus is huge. You do your thing, and I'll do mine," I yell at him. I don't mean the ridiculous words. But I am not ready to talk about the past.

In a split second, my ass is pushed up against the wall as Cole's huge arms box me in at both sides. His eyes command me to look into them. Something I've tried to avoid since we reconnected.

"Look. At. Me," he demands through gritted teeth.

I try, but the tears burn the backs of my eyes, threatening to come out. Tears I've worked so hard to keep inside. I'm not ready for them to spill out now. Then, *he* will win.

"Cole, please stop. I'm …" My voice breaks slightly. "I'm begging you."

The tears fall—oh, do they fall. Tears that have been bottled up inside for far too long. But that's what he can do to me—he has the ability to break me down, brick by brick.

Taking his hand, he tilts my chin up. "Please, Ally. Please look at me. I don't know what I did or what I didn't do. But I need you to look at me. Look at me like you used to." His voice is much softer now.

I do as I was told. But it only makes the pain worse. "I am."

"You're not." He flinches. "Not really anyway. Not like you did before."

That's because I was a different person then.

"I can't. Please, Cole. Stop," I plead.

His forehead leans against mine, and our hearts beat together as one. And I swear, it feels like the first time my heart has beat inside my chest since I left him.

"I can't fix it if I don't know what it is, Ally," he says, his voice filled with frustration. "Let me fucking fix it."

Bending down, I sob into his chest. Something I haven't allowed myself to do in months. Still, I can't stop the tears from falling. "Don't you get it, Cole?" I snap. "You *can't* fix me this time."

"Why not?!" He's quiet for a moment. "Did something happen while I was away at football camp? Is that why you left?"

"No," I lie, fiercely shaking my head.

Something did happen. Something pretty crappy. But it's my secret to keep.

Cupping my cheeks with his hands, he forces my eyes to his. "You don't have to lie, Ally. Not to me, not ever. I've got you. Always."

"Do you now?" I say, pushing him away from me and ducking underneath his arm. "Because it hasn't seemed like it. And to think, I've waited for *you* all this time. Not so much as sparing a glance at another guy."

His hands grab my waist, turning me to face him again. "But you said—"

I know what he's going to say—how I mentioned I'd seen way bigger dicks than his.

"I lied," I admit, cutting him off. "I can be a bitch. We both know this."

He eyes me cautiously. "You really haven't been with anyone else?"

I look down for a second before back up at him. "No. Just you." I laugh bitterly. "Wish you could say the same, playboy."

Relief covers his face. Pinching the bridge of his nose, he shakes his head. "I haven't been with anyone else either, Al."

"Wait, what? What about the girl at the—"

He grimaces. "I wanted to hurt you. So, I took her in the restroom. I even told her why I was doing it."

I'm confused and a little irritated that he lied. But mostly, I'm just relieved. We were each other's first. I thought we would be each other's only. When I thought he had been with that girl, well, it felt like everything was ruined.

"So, you did nothing with her? Nothing at all?" I question him.

He shakes his head once. "Nothing."

"No blow job? She didn't touch your dick? You didn't finger her or—"

"Ally, Jesus, no. Nothing means nothing. She knew I was using her to piss you off. She tried to talk me into fucking her when we got into the restroom. I said no. That was that."

"Okay then ..." I say awkwardly.

His lips form a grin. "I know one thing though."

"What's that?" I ask.

"You just admitted you can be a bitch. At least we can agree on that." He tries to keep a straight face.

I roll my eyes and flick him off. "Oh, fuck right off. You can be a dick too." I pause. "No, you are *always* a dick."

"Yeah, right. I might be a dick sometimes, but we both know I made you happy." He rolls his tongue over his bottom lip. "Really fucking happy."

My insides tingle at his words. We certainly did know how to make each other happy and how to take the pain away momentarily. They can say sex isn't a good coping mechanism, but I beg to differ. Cole showed his love in so many ways while we were intimate. It was never just about the sex. It was about experiencing something with somebody you loved. Somebody you trusted.

His voice breaks me from my thoughts. "All joking aside, I know I can be a dick. But you and I both know we needed to have that toughness inside of us. Without it, we never would have survived this life."

I smile sadly, my shoulders slouching. "I'm barely surviving now," I admit.

"Everyone is barely surviving," he says quietly. "All everyone is trying to do is just survive. That's life."

Finally looking him right in the eyes, I gaze into his stormy-blue color. "Cole?"

"Yeah?"

"I'm tired of just surviving."

Pulling me to his chest, he kisses the top of my head. "I know you are. Just hang in there a little longer, angel. I'll be in the NFL, and you'll be one of the country's most famous singer-slash-songwriters."

"I hope so." *I just don't know if you'll be next to me.*

It isn't about the fame for me. Not in the way it is for Cole anyway.

He'd never say it out loud, but he wants his name known because he wants his mother and all the others who left him to realize how much they missed out on. I know that's a huge part of his need to be the best.

For me, I just want to help other people who feel the same way I do. Or who hurt the way I've hurt. Music has saved my life time and time again. The lyrics quiet my mind, reminding me that I'm not alone in the struggles I've had and that I'm not the only one whose been dealt a shitty hand. I want to write a song expressing all of the pain that lives inside of my soul. Buried so deep that I'm not sure I'll ever fully cleanse myself of it. And truthfully, if one person listens to those words and they realize they aren't alone, well, then I will have done what I set out to do.

"I'll be here whenever you're ready to talk to me." His deep voice vibrates against my ear.

"Okay," I croak out. Knowing his words to be true.

No matter what, I know this boy—no, this man will always be here for me.

"You should get going. It's late," I say softly.

I'm tired, and as much love as I have for this man, I'm not ready to be with someone I have to share with the entire campus. It feels so different.

"Yeah, I guess I probably should," he says, but his eyes move to my lips, and he shows no sign of leaving.

I can tell he wants to kiss me. And I don't think I'd even try to stop him if he did.

Reaching out, he tucks a strand of hair behind my ear before gliding his thumb down my cheek. Stopping at my mouth, he rubs the pad of it against my lips. His touch causes a shiver to run down my body.

"Cole," I moan, succumbing to him like an ice cube being melted by the sun.

"Ally," his voice rasps.

Dipping his head down, he slowly runs his lips up my neck, breathing me in. Before finally pressing them to my own.

It's been too long since I've felt the softness of his lips against mine. How they fit perfectly with mine. Almost like they were made just for me to kiss. Somehow, it feels that way.

Greedily, my mouth opens, welcoming him inside.

His tongue slips into my mouth, and shit, I feel dizzy. I've missed him so much. So fucking much.

I know I haven't given him jack shit when it comes to information about me or where I've been all this time. And yeah, I suppose I have been a bit hard on him as well. I'd say something like, *I can't help it; it's just the way I am,* or shit like that, but those would just be excuses.

So, maybe I don't deserve this from him right now. But I'm going to take it anyway. Because I need him. And I think he needs me too. He's the only one who can make me feel something, anything, even if only for just a short time.

I might not be ready to give him what he needs from me. But I am sure about one thing: I need him inside of me.

Right now.

XO

COLE

I pull back and look down at her. My girl. My angel. My addiction.

If she were a drug, I'd shoot her straight into my veins. If she were a shot, I'd toss her back with ease and let her burn the whole way down. And if she were a smoke, I'd inhale her slowly, letting her reach every single part of my body before exhaling.

I. Can't. Get. Enough.

The way she's looking at me, I know exactly what she wants. But the problem is, I don't want to just fuck Ally. I want her to talk to me. I want to know what she's hiding. Shit, what I want is for us to go back to the way it used to be—when I was her everything.

She won't give me an inch, yet right now, she wants me to give her a mile.

Fearlessly pulling her shirt over her head, she throws it on the floor. Exposing her full, creamy tits. I haven't seen those beautiful works of art in too damn long. My dick strains against my zipper, just at the sight.

How the fuck is a man going to say no to that?

She's so bold and fearless with me. Letting me see her this way, just like old times.

She knows what she's doing, tempting me like this. She knows I could never tell her no. I'm a strong man but not *that* strong. Even the great Achilles had a weakness.

I take in her body. Her perfect, goddess-looking body. Her ass and thighs are still slightly curvy. Her stomach still toned and flat and her tits still more than enough for me. I've jerked off more times than I'd ever care to admit to this image right here. And now, she's mine for the taking.

Reaching down, I cup her in the spot she needs me the most. "Why should I give you what you want, Ally?" I question her, narrowing my eyes.

"Because you want it too—that's why," she answers matter-of-factly.

Of course I want it. I'd be a blind fool not to. The question is, is it the right thing to do? Especially when I want more. So much more.

Strumming my fingers on my chin, I think about it. I do want it. I want it with everything I am. It's not enough for me though. But it's a good fucking start.

Pressing her against the wall, I start by cupping her cheek and then move to her sexy neck, soon gliding my hand down to her breast. Her breathing intensifies the further down I get. Right to that perfect fucking place between her legs.

"You piss me off," I murmur into her ear. "I don't like being kept at arm's length."

"You piss me off more," she hisses back. "But I need you. Right now." Her voice is filled with pure desperation.

"You need me to fuck you? Is that it, Ally?" I want her to want it. But I also want her to want the rest of me too. "You need me inside of you?"

Biting down on her bottom lip, she nods. "So badly." She licks her lips. "But I won't beg. You know I won't."

I chuckle. No, she certainly isn't the type to beg. Never has been.

Still gazing up at me, she tilts her head. "But something tells me I won't have to."

Of course she won't have to beg. How could I deny such a beautiful mess? Especially knowing I'm the only one who can give her what she needs. Besides, she's finally looking me in the eyes right now. She's finally looking at me like she used to. Something she hasn't done since I first saw her here, at Brooks.

"One truth, Ally. One truth, and I'll give you what you need."

"Cole ..." She hesitates, but when I pull my hands away from her body, she sighs. "Fine. Fine. One. Fucking. Truth."

I nod. "Just tell me one, and I promise, I'll fuck you exactly how you like."

Glancing down at the floor, she softly shakes her head. "I didn't leave because I wanted to. And I didn't have a new family."

She might not realize it, but she actually gave me two truths. Anything that she shares with me is crucial. I want to know everything that's happened since she left.

"You've been on your own?"

She nods.

"Where?"

"One truth," she answers me.

Fair enough. I guess a deal is a deal. And she told me what I asked of her.

Pushing her thong to the side, I dip my fingers into her. Leaning my head down, I take her left nipple into my mouth. Swirling my tongue around it, causing her body to jolt.

"Yes," she pants in an incredibly sexy tone, making my dick grow harder, if that's even possible.

Tugging on my shirt, she lifts it over my head. Her eyes instantly find her signed name on the inside of my arm.

Reaching up, she runs her hand over it. "When did you get this?"

"Not long ago."

"Why?" she says softly.

Taking my hands, I push her to her knees. "If you want this, tonight isn't your turn to ask questions."

She gazes up at me, her dark hair flowing down her back, her eyes wild from being so turned on. Ready to take anything I give her. Greedy as ever.

She licks her lips before unbuttoning my pants and pulling them down. Followed by my briefs.

"Tell me what you want," she whispers, wanting me to tell her exactly what I expect her to do.

"Your lips wrapped around my cock. Now," I demand. No sweet tone in my voice, no romance.

She might be a queen who has the ability to hold my balls in a jar. But when it comes to this, I can tell she loves being dominated.

"Make up for being a traitor and leaving. And maybe then, I'll fuck you."

Her eyes burn with even more need. Moving her head forward, she runs her tongue up my length. Stopping at my head, she swirls her tongue around before pulling back and looking up at me. "Mmm … I've missed the way you taste." A small moan escapes her throat.

Gripping her hair tighter, I tilt my chin up. "And I've missed the way you suck my dick." *Fuck, her mouth feels good.*

Those blue eyes with swirls of yellow gaze up at me before she dives back in. She sucks and licks and hums. It's all too fucking much. My dick hasn't felt her mouth or her pussy in too damn long.

Jerking my hips back and forth, I fuck her mouth. And she takes as much as she can.

Pulling out of her mouth, I bring her up to stand and flip her around so that her ass is against me and her face is against the wall.

When I crash into her with no warning, she moans. Loudly.

No condom between us. Likely irresponsible. But I can't fucking help myself. I'm greedy with her, and I always will be.

Snaking my hand up around the back of her neck, I pound into her harder. "So tight. And all mine. Right, Ally?"

She doesn't answer, just moans again.

"Say it, angel," I hiss, tightening my grip on her. "Now."

"No," she answers sharply.

"No?" I growl. "What the fuck do you mean, no?" I still inside of her. "I guess you don't need this that badly then, do you?" I toy with her. Knowing how desperately she needs this.

Her head points down as she shakes it slowly. "I can't be yours anymore. Not when you're not mine." Her voice sounds defeated.

Pulling out, I flip her around. When I pick her up, she wraps her legs around my waist and puts her head against my shoulder. She's not a girl who likes to show emotion, but I absorb hers instantly.

Tipping her chin up with my thumb, I look into her big, sad eyes. "I've always been yours. I *will* always be yours. You should know that by now."

She tilts her head to the side. "Do you mean that?"

"Ally, there's no place either of us could ever go that would keep us apart." Moving my mouth to her neck, I murmur against her skin, "My soul belongs to you. Even if sometimes, I wish like hell it didn't."

I don't know whether I mean that or not. Sometimes, it probably would be easier to be free from her. With us, there is so much emotional baggage. But it's like I am a genie stuck in a bottle. My soul is a slave to hers, unable to leave. All she has to do is swipe her hand across that lamp and bam, I'll do anything she asks of me.

But on the other hand, I don't want anyone other than her. She is it for me, hands down. Even if she is a pain in my fucking ass, at the end of the day, she is the one and only thing the universe has ever gifted me.

I lay her down on the bed. Wrapping her arms around me, she drags me toward her. Silently telling me that she wants to finish what we started.

"I want nothing between us. I want to feel you and only you," I tell her, hoping she doesn't demand I use a condom.

Gazing up, she nods. "Me too. I'm protected. I have an IUD. Please, just give me you. All of you."

Not needing to be told twice, I part her legs and dive inside. Not slowly either—fuck no. I give her all of me, all at once.

Her nails feel so fucking good, digging into my back. But even she knows not to reach down to the bottom right side of my back. She was trained that way.

Her legs tighten around me, bringing us as close as we can possibly get. Yet I think we both feel like it isn't close enough.

It will never be close enough.

Buried deep inside of her is the only place I want to be in this moment. Fuck the past.

She watches me as she moans and bites her lips. She doesn't have to talk for me to know she's close. I don't have to either. We can just look into each other's eyes and know that we are both there. After waiting for all this time, neither of us can last long. But that's okay because in no time, I'll be ready to go again.

She's the only one I have ever been with. She's the only one I will ever be with. I can't even stand the thought of being with another woman who isn't Ally.

Anyone else wouldn't read my mind without hearing me speak. She and I, we get each other. We both came from the grit. Something not everybody can comprehend.

Make no mistake, just because she came from the grit doesn't make her anything less than gold.

When we finish together, it's complete and pure ecstasy. Until we both come back down and I look at her messy, dark hair and beautiful-as-sin body. And then I realize, she owns me. Again.

But who the fuck am I kidding? She never stopped.

fifteen

COLE

Feeling Ally's warm body, hearing her breathing as she lies peacefully in my arms, I feel better than I have in a long time.

I'm thankful that once her roommate knew I had stayed, she texted Ally that she was going to stay with some friends and gave us some time alone. We needed it.

My eyes grow heavy as I feel almost as light as a cloud. Sleep isn't something that typically comes easy for me. Normally, I have to run myself ragged until I am so exhausted that I can sleep. Then again, not only did I have a game tonight, but I also made love to Ally for as long as we both could stand it. It's no wonder I'm feeling so tired.

Glancing down at her, I smile and kiss the top of her head. *My angel.*

"I told you, stay in your fucking room! You little fucking shit!" my dad stumbles over the words. He's too high to form a sentence without his eyes closing as his body sways back and forth.

"Sorry, Daddy," I plead. "I just ... I just really need some water."

I haven't had anything to eat or drink in two days. I knew the risk of going out there while his friends were over, but I chose to do it anyway. And now, I'm going to pay for it.

"Hey, you guysss." My dad smiles a sick, demented smile. Showing all of the teeth he's lost since he started putting that stuff into his arm. "Want to play a game called Who Can Land a Knife the Closest to the Disrespectful Kid Without Killing Him?" He laughs a raspy smoker's laugh before grabbing me by my dirty T-shirt and throwing me against the wall.

Leaning down, he puts his nose to mine and points his bony finger. "Stand still, boy. Or you will die."

One lady tries to stop it. She comes here now and then, and she's nice to me. Sometimes, she even brings me a Nutty Bar and leaves it outside of my door. She uses the poison too. I've seen her do it. But the poison doesn't make her mean like it does to my dad.

"Ralph, no. Don't be fucking stupid," she yells to my dad, blowing smoke from her cigarette out of her mouth and into the air.

"Shut the fuck up, Vick," he yells over his shoulder as he digs knives out of the drawer.

Stepping in front of him, she tries to grab the knives. "No! I won't let—"

Grabbing her by her throat, he shoves her against the refrigerator. As he continues to squeeze, her face begins to turn blue, and her cigarette falls to the floor.

Finally, he releases her, sending her into a pile on the floor at his feet. She coughs and wheezes. I should probably go see if she's okay. That's what a good boy would do, but I'm too scared. Scared of my dad and his other friends.

He kicks her once before turning toward his mangy-looking friends. "Get her the fuck out of here. And tell her to never come back."

Her eyes are barely open, yet they find mine for a brief moment as they carry her toward the door. She mouths something. I think she says that she's sorry. But it's okay. She tried to stop my daddy. That's more than anyone else has ever done for me. Besides, she brings me Nutty Bars. Nobody has ever done that before.

Pointing the knife at me, my dad snarls, "This will teach you to hold still, you good-for-nothing sack of shit."

Positioning himself in front of me, he drives a knife up and reaches his arm back.

I'm scared. I'm so scared. I'm eight years old, and my own father is going to treat me like a human dartboard. But if I don't stand here, he might kill me. He has threatened to before.

I should be brave, not a baby. I should be a big boy and not be scared. But I don't want to die. I want to play football.

He tries to keep his eyes open, but because of the drugs, it isn't easy.

The same time the knife flies out of his hand, I turn to run away. Feeling the blade pierce the skin on the bottom right side of my back, I squeeze my eyes shut so hard that it hurts, and I pray that an angel comes to my rescue.

Maybe not today. But one day in the future.

"Cole! Cole!" Ally shakes me. "Wake up. You're okay. Shh, you're all right. It's all right."

It always takes me a few minutes to form a thought after I dream of the day my own father tried to kill me. This is a dream I typically have once or twice a month. Ally is used to it though. She's been around long enough to know these nightmares are something I deal with.

She knows how I got my scar and who gave it to me. That's why she never touches me there. But she also knows that the memory of it isn't something I want to revisit often. So, she never pushes me to talk about it.

We both have dark parts of our childhood that we like to keep buried. We unveil secrets when they are weighing us down, yet we also understand that some things are too painful to say out loud. Even so, we hold on to each other during the times when our monsters come back to haunt us. That's what makes our relationship so sacred.

"I'm all right," I tell her before pulling her on top of me. "I'm all right now."

Pressing her forehead to mine, she sighs. "Is there anything I can do?"

I shake my head once. "Just be here with me. That's enough to help."

Throwing her arms around me, her tiny body hugs me as tightly as it possibly can. "I'm right here."

I thank the fucking Lord that she is. Because having Ally around makes even the worst days better. But there's a part of me holding my breath, scared shitless that she's going to leave … again.

sixteen

COLE

"Where the fuck did you take off to last night?" Knox gripes during practice the next day.

"You did take off rather suddenly, man," Weston chirps up. "What, did you find yourself a sweet little something to take home?"

Lifting my shirt up, I wipe my face. It's fucking hot out here today, and my friends are nosy.

But I'm glad I left. Not only did I get to sink myself deep into Ally again, which is worth far more than going to a party, but also, apparently, some of the guys on the team got into a fight at the party last night, and word got back to Coach. And now … well, now, I'm pretty fucking positive he's going to run us until we die.

"I had something to take care of," I huff out. "I'm glad I wasn't there. Sounds like it was a fucking mess."

Knox nods, his eyes wide. "You fucking know it, bud. Straight-up fucking shitshow is what it was."

"What the hell happened anyway?" I ask him just as Coach blows the whistle. "Fuck. Back to running, I'm sure."

We make our way back over to Coach as Weston scowls.

"A few of our teammates fought some of the baseball players," Weston gripes. "Fucking idiots."

"Were either of you involved?" I shoot them a hard look.

They both hold up their hands.

"Fuck no. We stayed the hell out of that disaster," Weston says.

"One of the fellas on the baseball team diddled Dex's girl." Knox shrugs. "Guess Sexy Dexy was mad."

"Diddled?" I shake my head. "The fuck does that even mean?"

"Means he gave her the meat. You know, the D," Knox says, serious as can be.

"I can fucking hear you, asshole," Dex growls from behind us.

"My bad, man. She was probably a lousy fuck anyway. You're way better off without her," Knox tells him.

I wait for Dex to punch him in the face. Only he doesn't. He just grumbles.

"Dude, why not just say *fucked?*" I laugh at his word choice of *diddled*.

He shrugs. "In Maine, we say diddled. Besides, it's less crude, ain't it?"

I can't help the stupid-ass grin that spreads across my face. "I mean, yeah, I guess. But since when are you concerned about being crude?"

That fucker is one of the crudest dudes I know.

We stand there, waiting for Coach to tell us to run, and I'm just counting my lucky stars for this short break. He has half of the guys puking.

"Guess you have yourself a point there, ol' boy," Knox answers nonchalantly. "But back to you. Where were you last night?"

"Sloane told me that Ally was working. I know she doesn't have a car, so I didn't want her walking home in the dark."

He smirks and looks at Weston. "Bet he got some good ol' lovin' for being such a gentleman. What do you think?"

Weston laughs. "Nah. If it's the girl from the diner, she definitely told him to go fuck himself." Looking at me, he crosses his arms over his chest. "That chick don't play. I was a little frightened of her myself."

"Same." Knox nods. "Then again, she's hot as fuck. I'd let her punish me."

"Watch yourself," I growl. "You like running, right? So, you really don't need your legs broken."

Best friends or not, they will know better than to talk about my girl that way.

Just then, Coach yells, "Back to work, boys. You want to go act big and tough, fighting and shit? Well then, be prepared to run. Head back to the field for round two."

Glancing at the scoreboard clock, I see it reads four o'clock. Ally is working a double today. She won't even get out until eight tonight after being there at six this morning.

"Hey," I yell to my roommates as we make our way back onto the field. "Can one of you pick me up at Lenny's after practice?"

"Yeah?" Confused, Knox says, "Why though?"

I know I'll catch shit when I tell him my plan, but I don't really give a fuck.

"I'm going to drop my truck off there. Don't need Ally walking home late," I tell him.

I'd offer to get her, but we have a team dinner tonight as a bonding exercise. I'd not go, but because I'm the one who planned it, I can't ditch just to give Ally a ride.

"Ohh shiiiit. Storm is whiiiipped!" he yells obnoxiously to Weston, who pretends to be holding a whip in his hand.

"Oh, fuck off. You're just pissed because Blondie saw how small your dick was and ran away," I say to Knox.

"Yeah, right. She hasn't seen my dick yet. If she had, she'd be texting and calling nonstop." He tries to laugh it off, but I'm sure I struck a nerve. He was interested in that girl, and she didn't give him the time of day. Nudging me, he grins. "And if she had touched it, well, fuck, man, she'd be stalking me."

"Keep telling yourself that, man," I say, shaking my head.

I'm sure it seems like overkill, letting Ally use my new truck. But she isn't just some random chick. She's *Ally*. She's my family. She probably won't take me doing this lightly. It'll just be another way she thinks I'm taking her independence away. But that isn't it. She's mine to take care of, just like I'm hers. If I needed something, she'd be there, no questions asked.

It doesn't matter that she doesn't think we're actually together right now. Besides, soon enough, we will be.

Coach blows his whistle, and no matter how much I don't want to run, I know I'll see her face when I drop my truck off, so that makes this punishment a little less shitty.

ALLY

Today has been crazy at Lenny's. Sundays are always our biggest days. Lots of families going out to breakfast and lunch. But now that I'm going on hour eleven of being on my feet, I'm fucking tired. But my pocket is filled with cash from tips, making the long-ass day worth it.

"Al," Lenny says while looking out the front window, "that *nobody* boy is back."

Knowing exactly who he's talking about, I walk over to stand next to Lenny to see what he sees.

Cole steps down from his truck. Knox pulls up next to him with a guy in the passenger seat, who I learned is Weston.

My frosty heart melts a little as I watch Cole strut toward the front door. *My God, he's sexy.*

All of the memories of what we did last night play through my mind. It felt so good to be with him again. My insides flutter like a little bitch at the images.

Opening the door, he spots me right away. Flashing me one of those signature grins, he comes to me.

"What are you doing here?" I ask.

I know last night, I had a moment of weakness and jumped his bones, basically begging him to screw me. *Talk about embarrassing.*

But that doesn't mean we can jump right back in, does it? No, there's no way we're ready to just be together. I mean, aside from *together* in a sexual way. And I should really try to put the brakes on even that. But he makes it so goddamn hard not to want to turn into a damn porn star when he's around.

Rubbing his hand on the back of his neck, he uses his free hand to hold out a set of keys, placing them in the palm of my hand.

"What is this?" I glance down, confused.

"My truck keys."

"Why?"

"Because even though I'd love to pick you up from work, I have a team dinner in the cafeteria at seven, so I doubt I'll be done in time."

Looking up at him, I narrow my eyes. "I have legs. They can even move. Which means"—I try to sound surprised—"I can even walk!"

"Quit being a pain in the ass. Besides, I gave you what you asked for last night." His eyes glimmer with amusement along with something else. Something dirty. "This is what I'm asking for. For you to just drive my truck and not walk in the fucking dark."

"Cole …" I sigh, looking at the keys.

Reaching down, he rubs his thumb against my cheek, causing my traitorous body to lean closer to his touch. "Please. I don't want you out there, walking at night. Could be a bogeyman or some shit."

"A bogeyman?" I laugh.

He shrugs. "I mean, yeah. Or Sasquatch. Haven't you ever seen *Finding Bigfoot*? That shit is real."

Looking down at the keys again, I sigh. "This is really thoughtful of you, but I'm okay to walk. This truck is big and expensive. Very, very expensive."

"I'm sure the new Mom and Pops have decent insurance. Which is probably good since, well, your driving is shit," he whispers the last part, widening his eyes.

"Oh, piss off. You're the one who ran into the neighbor's mailbox," I point out.

"I did do that. Thankfully, she was a pervy, old woman with tits down to her knees, and she liked the looks of me."

I laugh at the memory. That old woman was obsessed with Cole. Good thing, too, because it saved his ass from getting into trouble for taking out her mailbox. All he had to do was flash her a few grins, help her move some stuff around her house—shirtless—and the mailbox was long forgotten.

"At least I wasn't like you." He nods his chin at me. "You backed into Natasha Hill's BMW."

I totally forgot about that. Cole had an old piece-of-junk truck that he had saved all of his money from working in the tattoo shop to buy. The one time I finally dared to drive it, I ran into none other than Charlotte's Fall's very own mean girl, Natasha Hill.

"Shh," I say, looking around. "Nobody ever found out it was me."

That girl had already hated me. She had the hots for Cole, and, well, I was standing in her way.

"We're a long way away from Charlotte's Falls, sweetheart. Don't think you have to worry about anyone finding out about the shit we did."

"I guess you're right." I smile at him, thinking back to all the memories we had in that town. I might have left that place on a bad note, but I also had a lot of really happy times there too.

"Please take my truck. I'll walk to your dorm after the dinner and pick it up. If you aren't home yet, I'll wait outside."

I ponder on debating it further, but I know this is a losing battle. Cole doesn't take no for an answer.

"All right, fine." I give in. "Thank you, Cole."

It would seem so natural to lean up and plant my lips against his mouth right now. It would be so comfortable and familiar.

He showed up here to let me take his very nice, very expensive AF truck home, knowing I am likely the world's shittiest driver. But he did it anyway. No, demanded it. He's swoonworthy—no doubt about that. He's always loved doing kind things for me. Though he never had a role model to show him how to be good, he learned it on his own. When I say most guys his age aren't half the man he is, I mean it. One hundred and ten percent.

When I first got my period, without asking, he ran to the drugstore in town and got me tampons and pads—he wasn't sure which I needed. I swear he spent his entire earnings that week on just feminine products.

And one time, when I got a nasty stomach bug and puked for two days straight, he never left my side. Not once. He even held my hair while I threw up and forced me to drink Gatorade, so I wasn't dehydrated. He's everything in a man that any girl could ever want.

Yet somehow, here at Brooks, it no longer feels like it's us against the world. It feels like it's the entire campus standing with him. And I'm awkwardly off to the side, trying to find where I fit.

My whole life, I always felt like I had been born at the wrong place, at the wrong time. I felt like I didn't belong where I was. I didn't belong anywhere at all. But when I met him, although I still felt like I didn't exactly belong in this world, I harmonize with him. It sounds crazy, I'm sure. But for me, my mom dying was one of those *everything happens for a reason* moments. If she hadn't died, I wouldn't have moved in with Marion and Dave. And if I hadn't moved in with them, I wouldn't have met Cole.

Truthfully, I'd choose him over my mother—*my own blood*—any day of the week. And seeing as I don't even have a clue who my dad is, I'd take Cole over that guy too.

"You can repay me later." He winks.

"Perv." I grin.

"Get your mind out of the gutter, babe. I don't want you to fuck me. I want you to sing for me. It's been too damn long since I've heard your voice doing what it was born to do." With that, he turns and walks off.

I watch as he struts out to Knox's truck. All six-two, two hundred pounds of solid muscle. He's beautiful.

Really fucking beautiful.

Last night felt like old times with Cole. It finally seemed like we were connected once again, like we used to be. He knows my body as well as I do. And I could sketch his with my eyes closed.

It's odd. I expected that once we were intimate again, the floodgates of bad memories would come rushing in. But they didn't. In fact, it just felt really damn good to be held by someone who I know loves me. Heart, soul—everything. I'm not pretending to be anything with him—he knows it all. Even the darkest, ugliest parts of my being, he's seen them. Yet he loves me anyway.

There's never been a doubt in my mind that he doesn't love me. I know he does. Things are just messy. And the worst part is, he doesn't even know why. He knows I'm different, and he knows something happened. But he has no idea what. I know eventually, I'll need to tell him. But I haven't got a fucking clue how I'm going to do that. It will be so hard to bring up. And the last thing I want to do is taint him with my words.

"The *nobody* boy left minutes ago. You can wipe that drool off of your lip, Al," Lenny says from behind me.

Whirling around, I flick him off. "Oh, cut it out, Len." I wiggle my eyebrows. "Or else I'll tell those old biddies who come in here just for you that you were asking about them."

Lenny is an attractive, older man. I mean, I'm not going to say he's hot. But for being in his seventies, dude's still got it.

"You wouldn't." His eyes widen.

Turning the side of my lip up slightly, I tap my pen to my chin. "Or ... would I?" I say.

He's scheming something in his head—no doubt about it. He's quiet for a moment longer before his mouth opens. "Fine then," he says nonchalantly. "I'll tell Lucinda to stop bringing the cinnamon buns. Seems as though only you benefit from them anyhow." He drops that major bomb.

Threatening a girl's cinnamon buns? Oh, hell no.

Lucinda does all of the baking for Lenny's. Pies, cakes, eclairs, cookies. You name it, and she makes it. And it's de-fucking-licious. But the cinnamon buns? They are out of this world. And I eat way too many of them a week.

"Fine, asshole. You win." I sigh. "A girl can't go without her cinnamon buns."

Satisfied with my response, he grins and starts to head back in the kitchen when, suddenly, Carla comes from taking an order.

"I heard you call that fine specimen a boy, Len. I have to tell you, that ain't no boy. That there was a man." Fanning herself with her hand, she widens her eyes. "A man whose hands I'd love to have all over my body."

Lenny only shakes his head and grumbles something inaudible before shutting the door to the kitchen.

I burst out laughing. "Easy, killer. Aren't you married with, like, fifteen kids at home?"

"Three, not fifteen—thank fuck for that." Grabbing my arm, she looks around to make sure no one is listening. Luckily, we've finally slowed down after an entire day of craziness, leaving only a few tables in here. "Bitch, have you seen that hunky piece of meat naked?"

I grin but try to hide it by grabbing a menu and holding it in front of my face.

Pulling it down, she gives me a pointed look. "Okay, dimple, spill."

"So, that's Storm … from Ohio," I tell her, cringing at the response I predict is coming my way.

She wasn't here the other times he came in when I was working.

"Waaaait, that guy, who just came in here, he's the infamous Storm? I've seen him in here before, eating."

"Yep." I nod. "Cole Storms. Also known as Storm," I explain.

"Wow. He's … yeah, he's … really something."

I haven't told Carla much about my childhood. She knows my parents aren't in the picture. And she knows I lived in a foster home with Cole and that I left. But she doesn't know why I left. I don't think she ever will.

"He is, and the dickhead knows it too." I sigh.

How could he not know it? He looks like he just walked out of a damn magazine with the headline "Sexiest Man Alive." With those blue eyes that change color with whatever he's wearing and sometimes even with the weather. Or his brown hair that always seems to lie perfectly messed up, as if he did it on purpose. When I know he didn't. It's just literally how he wakes up.

Lucky fucker.

"Well, I'm a married woman. I need all the deets," Carla says, leaning over the counter. "God love Tommy, but I've been looking at the same dad bod for twenty years now." She stops for a second before muttering, "Hairy dad bod."

I stifle a laugh. Tommy is her husband, and even though she says things like that, she loves that man more than life itself. She's just that middle-aged woman who loves to ogle younger men.

"One day, Ms. Carla," I chime as I walk away, "I'll fill you in on it all. Promise."

"Baby, I'm gonna hold you to it!" she chimes from behind me.

Somehow, I know for a fact that she will.

$$XO$$

When I turn the key, the truck roars to life. Loudly. And yeah … it's hot.

There are more controls in this bitch than a damn rocket ship.

How can there be so many buttons? And what the heck do they all do?

Papa Roach's "No Matter What" fills the cab of the truck. Causing my heart to melt inside of my chest.

Laying my head back against the headrest, I close my eyes and soak in the words. There's not a song that sounds more like my and Cole's relationship. The words talk about having each other's backs, even at the expense of taking a bullet for one another if it came down to it. That's us. That's how we've been since we were just two kids in tattered clothes with hungry bellies. It's how we will always be—I know it.

A memory filters through my mind of the two of us stealing candy bars from the little store in downtown Charlotte's Falls. The owner, Pauline, an older woman, was the sweetest thing. Yet we stole her candy.

We were fed just enough to keep us deemed healthy. So, if we wanted an extra treat, sometimes, we had to do horrible things, like steal. I vowed to myself that one day, I would go back and apologize to that lady.

The song ends. The song that I know wasn't playing by coincidence. I'm sure he put the CD in when he dropped his truck off. He likely had it, so this would be the next track to play. He knows how important music is to me. And how much I love Papa Roach.

I maneuver the seat forward until I can reach the pedals. I adjust the mirrors to make sure they are positioned right, and then I frown. The mirrors are fine. The problem is, I still can't see shit. Number one, I'm five foot three, and this truck was built for a giant. Number two, the windows are tinted so dark that it's like a goddamn cave in here.

"This is a bad idea," I mutter to myself. "What the hell was he thinking, letting me drive this thing? He's right; I do suck at driving."

Ever so slowly, I pull out of the parking spot. Praying I don't take out anyone else's car in the process.

The drive to campus is so fast that I don't even have time to get comfortable with driving Cole's truck. But I have to say, I feel like a badass in this thing.

Gradually and carefully pulling into a parking spot lit by streetlights, I turn the truck off and climb out. My feet ache from being on them all day, and I stink like a fryolator and stale coffee grounds.

"Daaaamn, Ally. You look sexy in a truck." Cole's voice flows smoothly out of the darkness. "When I make it into the NFL, first thing I'm going to do is buy you a truck of your own, any color you want." He slowly struts into the lit parking area, and the sight of him causes my heart to skip a beat. "Dinner got done sooner than I'd thought, but I figured I'd just meet you here instead of at Lenny's."

"You don't need to buy me a ride, Cole," I say sharply. "I'm not your orphan to take care of."

The closer he gets, the more steps I take backward. Eventually, my steps run out, and I find myself against his truck.

Stepping into me, he dips his head forward and hovers his lips over mine. "I'm getting real sick of you saying you're not mine, angel." Moving his mouth to my neck, he nips my skin with his teeth, causing me to hiss. "I'll remind you just how much you belong to me. And I'll do it right against this truck."

"I dare you," I say cuttingly.

I know he won't. Even if I sort of wish that he would.

He chuckles, causing his chest to vibrate against mine. Somehow feeling his heart that close to mine makes me feel like I'm actually alive.

"Oh, Allycat." He smiles against my neck. "You should know by now that I would never risk anyone seeing what's mine."

"Yeah," I say flatly before ducking underneath his hold and walking toward the dorm. "I knew you didn't have it in you."

Scooping me up from behind, he flings me over his shoulder like I'm as light as a feather. He runs his hand up the back of my leg until he has ahold of my ass. Lifting his hand up, he springs it down quickly, giving me a slight spank. "Stop fighting me. You know you won't win. Then again, you can get mad all you want. You're hot as fuck when you're angry."

I'm not mad. Not at all. I'm dog tired. But for this man, I can muster up some energy.

"My roommate is home," I tell him. "Do I need to remind you, we share a damn room? We don't have special dorms like you lucky assholes do."

Pausing, he turns back around, walking us to his truck. Opening the passenger door, he sets me inside before leaning into me. His mouth captures mine, and we do something we haven't done in a long time—we just make out. Aggressively.

His lips devour mine like he's starving and I'm a damn cupcake, leaving my lips deliciously sore.

Pulling back, breathless, he reaches between my legs, cupping me through my jeans. "Making out is hot and all, but I need in. *Now*," he growls the last part.

"Then, take me somewhere. Anywhere," I breathe out.

His eyes look like a lightbulb went off. As if he knows exactly the right place for us to go, so we can get as close as we can. Something we both always seem to crave with each other.

xo

COLE

When she said to take her somewhere right away, I knew where to go. The first week here, sometimes, I just drove around. Oddly enough, I was trying to find places that made me feel closer to Ally. Closer to my *home*. One day, I ended up here.

We drive on the grass path for a quarter of a mile until we come out to a small pond that is surrounded by a wooded area.

It reminded me of the pond we'd found one day when we were exploring for hours in the woods, neither of us wanting to go home. We were only fourteen at the time, and I remember we were both sweating after walking so far. The water looked like heaven, but neither of us had a swimsuit.

I went in my boxers, and she was in her tank top and panties. I think it was then that she finally saw me as more than just a friend. She saw me as hers.

I was already *head over heels, completely fucked up dumb* in love with her. It took her a little longer to figure that out. At least, I think it did. She's always hidden her feelings and emotions. With her, I've always laid it all out there, take it or leave it. What you see is what you get.

Gazing out the front window at the headlight-lit pond, she smiles. "This is perfect."

"Remember that place we found when we went on one of our infamous adventures," I ask her, reaching my hand over and resting it on her thigh.

She laughs lightly. "Yeah, I do. Except the water in this pond looks a little cleaner. But that place was still perfect."

"Way better than going home."

She nods in agreement. It was muddy in that pond and far from clean. But after hiking through woods for three hours, it looked perfect. Besides, like I said, it was way better than being at home.

We always stayed out of our foster parents' home as late as we could. Just the two of us, often huddled in some weird place. Maybe the bleachers after football practice, a random riverbank we'd found, or a dugout when there wasn't baseball going on. It wasn't ideal, but we had each other.

We came back to that same place all throughout high school. Strange enough, it's also where she gave me her virginity—in the grass, under the stars, on a night in July. Two kids who had no fucking idea what they were doing but couldn't get enough of each other from that point on.

I'd like to get her to talk to me tonight. Make her tell me about whatever happened while I was at football camp. And to hear each and every detail in between. I want to know where she's been, who she's been with, if she was taken care of. I want to know everything.

But just like a stray cat, all alone in an alley, she's skittish. Even more so than before. I need to take my time in finding out whatever she's hiding. She isn't just going to open up to me right away. She needs to know I'm still the me I was before she left. I gained her trust when we were twelve. I'll do it again now, no matter how long it takes. She's worth the wait.

Reaching out, she slides her hand up my shirt before tugging at it, eventually lifting it over my head. When she leans her head in, her lips find my neck, and slowly, she works her way up to my jawline and finally to my mouth.

Her hands never touch the bottom right side of my back—she makes sure of it. She knows it's a trigger for me, and she respects that. Any other girl would want to ask me five hundred questions about this scar. But she knows I don't want to talk about it. Her scars are invisible to the naked eye, but that doesn't make them any less than this scar on my body. I've come to realize, some of the most agonizing pain cannot be seen.

Her tongue clashes with mine, and I devour her lips until I'm certain they are bruised. Her kisses always taste like Juicy Fruit gum because I swear, she chews that shit all the time.

Grabbing a handful of her shirt, I tug. "Need you to take this off."

She eagerly does so, followed by her bra, exposing her perfect chest to me.

Taking her nipple into my mouth, I lick before releasing it with a popping sound. "All mine," I murmur between her tits before continuing downward and unbuttoning her jeans and pulling them down. I cup my hand between her legs.

She greedily grinds herself against my palm before reaching down, unbuttoning my jeans, and sliding them and my boxers down just far enough for me to spring free.

Leaning her head forward, she gently bites my bottom lip while looking me in the eyes. She takes my dick into her hand and pumps slowly. "All mine," she growls back at me.

I can't help the smirk on my face. "Demanding little thing, aren't you?" I murmur against her skin.

I fuck her with my fingers while her hand works me until I've had enough of it. I need to be inside of her. I can't wait another fucking second.

Reclining my seat, I roughly pull her onto me, landing her right on my dick. She hisses but instantly starts moving up and down. Her beautiful face is lit by the moonlight shining into the truck cab.

She rides me hard, her tits moving up and down. The sexiest noises escape her lips, driving me mad.

I know she's close.

"Should I pull out?" I choke the words out, praying she says no.

Last night, we got caught up in the moment, and she let me go bare. I'm sure some might think it's irresponsible to not use a condom, and with anyone else, I would have to agree. But this is Ally. And the thought of anything being between us, I can't stand it. Besides, we've only ever been with each other. Something that is so fucking sacred to me.

She shakes her head.

Thank fuck.

"Remember, I have the IUD. Please, I need you. *All* of you."

She puts her forehead to mine, and our lips linger over each other as we both come undone. I feel her tightening around me. Her sweet breath hitting my mouth as she breathes erratically.

"I love you … so damn much." I wrap my arms around her, digging my fingers into her back, not wanting to let her go. Never wanting to let her go.

"I love you too. Thanks for always being the storm, my happy place."

"And a damn good lay, right?" I tip my chin up at her. "You sure sounded fully satisfied," I say, reminding her of the bullshit she said at the movie theater. *Partially satisfied, my ass.*

She laughs against me. "You're all right, I suppose."

"All right? Pfft. This dick is some grade-A shit," I scoff.

Tilting her head to the side, she bites her bottom lip. "I'm not sure yet, but I'd be willing to go another round to see."

Since I first met Ally, my heart has been outside of my body and with her. Until the day I die, that's the way it's going to be.

The wildest part? I wouldn't want it any other way.

seventeen

COLE

On my way to class, my phone vibrates in my pocket. Pulling it out, I see Jenn, my adoptive mother's name, on the screen.

I debate on not answering, but I've been dodging both her and her husband's calls a lot. Fuckers might be using me to be the next *Blind Side* movie or some shit, but they haven't treated me badly. In fact, they treat me basically like their own kid. So, I guess I can't be a complete dick to them.

"Hello?" I answer.

"Cole, hi. You picked up." She sounds both surprised and relieved.

I'd rather talk to Jenn than Matt. He's nice and all, but it's easier for me to be a dick to another dude. Jenn is a sweet lady who likes to talk and bake lots of shit.

"Uh, well, you called me. So, yeah, I picked up."

"Oh, right, right. You are absolutely right."

How many times can someone say right *in one sentence?*

"Matt and I, well, we wanted to come up for your next game. If that's okay." She pauses. "It's all right if it isn't. Although we'd be so bummed. But, like I said, it would be all right. Whatever you're most comfortable with, Cole," she stammers and trips over her own words.

I have no idea why I hold the ability to make this woman so nervous, but all I know is that I do.

They asked to come to my other games and get dinner after, but I gave them the cold shoulder. I turned eighteen in July, so technically, they aren't really my adoptive parents anymore. But they keep trying to stay in my life.

I'm sure it's just for the chance when I make it into the NFL and they can point and smile, nodding their heads, like, *Yep, we did that. We're responsible for making him great.*

And to that, all I have to say is, fuck that. *I* made myself great. The coaches I've had made me great. Not them.

"Uh …" I scratch the back of my neck, not really wanting them to come, but also not loving the idea of having to tell her that. "Sure," I say nervously, clearing my throat. "I, uh, I guess."

"Really?!" her voice squeals. "Oh goodness, I'm so excited. Wait till I tell Matt. He has been dying to get out there and watch you play. I even got a jersey with your name on it!" She giggles. "But I totally don't have to wear it if it will make you uncomfortable, I mean," she says when I don't reply. "I can leave it in the closet."

"No," I croak. "That's fine. Thanks for the support."

"Woohoo! We will be there!"

I think she's a talkative lady anyway. Couple that with being nervous, and she doesn't shut up. She and Matt helped me move up here, against my protests. Knox saw them and teased me nonstop about how hot my mom was. I didn't correct him that she wasn't my mother. That would have made it awkward.

He's not wrong either. She's young, in her mid- to late-thirties. She's a blonde bombshell.

"All right," I say dryly. "I have to get to class. But I guess I'll, uh … see you guys this weekend?"

"Sure will. We'd love to take you out to dinner afterward. Since it's an early game and all."

"Yeah, all right, I guess."

"I'm sorry. I'm being too pushy again. Have a good day, Cole."

"Thanks. You too," I mutter into the phone before hanging up.

I know one thing: if I have to sit through a dinner with two people I barely know, I'm bringing Ally with me. Best they get acquainted with her now since she's here to stay.

She's still keeping me at arm's length. I can tell she isn't letting me completely back in yet. But the sex … we've some kick-ass sex. And that's a start.

eighteen

ALLY

The thing about football games … the energy is always explosive. I thought football games in high school were a big deal, but they don't hold a candle to football at Brooks. This shit is always crazy.

"Astronaut in the Ocean" by Masked Wolf fills the stadium as the players run through the tunnel and onto the field. Jumping into the air while they pump their arms up and down, yelling at the crowd.

Instinctively, right away I spot *Storms* on the back of jersey number twenty-two.

Even in his uniform, face covered by his helmet, and hundreds of feet away, he still makes my heart do that annoying fluttering thing it does that makes me feel like a damn butterfly is attacking my stomach. The way he moves, the way he walks, the way he commands attention with all eyes on him—it's just mesmerizing.

How can someone who is fighting so many battles inside move through life with so much grace? It's actually maddening, knowing all these other bitches are likely watching him, salivating.

I know his adoptive parents are here somewhere, in their designated family seats. I don't want to meet them without him here; it doesn't seem right. So, instead, I agreed to dinner with them after the game. I could tell Cole was anxious about meeting them alone, so when he asked me, I instantly said yes. Anything I can do to make him more comfortable, I'll do it.

Well, other than agreeing to never walk home from work in the dark. Because come on, I'm a grown-ass woman.

He warms up, throwing the ball to a teammate. I'm pretty sure it's his roommate Weston. Though I can't be positive. I have Cole's ass down pat. I'd know that beautiful piece of meat anywhere. But this guy, nice as his butt might be, he isn't my Storm.

After he fires the ball to his teammate, his gaze turns to the stands, finding me. Reaching into the small, hidden pocket in his football uniform pants, he pulls out a folded-up letter before holding it to his heart.

Even from my seat, I can tell the letter is tattered and worn from years of carrying it around.

I know what it is without even seeing the words inside. He carried it around for years after I gave it to him, and I guess he's never stopped. And that makes my damn heart squeeze inside my chest. I'll never know what I did to deserve him. He could have anybody in the world, yet he chooses me. Every single day.

Smiling, I nod and blow him a kiss. And then … I swoon. I swoon because he's a six-foot-two, two-hundred-pound giant, made of pure muscle, and he's comfortable enough to hold up the damn letter I wrote him when we were sixteen. I swoon because he's comfortable enough to not give a shit that we're surrounded by a stadium full of people and many of them have their eyes on him. To Cole, it's just us.

Tucking it back into his pants pocket, he goes back to warming up. Though I don't miss his head turning in my direction occasionally. Almost like he wants to make sure I'm still here, that I haven't left him again.

"Um … what the hell was that?" Sloane says with her mouth wide open, completely gawking at my man.

"What?" I play dumb.

When she stares at me with her mouth hanging open, I shrug. "Just a thing. Between Cole and me."

"Ohh, now, he's Cole, not Storm. When you called him Storm, it seemed so less personal than *Cole*." She says his name in a low, seductive tone before swatting me on the knee. "For real, what was that? I need some sweetness in my life. And that looked sweet."

Playing with the torn fabric around the hole in my jeans, I mindlessly pull the loose threads between my fingers as I tell her what he just held up. "It's just a letter that I wrote to him before his team got on the bus and headed to state for the championship. He was only a sophomore and already captain and starting quarterback—he was that good. But he was nervous. It was his first time going to state, and I wanted to make him feel better." I smile at the memory of sneaking into the locker room before the team was in there. I stuffed it into his uniform and ducked out of there minutes before all of the guys filed in.

Her eyebrows pull together as she puts her hand on her chest. "And he kept it?" She shakes her head. "He freaking kept it? You're kidding me."

Looking back at the field, I smile. "I guess he did."

I think back to the letter and when I wrote it. English class, block B, right before lunch. Watching his nerves get to him got to me too. I hated to see him doubt himself so much.

To my Storm.

I know you're nervous for tonight. But trust me, you don't need to be. You have more talent in one of your testicles than the other guys have in their whole bodies.

You are so much better than you know. You are so much more than you know. Just remember that.

You've got this game. I'll be there, cheering you on, just like I always do—loud and annoying. And I promise that I always will. I also promise to forever be your biggest fan, to always believe in you, even when you don't believe in yourself, and to love you and never leave. Who could leave such a fine ass?

I love you so much more than I could ever write on this damn paper. Thanks for putting up with my moody self.

Forever and always. In the good and in the grit.

Love,

Ally

xo

XO

COLE

Glancing up, I see there are seventeen seconds left on the clock. What a beautiful sight. We're up two touchdowns and about to score again, if all goes as planned.

Knowing Ally is here always makes me play better. She's like a good-luck charm. And not because I'm trying to show off for her, but because she gives me confidence.

Our opponents will all be looking at Knox, thinking I'll throw the ball for him to run it in. But joke's on them. I'll be running that bitch in myself.

I call out the play, "Green twenty-two."

I step back, appearing like the ball will be fired at any second. Everyone around me starts to move to stop something before it even happens.

I turn to my left, rolling off of one of their defensemen. Tucking the ball under my arm, I run like hell the short distance into the end zone, and I dive into it. That puts us up by three touchdowns, and the clock runs out.

Once my teammates are done smashing their helmets and chests against mine, my eyes find Ally again, and I point to her and then pat my heart.

All for you, is what I want to tell her. Every single thing I do is for her.

Her face breaks into a smile as her dark hair blows in the wind, some pieces flying over her face.

Fuck me, she's so beautiful.

I wish I could celebrate this win by taking her back to my dorm and devouring her body. But unfortunately, we have an awkward-as-fuck dinner to get through.

Moving my eyes further down, I see my adoptive parents waving to me. Jenn's blonde head shakes as she jumps up and down, smiling at me. Matt gives me a cheesy thumbs-up. Both are wearing Brooks University jerseys with my last name on the back, undoubtedly.

In a little while, Ally and I will be going to dinner with them, and while I'd rather celebrate my night by being buried balls deep inside of Ally, I'm just glad she's going with me so that I won't be alone.

nineteen

ALLY

Twisting my spaghetti with my fork, I take a bite and wipe my mouth. Whatever this restaurant is, it's fucking delicious but also stuffy as hell, and I feel like I stick out worse than a sore thumb.

"So, Ally, what are you studying?" Jenn asks sweetly.

She seems nice enough. And Jesus almighty, she's beautiful.

Both look awfully young to be the adoptive parents of a teenage boy, in my opinion. I'm guessing they are in their late thirties.

Her blonde hair is cut in a perfectly styled bob. And she has honey-brown eyes that are warm and comforting. But I know more about them than I've ever let on. Like how they paid just to have Cole in their family. Shady.

"Music technology." I smile, trying not to sound nervous. "I'd like to be a songwriter."

"Do you sing too?" Matt asks.

He's the same height and build as Cole. His hair is dark brown, and his jawline is sharp enough to cut the steak on his plate.

Turning toward this complete and total DILF, I nod. "I do sometimes. But I'm not sure if I want to be directly in the limelight. I care more about getting my words out there." Suddenly feeling like a dick, I shake my head. "Not that I'm good enough to even make it big time. I was just—"

"Oh, you're good enough," Cole says. "Future Halsey right here." He grins, jerking his head in my direction.

They both laugh at his completely ridiculous comment.

"Well, whatever you decide to do, I'm sure you'll do great," Jenn says. Suddenly, her eyes grow misty. "The fact that you two are as good of kids as you are is crazy. You're both an inspiration. Rising above isn't an easy thing to do."

"Jenn," Matt warns.

She shakes her hand in front of her. "I know; I know. I'm not trying to make anybody feel uncomfortable. It's just how I feel." She looks between Cole and me. *Sorry*, she mouths.

"It's all right," I say before taking a sip of water. "And thank you." I offer her a small smile.

Cole doesn't respond. Instead, he stands up. "I'm going to use the restroom. Be right back," he says, looking at me and me only.

I give him a nod, letting him know I'll be fine. I'm sure, knowing Cole, he probably just needs a minute. I know he was anxious for this dinner. He has no idea I was more so than he was.

Making sure he's gone, I look at the perfect couple seated across from me.

Leaning forward, I waste no time. Dropping my voice lower, I say, "I know you paid our foster parents, so you could adopt him. I haven't told him. But I'll tell you this right now: you will not use him for his talents." Looking between the two of them, I snarl, "Or else I promise you, I will have both your asses arrested. Are we clear? Because if we aren't, I'll have you know that I have evidence against you." I'm lying. "Hard evidence. Jenn, you'd be looking at years in a cell next to a brute chick named Norma, and, Matt, you'll have to worry every time you shower, constantly gripping the soap extra tight."

I don't actually have evidence to back it up. But I found out about their arrangement with Dave and Marion while Cole was away at camp, and I needed to get to the bottom of it. Because I can tell that even though he avoids them, Cole cares about them a little. If they hurt him, I'll hurt them harder. Guaranteed.

Both of their faces pale, which only brings a smirk to my lips.

"Ally—" Matt starts to say, but his wife holds her hand up.

"No, let me." She turns toward him, her eyes filled with sadness along with what appears to be shock. "Please?"

Reluctantly, he nods.

"I promise you, it isn't what it seems." Reaching over, she takes my hand, causing me to flinch. "Just allow us a little more time, and then we can explain it all to him. And to you."

"Explain what?" I glare at her. "And why should I grant you more time before I tell him?"

Glancing at Matt, she sighs. "We know things. A lot of things. And while I'm sure we look like we're the bad guys, we aren't. We just ... need more time." Pulling her hand away, she wipes her eyes. "We aren't dumb. We know he's an adult now. He could cut us off at any point."

"He could," I say sharply.

"But he hasn't," she points out. "And we thank God for that. We enjoy time with him so much. We aren't ready for it to end." Her eyes stare right into mine, and fuck me sideways, I believe her.

"And, Ally?" she whispers.

"Yeah?" I say dryly.

"For what it's worth, we wanted you too, Ally. We knew how much you meant to him. But when we came back for both of you, they told us you had left to be with another family."

I'm blown away by her words. If they are even true. How the hell would I know?

"I-I don't … I'm—" I stutter over my own words. My brain feels fuzzy and overwhelmed from this conversation.

"Just trust us." She touches my hand again. "I know it's hard to do. I understand this is an astronomical thing for me to ask of you. But we're begging you—I'm begging you for a little longer. Please, just trust us."

"Fine," I answer, pulling my hand away. "But figure it out soon. Time is ticking. I don't keep secrets, especially from Cole."

They quickly look at each other before nodding.

"Thank you, Al—"

"Don't thank me. I'm only doing what I think is right for Cole," I cut Matt off.

"Right. Okay," he murmurs, eyeing me nervously, like I might take his steak knife to his nutsack.

Trust me, motherfucker, you hurt Cole, and it's on.

My phone vibrates in my pocket. Checking it under the table, I see it's a message from Cole.

Cole: Tell them I'm upset and I need a few minutes. Come to the door next to the restroom. It says Staff Only. Knock six times.

Holding my phone up, I offer them an apologetic smile. "So … Cole's been having a rough few days." Pausing, I shrug. "With personal stuff," I lie. "He just needs to talk to me for a few minutes. Why don't I go help him, and once we get back, we can all order dessert?"

I'm nice to their face so that they don't follow me, but truthfully, if Cole says he wants to get out of here, I'll drive the getaway car. And I'd do it with a smile, if that's what he wanted to do.

They both look nervous, and Jenn's eyes widen. "Are you sure he'll be all right?"

I nod. "Oh, yes. Please just allow me to go talk to him. Be back in ten minutes."

They look at each other and then to me. "Okay." They both nod in agreement.

xo

COLE

I'm not having a hard time. I don't need to talk. I just can't stand Ally's sweet scent of vanilla or being so close to her bare legs and not being able to reach over and run my hand up her thigh and continue on up to that beautiful place between her legs.

When I picked her up after my game, she had changed into a skirt that showed her toned, tanned legs, paired with a tight-ass top that her tits strained against. I knew right then that I wouldn't be able to concentrate.

She straightened her long, dark hair tonight, making it flow damn near to the bottom of her back—the perfect length for me to fist while she rode my cock. These filthy images are basically all I've seen since she climbed inside the cab.

She's spellbinding. And I couldn't sit there another minute without touching her.

Add having her so close and the awkwardness of this dinner, and I need a fucking escape. An escape only she can grant me.

Maybe that makes me a fiend, but I'm okay with that. I don't need booze in a bottle or a needle in my vein, a line of white powder, or any of that shit. She's my addiction. And I can't fucking get enough.

A minute later, six knocks sound against the door.

When I open it, she rushes in, a confused look on her pretty face.

"Are we actually going back to dinner? Or are we going to blow this fucking Popsicle stand?" she questions me. "I'm totally game for whatever you want to do, babe. But just so you kn—" Her voice dies in her throat as she watches me turn the lock on the door.

It's a small room with a handful of tables and chairs in it. I would say they use it as a break room or something. The second I saw the tables, I knew I wanted Ally's naked body on top of one.

"Ally," I say, stepping up to her and sliding my hand up the back of her neck, pushing her mouth toward mine. "I need to feel you. Is that okay?"

Instantly nodding her head, she moans into my mouth when I glide my hand up her shirt and cup her breast.

"I love you," I tell her before pushing her back onto the table. "But you are driving me fucking insane tonight."

"Wh … why?" she says, her voice shaking slightly from my touch.

"Because you smell like vanilla and you look like sex."

"Wait, are we going to bang in here?" Her eyes gaze around the room, and I can hear the excitement in her voice.

Hiking her skirt up, I pull her thong over. "Going to have to do this quick. We only have six minutes before we look suspicious."

Her blue eyes gaze up at me, those rays of yellow swirling through them as her pupils dilate. Biting her lip, she nods. "Okay."

Pulling my jeans down just enough, I take my painfully hard dick out and stroke myself. Her eyes watch me, and I see how turned on she gets as her nipples harden beneath the thin fabric of her shirt.

"You ready for me, sweetheart?"

"Yes," she hisses. "Always."

Before she can so much as blink, I thrust into her, causing her to cry out.

Putting my mouth over hers, I nip her bottom lip. "Those cries are for me and me alone, angel." Pumping into her again, I lean up and glare down at her. "Need you to keep quiet. I can't have everyone in the restaurant hearing what's mine. Got it?"

Biting her lip again, she nods once.

"Good girl."

Hard and fast, I fuck her with everything I have. And she greedily takes it, doing a good job of keeping quiet too. Though I can tell by watching her, she's dying to let out a scream. And I'm dying to hear her sexy, tortured cries.

It doesn't take long for us to be staring into each other's eyes, both so high that I think we might leave this planet. And for that short period of time, it's only us in our own world. No strange adoptive parents waiting outside the door, no football team and responsibilities to fulfill, and no secrets hidden and buried in her past. Just us. Just two kids who can't get enough of each other. Two bodies who need each other to survive, to feel, to live.

Just me and the person I want to give the world to.

Until it's over and it's time to go back and eat some awkward-as-fuck dessert. I would much rather have her instead of anything on their menu.

twenty

ALLY

It's been a week since Cole and I went to dinner with Matt and Jenn. A week since they told me to not tell him that they'd paid for Cole to live with them. A week since we had some really hot sex in a staff-only room at the restaurant. So, in other words, a week ago was a shitstorm.

How we got away with banging in a locked room before returning for some dessert, all like, "We'll have the tiramisu, please," like we hadn't just banged on a damn table minutes before, I have no idea. Either Matt and Jenn are great actors or they really had no idea what we'd disappeared to do. Either way, I don't really care. It was worth it. There was just something so thrilling about doing that in such a forbidden place. I sort of want to make it a weekly occurrence.

Cole and I have always had a hard time with keeping our hands off of each other, and at the restaurant was no exception. I can't resist him. And lately, it's as if we're making up for lost time and have turned into damn bunnies.

Oddly enough, a voice inside of me is telling me that Jenn and Matt aren't the bad guys. I have this strange feeling, like whatever they did, they did it for a reason. I also think that maybe, just maybe, more is to come. It seemed like they desperately needed me to keep this secret for just a little longer. And even though it means keeping more secrets from Cole, call me crazy, but I plan to do just that. I can tell he enjoys having them around. Not that I can blame him. It's nice to have someone—*anyone*—after years of radio silence from any parental figure. I think it's that void that you feel when you experience a thing like your parents not wanting you. You just want someone to care. To see you. To acknowledge you're there.

Their words filter through my mind over and over. "*We wanted you too, Ally.*"

I think of how differently things would have turned out if only Marion and Dave had let them take me. I can't seem to find a motive for why they wouldn't have.

I have other secrets I'm keeping from Cole too. Just keep adding them to my list. This bomb I'm going to have to eventually drop on him, I'm afraid it will fuck up his line of vision. And if I know Cole, he'll want to hurt anyone and everyone who hurt me. I can't let him do that. It will tarnish his name and ruin his future. I love him too much for that to happen.

But Cole can be as stubborn as they come, and I'm afraid no matter what I say, he won't listen.

"Do you have to work tonight?" Sloane asks while curling her hair.

"Nope, first weekend off in a while."

I'm a little bummed. I like making the cash. But it's been slower than usual, so Lenny only wanted either me or Carla on. And since she is the one with three mouths to feed at home, I told her she could have the shift if she wanted it.

"There's an open mic night at the bar in town. I hear they never even card. Can we go? Please?" She sticks her lip out. "I really want to hear you sing."

"Depends. Are you going to sing too?" I ask, raising an eyebrow.

"Girl, my voice is shit. But if it gets you up on that stage, you bet your ass I will."

Clapping my hands, I jump up to change, actually excited to sing in front of people. It's been a while. "Let's do it."

Rushing over to our mini fridge, she pulls out a six-pack of Smirnoff Ice. "We'll Uber over. Let's get buzzed first. That way, I don't freeze up onstage." Taking one of the bottles from the pack, she giggles. "A few of these babies, and I'll be singing so loud that you'll need earplugs. You'll probably pretend like you don't even know me."

"You'll do just fine, I'm sure," I assure her before looking at her drink selection. Wrinkling my nose, I push past her and grab my new bottle of Crown Royal Peach. "I can't drink that shit, but I'll take a few shots of this." Looking it over, I frown. "Besides, to sing in front of people again, I'm going to need something stronger than your bitch drinks."

"Hey! These are yummy!" she whines.

"Different strokes for different folks." I shrug. "Drink up!" I say, pointing to her bottle. "We've got singing to do."

COLE

Staring down at my phone, I read Ally's reply again, my body slowly filling with irritation.

I asked her what she was up to, and she told me it was a secret. With a laughing face emoji. It instantly irked me, given our history of her leaving and shit.

Hitting her Contact for the third time, I try to call her. Yet again, I get her voice mail.

Stomping on the gas, I drive toward her dorm.

"Dude, I thought we were going to go find a party. Why the fuck are we here?" Knox bitches.

"Yeah, man, what the hell's going on? We got beers to drink and ass to find." Weston hits my headrest lightly. "No particular order either," he says, wiggling his eyebrows.

Football players basically get any chick thrown at them. We're at the top of the food chain even if I don't understand why. We can throw a ball? Sweet. Somehow, I know that even if I wasn't the star player I am—hell, even if I'd never picked up a football in my life—Ally would still love me.

"Ally isn't answering. I just want to see if she's home. Calm your dicks down," I huff.

"Oh yeah, we're the ones whose dicks needs calming," Knox mumbles under his breath.

Throwing the truck in park, I glare at him. "Chill the fuck out, or I'll have Ally come after you."

My threat has him shutting his mouth real fast. For whatever reason, these guys are intimidated as shit by her. I suppose I can't blame them. She'd scare me, too, if I didn't find her so fucking hot when she was annoyed.

I walk up the stairs and to her dorm room. "Ally?" I knock a few times. "Ally?"

A chick with the blondest hair I've ever seen—so blonde that it actually burns my eyes a little—pops her head out of the dorm next to Ally's, attempting to put an earring in.

She looks me up and down. "You lookin' for someone, sugar?" her thick Southern accent drawls, and I can tell by the way she's looking at me that she's getting the wrong idea.

"Yeah, Ally," I answer back shortly. It doesn't take much for people to get the wrong impression these days. The last thing I want is this girl to think I'm coming on to her. "My girlfriend."

That last part might be a stretch. I've never once asked her to be my girlfriend. Even as kids, we just knew we were together, and that was that. Things are different now. She seems to forget some days that she belongs to me.

I'm going to remind her of that real quick.

"That lucky bitch!" She rolls her eyes. "My girls and I are headed to meet her and Sloane in a few minutes. We're running late."

"Where?"

"They went to open mic night at Club 83."

"Thanks," I yell as I jog off.

Why would she need to go there and keep it a secret? Doesn't she know how fucking sleazy college guys can be? Not to mention, the creepy fucks who hang out there?

"So, what'd ya find out, Cappy?" Knox says from the passenger side.

Pulling away from the curb, I grip the steering wheel with one hand. "Club 83. Open mic night. Her and Blondie."

"Shit, man. Really?" He groans. "I haven't seen that chick since they came over and watched a movie. Do we really need to roll up there? I'm not trying to have her up my ass tonight."

"Holy fuck." I laugh. "What are you smoking, man? Because I want some."

"What do you mean?" Knox frowns, confused.

"If you really believe that chick is going to be up your ass and *not* the other way around, you're on something."

"Am not!" He pouts. "I thought we were going to a fucking party or something."

"You can go home. I can drop you off. Both of you," I say. Keeping my eyes fixed on the road. "You can paint each other's nails and talk about who has the biggest vagina."

"Fuck no. A chance to see people sing and bomb it? Hell yes, I'm going." Weston cheers from the back.

Knox is quiet for a moment before finally shrugging. "Fine. Me too, I guess."

I knew he wouldn't miss out on going to an open mic night. And I know he's avoiding Sloane. He likes her, but there's something holding him back. I don't know what it is, and it's not really for me to figure out. Besides, I have enough fucking drama with my own girl.

The thought of hearing Ally sing makes me slightly less pissed at her. Aside from the night I gave her a ride home and she quietly sang along to "Broken," I haven't heard her sing in too damn long, and I miss it.

"What happened with you and this Sloane chick anyway?" Weston questions him. "Seems like she really bent your dick out of shape."

Turning toward Knox, I grin. "Did Knoxy get his heart broken?"

"Fuck no," he grumbles. "It's just … complicated."

I chuckle. "All women are, brother. All women are."

"Isn't that the truth?" he mumbles before laying his head back.

XO

We strut in through the doors at Club 83, and just like every other place, everyone stops what they're doing just to watch or say hello, fist-bump, purr like a cat, or thrust their titties at us. You name it, and we see it.

Some of the guys eat it up. Not me. I fucking hate being surrounded all the time. It makes me feel so claustrophobic. There's no escaping it either. If we get up and go to a new seat, the vultures follow. We can tell them to fuck off, but even I don't like to be a prick.

I'm an imposter. In this group of normal college kids, many who are rich or come from nice homes, I know I don't belong. That's why I'm most myself with Ally because we know where we each came from. It isn't some hidden, dirty secret. As her note said, *In the good and in the grit.* Because it doesn't matter which, we'll have each other's backs.

I look around the room for her but don't see her anywhere. Shrugging off the cling-ons who are rubbing against my arms with their long, pointy, painted fingernails, I sense that feeling of suffocation coming over me. So many strangers, all touching me.

How the fuck will I make it in the NFL?

This is so small on the spectrum of attention. When I'm in the NFL, it'll be like this times one hundred.

That's really the only downfall to a future in playing pro ball. I want the world to know my name. I want my face and stats on the TV. I just don't *want* everyone all up in my space when it happens. Unfortunately, that isn't how it works. If you're a pro athlete, it is assumed that your life is allowed to be broadcasted.

"Wade," I call to Weston, "you see Al—"

I don't finish my sentence when I spot her up on the stage, all alone.

A slow beat starts, and soon, her beautiful, haunted voice sings the lyrics to "Landslide." Suddenly, every single person is quiet, watching her, completely captivated, including me. Abruptly, all the feelings I had about being annoyed that she snuck here without telling me are gone as she hypnotizes me with her voice.

Word by word, she rips my heart out and breaks it into more pieces. Not meaning to either. But she's that good that she can bring you to that place where you hear all of her pain as she sings. She isn't just up there, singing about cupcakes and rainbows. Fuck no. That girl has lived through hell, and it comes out in her voice.

Her eyes are closed for most of it. Something she does when she's really into what she's singing. And when she's done, nobody moves, and nobody talks. Fuck, I'm not even sure if anyone breathes.

We all just stand there, completely numb from her gift.

Her lips turn up slightly as she gazes around the room. "Thank you," she says before stepping down off the stage and walking over to Sloane.

Sloane instantly pulls her in for a hug and jumps up and down. Along with the rest of the crowd, who roars and cheers for her.

Within five minutes, she's already gained fans, just by showing herself to them. The real her. The raw her.

Her angelic voice has this uncanny way of calming even the biggest of *storms* down. I should know. I'm one of them.

She hasn't spotted me yet as I walk up behind her.

"Good job, beautiful."

She turns slowly, and her cheeks redden. "Oh fuck. You heard me?" Graceful angel to crude pirate in a matter of seconds.

Gripping her chin softly, I look down at her. "I did. And I was pretty pissed off that you tried to be sneaky with me." Moving my hands down her back, I cup her asscheeks and bring her closer. "You trying to piss me off, *Allycat?*"

"No," she says, her eyes dancing with fire. "I don't need a leash; you aren't my master."

Leaning my head down, I bite her neck before moving my lips to her ear. "You might want to rethink that, sweetheart."

"Or what?"

"Or I won't fuck you next time you're begging for it." I pull back, watching her reaction.

I don't mean it. She wouldn't have to beg much for me to give her what she wanted. But still, I'd like to try to instill some fear in her.

She only looks further amused as her lips twitch, and she laughs. "We both know I don't need to beg you to give me what I need." Standing on her tippy-toes, she wraps her arms around my neck. "Forgive me, master?"

She knows she's the one in control. I can play God all I want, but when she snaps her fingers, I'm a little bitch.

Her little bitch.

"I suppose. You'll just have to make it up to me." I run my thumb over her bottom lip. "With that pretty mouth."

She shudders before I lean down and put my mouth to hers.

When I kiss her lips, she tastes of Crown Royal Peach and smells of vanilla. A dangerous combination for my self-control.

Pulling back, I grin. "Thank your loudmouth neighbor for me showing up here."

She laughs, her whole face lighting up as she does. "Extremely blonde hair?"

I nod.

"That's Amber. She's nuts, but I like her."

"Oh yeah?" I ask her, unable to pull my eyes from her plump lips.

"Mmhmm," she says and nuzzles her face against my shoulder. "Takes a nut to know a nut."

"You have a point there." I chuckle before murmuring against her ear, "Speaking of nuts, mine are blue just from watching you tonight. You going to take care of that or …"

She swats my chest. "Is Knox here? Sloane is singing next." She giggles. "She said she's an awful singer."

"Oh boy. And yeah, he is. He seems pretty bitter over her. What even happened?"

She shrugs. "I really don't know. She makes it sound like he blew her off and just hasn't talked to her since. Who the hell really knows?"

I don't understand the pair of them. At. All. They are confusing as fuck. But I know he'll tell me when he wants to, so I'll wait until he's ready. God knows there's enough shit about me that I've kept to myself and away from him and Weston.

A song starts, and everyone's attention turns toward the stage, where Sloane stands with her blonde hair curled in waves, wearing a black dress.

She's beautiful, but she's not my type.

Pulling Ally's back to my chest, I murmur against her hair, "What the fuck is this song?"

Her body shakes with laughter. " 'Sorry Not Sorry' by Demi Lovato." She cranes her neck to look up at me. "She picked a good one. I'd say she's trying to send Knoxy boy a message." Ally nods her chin and points to the bar, where Knox stares at the stage with a grumpy-ass look on his face. "He looks super impressed by it." She giggles.

Turning my attention back to Sloane, I frown. "Ally … I know she's your friend and all, but—"

"She's fucking terrible," she finishes my sentence, staring at the stage like a zombie.

"Yep. Aw-fucking-ful," I agree with her, my ears literally burning inside from this chick's voice.

Sweet fucking Jesus, make it stop.

"It's so bad. But we have to make her feel like she did good," Ally says. Turning her body toward me, she grips my cheeks. "For real, she's been so sweet to me, and she was nervous about doing this. You need to tell everyone to be nice to her." When I stare at her, confused, she widens her eyes. "Well, what the fuck are you standing here for? Go! Go tell the guys to be nice."

Realization hits me. "Oh, right, right." I start to strut off but turn toward her and narrow my eyes. "What do I get out of it?"

"You get me not kneeing you in your nutsack. Now, go!"

Smirking at her, I wink. "I'll get something out of it. I'm sure of it."

She looks like she might actually cut my dick off and stick it in a blender. The thought makes me cringe as I head over to the bar, where the guys are seated.

"Yo." I take a seat next to Knox, whose eyes are still glued to the stage. "Going to need you to do me a favor."

"What's that, bud?" Weston peers around Knox at me. "Tell me quickly before I go cut my own ears off." He nods to the stage. "This chick sucks ass so bad. I might actually go jump off the roof."

Knox turns his head toward him and glares. "Fuck off. She isn't *that* bad."

Sloane attempts a high note, and holy fuck, my head hurts.

Knox sighs. "All right, she's awful." Punching Weston's arm, he shrugs. "But I'm bettin' it took a lot for her to get her sexy ass up there. So, be nice. None of us have the balls to do it."

"Yeah, that's why I came over here," I tell them, taking a swig from the beer the bartender just dropped off. "Ally says we need to be nice and act like she did good. So, spread the word." I smirk. "If not, Ally will probably have all of our dicks pulverized by midnight."

Saluting me, they both nod in agreement.

"You got it, Cap." Weston taps his beer against mine.

"Her voice might suck, but her dancing is fucking hot." Knox whistles under his breath. "That fucking black dress is sexy."

She does have moves, making this show a little less unfortunate. It also isn't fair that she had to sing after Ally. That right there set her up for failure.

"So much for her being up *your* ass, pussy," I tease him. "Seems like it might be the opposite, huh?"

He flicks me off and grumbles something. He makes it too easy to give him shit.

Ally is gone from the spot she was in earlier. I'm just about to go looking for her when a big commotion on the dance floor breaks out. Standing up, I push myself through the crowd. I don't need anyone accidentally hitting my girl.

Only, when I find the fight, I realize, it *is* my girl.

A big, preppy guy grabs his nose as bright red blood pours out of it, covering his white polo. "You fucking bitch! You broke my nose!"

Holding her arms up at her sides, one eyebrow arched, she only shrugs. "I told you to get your grubby fucking hands off of me not once, but twice. If your dumbass chose not to listen, well then, that now crooked-as-fuck nose is all on you, homeboy."

"What the fuck?! You're psychotic! It's my fucking nose!"

She smirks. "Oh, sweetheart. We all know you weren't headed for a life of modeling anyhow. You have to be attractive for that."

Anger fills every ounce of his face along with humiliation. Before he can say anything else, I interfere.

"Ally, what the fuck happened?" I grip her hips and pull her behind me.

Before she can answer, I turn my attention to the poor bastard whose nose is most definitely broken. I can feel the veins bulging in my neck after hearing Ally's words about what this fucker did.

"What the fuck is going on here, fuckface?" I growl. "Did you put your hands on my girl? After she asked you not to?"

Recognition flashes in his eyes. Holding his hands up, he shakes his head and looks like he might shit his pants. "Cole Storms, sorry, man. I didn't know she was your girl."

Stepping closer, I point my finger in his face. "Doesn't really matter if she's mine or not, asshole. A woman tells you to back off, you back. The. Fuck. Off," I roar. "But yeah, because she *is* mine, you really fucked up."

"I, uh ... dude, I'm sorry. I'm really fucking sorry," he rambles on. Nose still flowing like a goddamn river.

Ally must have clocked him good.

"You so much as look at her again, I'll bury you. Got it?" I glare at him before gripping his shirt and shoving him toward the Exit sign, landing him right on his ass. "Get the fuck out of here."

Normally, I'd light his ass up for touching my girl, but it looks like she had that covered.

He stumbles backward before taking off. He wasn't any smaller than me, but I know I could have taken him. Especially when it comes to my girl. I could easily defeat a thousand men if it involved my angel.

Turning around, I see Ally storming off.

Great, I've gone and pissed her off again.

And I don't even know what the fuck I did.

XO

ALLY

Pushing out through the door, I walk out onto the sidewalk.

"Ally," Cole's deep voice says from behind me.

Whipping around, I point my finger at the ground. "I had it handled. You don't always need to swoop in and make a damn scene." My voice begins to rise. "What the fuck is it with men needing to wave their dick around to prove whose more of a badass? Jesus fucking Christ."

He does something even more annoying. He laughs. He fucking laughs!

"Trust me, babe, I could tell you had it handled." Running his hand up the back of his neck, he rests it on the top of his head thoughtfully. "I think everybody in there with eyes saw you had it handled. Hence the fucking flood. I mean, for fuck's sake, Al, they'll probably need to hire someone just to clean that shit up."

"Not my problem," I quip back. "Guess he should have kept his sweaty-ass hands to himself, huh?" Letting out a groan, I sigh in frustration. "Either way, I had it handled, Cole!"

"Sweet thing, standing in the shadows, letting you take care of shit all on your own—well, that isn't how this works." Stepping up to me, he tilts my chin up forcefully. "And I think you ought to know that by now."

"You're the most impossible human being on the planet, Cole Storms."

"Yeah." He nips my lips playfully. "But you love me anyway. Let's get the hell out of here. Any more singers like your friend, and I'll likely let you cut off my ears."

Swatting at him, I point my finger. "Be nice. She's a good friend to me."

"Sweetheart, that's great and all. But it doesn't make up for the fact that her voice sounded similar to that time I heard a rabbit screaming in the woods behind my house."

Pouting, I shove him. "That's sad. Rabbits do that when they are being killed."

He widens his eyes and puts his mouth in a line. "Well, your friend sounded like she was slaughtering a pack of wild turkeys."

Throwing his arm around me, he drags me closer to him. "Let's go make sure the turkey murdering herself is all right to drive home, and then I can take you back to my place. Oh, and, Ally?"

"Yes?"

"For future reference, don't put up a fight when I defend you. That's a bad girl."

Turning, I lock eyes with him. "Then, punish me."

He grins. "I can't. You'd like that too much," he says against my ear, causing my entire body to tingle.

Maybe I am hot and cold. And maybe he is overbearing. I can't deny this gravitational pull that we have with each other. I'm not dumb. I know even an ocean couldn't keep us apart.

I need to keep him close enough for me to survive but far enough for him to not find out the truth about the day that I left.

twenty-one

ALLY
TWO YEARS BEFORE

"Twenty questions?" I ask Cole sweetly.

We've been together for four years now. I know him inside and out. I know his body, I know his heart, and I know his soul. But one thing he's always kept sort of hidden is his mind.

"Tell you what, angel. I'll give you five."

"Fine," I huff.

Five is better than nothing, I suppose.

"Do you ever wonder what it would be like if our parents had been normal?" I ask Cole as I lean against him while we sit with our legs dangling off the bridge up the road from our house.

"Nah," he says, throwing a rock in the water. "Wondering won't change it, Al."

I bite my lip and nod. "I know. I just ... can't help but wonder. That's all."

He gives me a knowing smile. "I know. But if my dad hadn't been an addict, I wouldn't have ever met you. And if I hadn't met you ... I don't want to even imagine that."

I jab his chest lightly. "Laying it on thick, aren't you, Stormy?"

"Just for you, babe." He winks.

"Do you ever miss them? Your parents?"

Leaning back on his hands, he shrugs. "I didn't know my mom. And my dad? Well, that man, like I've told you before, was a piece of shit. So, no, Ally. Not one bit."

I nod. "Do you wonder what your mom was like?" I ask this more for my own curiosity.

My dad has never been in the picture. I tried to meet him, and it was a miserable fail. Yet I still find myself wondering.

He's quiet for a moment before looking off in the distance. "In my head, I imagine that she had sunshine hair and smelled like chocolate chip cookies. I tell myself she left because she had no choice. My dad was a nightmare." He looks at me, his knowing eyes reading my every thought. "I tell myself these things to feel less worthless, unlovable, or damaged. But at the end of the day, I'm not the one who should be feeling any of those things, and neither are you." Reaching over, he cups my cheeks. "Both of our parents left their kids because of something inside of them, Al. Not because of us. It had nothing to do with us."

His answer hurts my heart. He always knows what to say to quiet my demons. The ones who make me feel everything and nothing all at once. The ones who drive me almost to the point of madness.

He's so reasonable and rational. Unlike me.

"Two more, baby. Time's a-wastin'."

"Where do you see yourself in ten years?"

"I'll be twenty-six. So, I'll be in the NFL, for sure. And you'll likely be a famous singer, and I'll be the lucky son of a bitch who's married to you."

My smile falters as I glance at the ground. "You'll have a lot of women throwing themselves at you and all that fame and fortune. You'll probably forget all about me," I say, my cheeks growing redder with each passing second.

"Never going to happen. There's nothing I'd put before being your man. No goal, no place of arrival, no amount of money, no woman, nothing. None of that is above me and you." He smiles as he runs his fingers down my cheek. "One more question, sweet cheeks."

"Why did you call me the angel when we first met?" I ask the question that has always been in the back of my mind.

Standing up, he pulls me up with him and scoops me up. "Because in the darkest of my days, I prayed for you. I just didn't know you yet. But I prayed for an angel, knowing one day, if I was patient, an angel would come."

"An angel." I smile.

"Yep. And I never want there to be a day when I wake up in a world where you and I are apart." His lips kiss mine, and after, the taste of mint lingers on my lips. "Understood?"

I nod slowly, wanting to taste his lips again. "Understood."

twenty-two

ALLY

"I think you're the only one who's ever scrubbed the legs of the chairs," Carla says from behind me.

Dipping the rag in the hot, soapy water, I wring it out before moving to the next leg. "Bitch, that's clear. These things were nasssty." I shake my head and tsk her. "You all should be ashamed."

The kitchen door swings open, and out strolls Lenny. "I'm too old for that shit, Al. And Carla here, well, she's too damn lazy."

All Carla does is shrug and lift her eyebrows up. "He speaks the truth. Ain't nobody got time for that."

"Well, I mean, it's slow as shit. I think we got a little time," I deadpan.

"You're not about to soon." She nods her head toward the front door.

Following her eyes, I watch the door to Lenny's push open, and in strolls Cole. A white T-shirt and faded blue jeans with a pair of Nikes on. And a ball cap that is pulled down low on his head, making my stomach do somersaults.

Pushing myself to stand, I walk over to meet him. "Hey, stranger. What are you doing here?"

He grins, those beautiful white teeth showing. "Just wanted to see my girl for a minute. Team's heading to the airport in a few hours for our game tomorrow in Massachusetts. I wanted to kiss you good-bye."

When I glance at our audience, Lenny quickly tries to busy himself. Pretending he wasn't just eavesdropping the hell out of this conversation. Carla just continues to blatantly stare.

"I'll be back in five minutes."

"Make it forty-five, Al," Lenny calls over his shoulder. "We won't have our dinner rush for a few more hours anyway, and I don't want to see Romeo here salivating over you. So, go, scoot, skedaddle."

Knowing I won't see Cole tonight, I don't need to be told twice. Forty-five minutes is all I need. Hell, I would have settled for five.

"Where do you want to go?" he says as we climb into his truck.

"That pond is what, ten minutes away?"

His eyes show the smile that he tries to keep from his lips as he backs out of the parking spot, doing that incredibly sexy thing where he puts his arm on my seat.

"So, while we're on our way there, I wanted to run something by you," he says, flicking his gaze between the road and me.

"What's that?" I ask anxiously.

"Don't be nervous," he says, reading my mind. "I was talking to Coach. I asked him if he could talk to the music director and get you to sing the national anthem at our next home game."

"Cole, you didn't …" I say.

I feel like I'm going to puke. Doing that in high school was no big deal. We had a small school. Brooks U is huge. That's a lot of eyes. A lot of judging eyes.

Wiggling his eyebrows, he grins. "I did. Because, babe, you love singing in front of people. I know at first, you always do this thing where you get nervous. And when you get nervous and stressed, you get bitchy. But then you fucking love it."

I frown and point to him. "You just said I'm bitchy."

He shrugs. Taking my hand, he presses it to his lips. "Well, sometimes, you are."

"This was really nice of you, Cole. It means a lot, really."

I'm nervous as shit about doing this. But he believes in me. If he didn't, he wouldn't want me singing in front of thousands of people.

"You can repay me when we get to the pond." He winks.

twenty-three

COLE

"Take your shirt off. Let me see all of you," I say in between kissing her. My hands find a long lock of her hair, gripping it back.

Then, I run my hands up her bare thighs as she straddles me. She moans, "Storm."

When she says my name, it finally sounds like the way she used to say it. "You're always so ready for me. Aren't you, baby?"

She groans before thrusting her chest in my face. Needing my mouth on her gorgeous tits.

I do what she's silently asking, earning me a hiss as she grinds herself against me. I love how she's always ready for me. Always wanting me.

When I glance out the window, I don't see a soul in sight. In fact, this place is so secluded that I don't think anyone even knows it's here.

Pushing the driver's door open, I carry her outside with my pants down around my ankles.

"Wh-what are you doing?" she says, excitement laced in her words.

"I'm going to do something I've always wanted to. I'm going to fuck you against this truck. Okay, sweetheart?"

She nods and greedily tightens her legs around my waist. Ready for more. Always.

As I push her down onto my cock, she cries out. And I'm okay with it because I know without a shadow of a doubt that we're alone. There might be bears or ducks or some shit around, but I'm okay with them hearing her sexy sounds. As long as it isn't another dude, I don't really give a fuck. Because hearing her makes me that much more turned on.

As I thrust into her over and over again, all that fills the air are the sounds of our skin smacking together and her cries.

Her dark hair falls down her back, cascading in an irresistible blanket of silk for me to grab on to. Pulling it slightly, I force her head up so that her eyes connect with mine.

"I love you," I tell her, as I've told her a thousand times before. And I'll tell her thousands of times again.

Her name will be on the last breath I take on this earth. I'm sure of it.

"I love you," she whispers back.

I drive myself in as deep as I can. Moving my hands down, I grip her ass, pushing her onto me harder.

She bites her bottom lip, her eyebrows pulling together as she does. "Cole."

"You there?"

She nods.

"I'm here too, baby. Right fucking here."

That's all it takes for us to finish together.

And I wish like hell I could do it again. But looking at the clock, I realize she's got to get the fuck back to Lenny's. Fast.

Sex with her, as many times as it happens, will never *not* leave me wanting more. It's far from just being intimate—I know this much. It's a spiritual fucking awakening. It's two souls connecting in more ways than one. And more than anything, it's my fucking addiction.

"Wait." Ally's eyes stare at the tattoo on my back—of the angel who looks like her—before I get my shirt over my head. "I've always loved this tattoo. You never did tell me why you got it though," she says softly, running her hand over the ink.

Turning around to face her, I pull her to stand between my legs, and I lean my back against my truck. "Because the thought of you, my angel, is what got me through, Ally. Then, before, and now."

"Does that mean you've forgiven me? For leaving you?"

I laugh. "I mean, the way we've been fucking, I thought that was a given."

"Fucking and forgiveness are two very different things, Cole," she says, leveling me with a hard look. "Have you actually forgiven me?"

"I am working on it," I tell her truthfully. "I really am."

It would help if she told me why she left me. I think that would give me the closure that I need to let the past stay in the past. But she dances around the truth about that day like she's doing the fucking do-si-do.

"Thank you for trying," she says softly before reaching up and running her fingers through my hair. "I don't want to live in a world where you and I are apart."

Her words, though they might seem small, mean so fucking much. She's always been so quiet with how she feels. I know she loves me. I know I'm the one for her. But she has a hard time saying the words out loud.

"Me neither, baby. But right now, we need to get your beautiful ass back to work." Spinning her around, I slap her ass hard. "Chop-chop."

twenty-four

ALLY

The next weekend comes fast, and here I stand, ready to go out in front of a shit-ton of people and sing the national anthem. I love that Cole did this for me, but at the same time, I sort of want to castrate him for it.

"Don't be so nervous, girl. You're going to totally kill it," Sloane says before giggling. "And remember, no matter what, you will never be half as bad as me."

My skin feels hot with anxiety; it prickles and feels itchy. My brain is in an almost-foggy state. I've never been this nervous to sing in front of people. But this is a lot of people.

I try to give her a smile to let her know I'm okay. Though I think it just comes out as an awkward, weird-as-fuck facial expression, of which I have no control over.

Damn Cole and his ideas.

"And now, our very own student, Ally Lee James, will sing the national anthem."

The words echo through the stadium, and I actually think my stomach might fall out of my butthole. But even still, I make my way to where I was told to go, and I take the microphone. And once I have it, that thing that always happens, happens again. I'm fine as the words begin to flow out of my mouth. I couldn't tell you how they sound because my heart is pumping so loud in my ears that I can't hear a damn thing other than that. But I know I'm singing the words.

When I'm done, I find Cole in the line of players, and I give him my best smile.

He did this for me. He gave me the honor of singing the national anthem at a college football game. And what an incredible thing that was to do.

He points to me and claps. Telling me he thinks I did a good job, and really, that's all that matters. The fact that he believes in me is everything.

XO

"Go down there and give your fine-ass boyfriend a kiss," Sloane says, shooing me away.

I roll my eyes but oblige. Secretly wanting to throw my arms around him and drink him in.

Cole poured every ounce of himself into this game. He was on fire, and it was a beautiful sight to watch. And the team won by a landslide.

"Hey, superstar." I wink. "Looked pretty good out there."

"Pretty good?" A wolfish grin stretches across his face. "I was fucking legendary."

"Eh … you were all right."

Scooping me up in one swift move, he presses his lips roughly against mine. "You're so full of shit. I'm surprised your eyes aren't brown."

"I'm just playing." I kiss him, tasting the mint gum he's been chewing. "You were *fucking legendary.*"

"Damn straight I was." Twirling me around in a circle, he puts his nose to my neck. "And you, Ally Lee James, were fucking incredible." The stubble on his face tickles my skin. "And unbelievably sexy. You were born to be on a stage, sweet cheeks."

Setting my forehead against his, I peer into his eyes that look more green than blue today. "I don't know about all that. But thank you for setting it up for me to do that. I was nervous, but I'm so glad I did it."

"Anything for my angel." He nips at my neck.

The truth is, as much as I love to sing, I'm starting to second-guess that I want an actual career in it.

"Yo, Storm, party tonight at Andrew and Asher's house. You coming or being a little bitch?" Knox calls out to Cole.

Usually, Cole wouldn't take being called a little bitch too well, but I can tell that anything that comes out of this guy's mouth is all in good fun. I've been around him and Weston since Cole and I have been spending more time together, and I have to say, I enjoy hanging around them. And I can tell they are good friends to Cole, which obviously seals the deal for my stamp of approval.

Setting me down on my feet, he looks down at me. "What do you think? You feel like partying tonight?" Pressing his mouth to my ear, he drops his voice low enough for only me to hear. "Or we could go back to my place and have a party of our own."

My lips curve up in a smile. "While the latter is rather tempting, I could actually go for a little Crown and a lot of dancing." I look at Knox and tip my chin up. "Sloane will be with me." I don't ask; I tell him.

"Perfect," he mutters before stalking off.

His body language tells me he isn't big on the idea. But oh well. Where I go, she goes.

"Who even are Andrew and Asher? No frat guys, right?" I ask Cole.

He shakes his head. "Fuck no. They are seniors on the football team. They have a place off-campus."

Tilting his head to the side, he tucks a strand of hair behind my ear. I don't know how he makes such a small movement seem so intimate.

"I hope we can have a place off-campus next year too."

Pulling my lips to the side, I hold my hands up and shrug. "We shall see."

His eyes narrow slightly as he watches me. "Yeah, we will."

He wanted me to give him more. To tell him, *Yes, yes, let's do it. Let's plan to move in together!* But the truth is, I haven't even come clean to him yet about all the secrets I've buried. I'm being disloyal, and I know that isn't exactly the best recipe for us moving into a place together.

Hopefully by next year, everything will be out on the table. But then again, what if Sloane wants to room together still? I can't be that girl who drops her one and only friend for a guy. But he isn't just a guy.

One thing I know for certain is, I am excited to tip back some Crown and shake my ass against Cole and Sloane. My experiences in the past shouldn't ruin my chances at being a normal college girl. And normal college girls get dolled up and go to parties. That's exactly what I plan to do tonight.

COLE

The music pounds through the speakers at the party, and I'm standing here, wondering why in the fuck Ally was so hell-bent on coming separately.

Because she lives to be a pain in my ass—that's why.

"Where's your better half?" Weston grins, handing me a beer.

Taking it gratefully, I take a long pull from it and frown. "She insisted we meet each other here. She wanted to come with her friend and 'run into each other.' Get the whole 'college experience.' " I shake my head. "Women are batshit crazy."

Clinking his beer against mine, he nods. "True that, brother. True fucking that. But I gotta tell you, that girl of yours, scary as she might be, she can fucking sing."

"Hell yeah, she can. She's going places. Big places."

He eyes me over. "That scare you?"

Playing with the label on my beer bottle, I shrug. "It never did before."

"And now?"

"And now"—I sigh—"I don't know. She keeps me at arm's length. I don't even know if she realizes she's doing it." I shouldn't be telling him any of this. My relationship with Ally has always been sacred to me. Yet here I am, spilling our secrets.

"Then, make her let you in. I've seen the way that chick looks at you, my man. She's ride or die, no doubt."

Finishing my beer, I set it down and run my hand over the top of my head. "Yeah, she is. She always has been. I just want to make sure she's riding shotgun because she wants to. And not because she's loyal to a fault."

He lightly slaps me on my back, and his eyes meet mine. "I promise you, a girl like her, if she didn't want to be riding in that car, her ass would have never gotten in the seat in the first place." He winks, and then he's gone.

I hope he's right. I've tried to push these feelings aside. Feelings of fear that I've had that she's going to leave when she finally figures out I'm not what she wants. That she can be a star all on her own, without me. Honestly, if I lost Ally, I'm not sure I'd survive it. That'd be like taking my heart out, and how the fuck could I live without a heart?

I smell some chicks perfume before she speaks, pulling me from my thoughts. It's obnoxiously strong and not welcome.

"Hey there, big guy," she purrs before dragging a nail up my arm and across my chest.

The last thing I want to be is rude, but Jesus Christ, I wish these chicks could understand the word *boundaries*.

When I turn toward the chick who is undoubtedly trying to be Cole Storms's fuck of the night, I remove her hand from my body. Which causes her to stick her lip out and pout.

"Come on, handsome. I promise you, I can be one hell of a good time." As she leans into my ear, her fake-as-fuck tits push against my side. "In fact, I can be anything you want me to be."

"While I'm sure that's all true and I have no doubt you're great and all, I'm going to have to pass." I attempt to smile, trying to at least treat this chick with kindness.

Her hand reaches up and touches my hair, causing me to flinch. It's never sat well with me when chicks think they can just put their hands on the football players simply because of the team's overall reputation of being fuckboys.

"I've been told I give the best head at this campus." She smirks proudly, and I'm suddenly so fucking thankful that Ally has a brain and knows not to tell people out loud how good she is at sucking dick.

That would be awkward.

"Wow … what an … accomplishment. That sounds wonderful, but I'm all set." Pointing to Dex, who's standing by the pool table, I nod my chin at him. "That guy right there will gladly take you up on your … talents."

"I'm also down to do *anything*," she says slowly. Not getting the hint. Not fucking getting it at all. "Even back door."

"What's going on over here?" Ally's smooth voice coos as she glances between us.

"Not a damn thing," I say, drinking in her body like water.

The girl who apparently can suck dick like a motherfucker snarls, "We were getting ready to go somewhere. Can I fucking help you?"

Her breath smells of cigarettes. Mix that with whatever perfume she's wearing, and it makes my fucking stomach turn.

It's like a slutty nana meets chain-smoker, sprinkled with a little bit of porn star. But *not* the hot kind.

Ally's eyes shift between us. "Were you now?" Her eyes finally land on mine.

"Fuck. No," I growl. "I was polite the first fifteen times you came on to me, and I turned you down, but now, I'm really fucking over this." Moving forward, I grab Ally's hand with no other intention, except to get the fuck away from this weirdo.

Leading her outside onto the back lawn, I see a few chairs next to the fire.

Pulling her down onto my lap, I grip her thigh. "Took you long enough to get here."

She doesn't look at me, and her body is rigid. "Seems like you were getting on fine without me," she answers bitterly.

"What the flying fuck, Ally? That bitch came on to me. It happens a lot here, and it means absolutely nothing."

Of course, at that exact moment, a group of girls decide to all take their clothes off and climb into the hot tub.

Leaning over the edge, completely topless, one slurs, "Storrrrmy baby, come in here and keep us company."

Ignoring them, I keep my eyes trained on Ally.

"Let's just go. This was a fucking stupid idea," I say through gritted teeth.

"Stooorrrm," she slurs again. "I promise you, I'll treat you way better than that frosssty bitch can." Her friends all giggle obnoxiously. "Bitch isn't even that good-lookinnng."

"She does not deserve a guy like him. I've heard his dick is huge," another gushes. "I can't wait till it's my turn to ride it."

"Wait … isn't that the girl who sang the national anthem at the game?"

"Yeah, she wasn't even that good."

Pushing herself up, Ally struts over to the hot tub. "Reeeally fucking classy, you dumb bitch." She tsks them. "Cole Storms doesn't sleep with bitches who have loose vaginas that are the size of the Grand fucking Canyon. So, I'm sorry to say, sweethearts, but you're shit out of luck." She shrugs apologetically. "Maybe you can get surgery to fix your pussies, just like you got surgery to fix your tits."

"Ugly bitch," one yells before splashing water.

"Slut!" another screeches.

"Enou—" I start to yell but am cut off when I see Ally pick up their clothes before throwing them into the fire.

Walking backward away from them, she smiles, holding her hands up. "Whoopsies! Hope that wasn't anything too expensive." Covering her giggle with her hand, she shrugs. "I'm just so damn clumsy when I get around thirsty bitches. My sincere apologies."

Once she gets away from them, she turns around and walks back into the house. Long, dark hair cascading down her back sways with every step she takes. Her hips moving side to side is a welcome sight.

"Ally," I yell, but she keeps walking.

Following her out the front door, I grab her arm. "What the fuck are you doing?"

A bitter laugh escapes her as she points her finger at me. "Is this just how it'll be? As in from here on out?"

"How what will be?" I grunt.

"Being around you. It's now you and the entire campus. You *belong* to them now."

"Fuck that. I do not belong to this fucking campus. Cut the shit."

"How would you like it, huh?" She levels me with a harsh glare. "How would you like it if every single time we went out, a dude was trying to fuck me?"

"Damn it, it's not the—"

"It is the same!" she yells, cutting me off and stomping her tiny foot. "It would be no fucking different! She said your dick is huge. What if that Kent guy had said my tits were nice? How the hell would you like it?"

I get it. I do. I would lay a motherfucker out for hitting on my girl. I know I would. And if Kent had said a word about her tits, he'd be receiving his meals through a straw. But I didn't ask for this type of attention. And truth be told, I *hate* it. I wish I could just go about life and be left the hell alone. But that isn't how it works now.

"You're right; it's the same. I'm sorry. I'll do better at trying to keep them away."

"How, Cole? How can you keep girls from acting like this? How?"

"I don't know!" I slam my hand against the wall, causing her to flinch. "It's just part of my life now, Ally! Shit's different than it was back in the Falls, Jesus fucking Christ!" I regret the words as soon as they leave my mouth and make their way into the world.

"Good to know that things are *different*." She moves back a step, trying to put a bigger gap between us. "You're the one who's different. Chilling with your buds, letting bitches hang all over you, walking around like you're God!" She holds her chest, and I watch as she crumbles before me. "It used to be us. Me and you, together."

"It still is us. I'm right here. I have been right. Fucking. Here." Stepping up to her, I glare down. "I am not the fucking one who chose to leave in the first place, remember that?"

"How could I forget?" she hisses. "You remind me every. Single. Day."

"Guess I haven't gotten over it." I shrug lazily. Being the resentful dick that I am.

"Good." Her venomous eyes narrow. "I suppose you never will either."

"How the fuck can I when you can't tell the fucking truth to save your life, Ally?"

She isn't a liar; she is just withholding information from me. Information I need in order to move the fuck on.

"Go fuck up more parts in your life with heated words, Cole."

Tears roll down her face, and I should want to stop them, but I'm too fucking pissed.

"You show up here, begging for me to fuck you. Giving me nothing in return, and I'm the one who is fucking things up?" I laugh. "What the fuck happened to you, Ally? Because you aren't the girl I knew before."

"You're right." She pounds her fist against her chest. "That girl is dead. And guess what, *Storm*. So are you and me."

"No surprise there," I say sharply. "You've been looking for a way to sabotage us since we started back up again. Congrats, Al. You've done it again."

"You don't know what the hell you're talking about, Cole."

She tries to leave, but something in me snaps.

Grabbing her wrist, I anchor her in place.

"Let me go! I'm not yours to control, Cole! I don't belong to you."

"Well, fuck you then. Because I belong to you. I fucking belong to you and you alone." I get an inch from her face, and my chest heaves with every uncontrolled breath that I take. "Rub that fucking lamp, Ally. Rub that godforsaken thing, and I'll be here, at your feet, chained to you for the rest of my miserable life."

"Don't you get it?" She shakes her head, wiping tears away with her sleeve. "I don't want to be your master. And you sure as hell aren't mine."

Dropping her wrist roughly, I glare down at her. "Good."

As she leaves, I can't stop myself from what I say next. "Don't come crawling back to me. Not this time." And then I say something that I'll soon realize are poisonous words that I'll regret for the rest of my pathetic life. "You want to treat people like dirt, Ally? Well, now, I see why every person in your life has left you. It's all crystal clear."

Turning around, she comes at me, fist flying as her tear-soaked face sobs. I catch her fist in my hands, holding it down.

"Fuck. You," she screeches in a high-pitched sound I've never heard come from her.

Slowly, she pulls her arm away, wrapping both around her own body. As if she's hugging herself. "I hate you. I fucking hate you." She cries harder, to the point of hyperventilating.

And then she says something that I'll never unhear.

"I wish I'd never met you, Cole. I-I wish I could erase every stupid memory I ev-ever had of you at all."

She's hysterical now, and I don't reach out and touch her or hug her. Nothing. I simply watch as she comes undone.

"I hate you more than I hate my own mother."

As she turns to leave, I don't have the urge to run after her. For once in my life, no matter how much it hurts me, I let her leave.

I let my angel walk home alone … in the dark.

twenty-five

COLE

"Run it again," I yell to my teammates, who all groan in obvious aggravation.

"Dude, I think we've got it down. We have run the same play ten fucking times now," Dex calls to me, wiping sweat from his brow.

Turning toward him, I march up into his space, holding my finger up. "What the fuck did you say to me?"

He grits his teeth, and his nostrils flare. "I said, I think we fucking got it, Storm."

"Oh, do you now?" I laugh. "Well, guess what. Coach left me in charge today, not you. Which means we can run it ten more fucking times if that's what I say we need to do," I growl like a fucking animal.

Looking around at my team, I hold my arms out. "Any other pussies want to cry about the plays I want to run? Speak now."

I'm being a dick. I know I'm being a dick. I'm in a shit mood today. As a matter of fact, I have been for the past nine fucking days.

Nine days. That's how long it's been since I've seen Ally. Why I let her back in so easy is my own fault. The crazy part is, I'd do it over and over again too. And I'd do it with a fucking smile. Which is absolutely pathetic. But she's going through something, and all I want is to be able to help her.

The boys can call me whipped, the world can call me dumb, but I don't give a fuck. When you love someone, you love them through the bad times, and you love them through the good. You don't give up on them. Good or grit, if your dumbass loves them, you need to stand by their side. Even if it's in the shadows. Watching like a fucking creeper.

I know about most of the lowest points in her life. If you ask me, the girl is doing good to even get out of bed in the morning. I'll never give up on her. But this being apart, it wears on me. And apparently, it turns me into a dick for my teammates.

"Hey, man," Knox whispers, gripping my shoulder. "You good?"

"I'm fine. Why?" I shrug him off.

"Well, uh, you're being a tad overkill. Actually, you're being a dick." When I send a glare in his direction, he holds his hands up. "And I can tell you that because we're best friends."

"Sorry, buddy." Weston appears at my other side. "I respect the hell out of you, and you know that. But I have to agree with Knox on this one. These guys are busting their asses out here. We've run that play flawlessly all ten times. What's going on with you?"

"I'm fucking fine. This next game isn't going to be easy. We need to be prepared."

Weston eyes me over before his mouth opens to speak. "And we *are* prepared, brother. If you want to run it ten more times, we'll do it. But only if you think we need to." He drops his voice lower, so only I can hear him. "And not just because you're in pain."

"I'm not in pain. I'm fucking fine," I snarl at him.

Leaning into me, he pats my shoulder. "I know a man in pain, trust me. Just because I don't talk about anything of substance doesn't mean I haven't felt some of the same shit you have. Man to man though, punishing your teammates isn't going to help."

I look around at my teammates and at Coach, who's eyeing me on the sidelines, no doubt about to step in and take this practice from me. I'm sure this was a test, and I likely failed. He wanted to see how I'd lead my team solo during practice, and I ran them damn near into the ground.

Jerking my chin at my team, I wave them over. "Everyone, huddle up."

They make their way over and form a circle around me, their body language far different than usual, and I can tell I fucked up.

Looking around at their faces, I pull my helmet off. "I'm sorry, boys. I know practice sucked ass. I know I was hard on you all. I can be intense when it comes to this game."

I get a few snickers and a few grumbles.

I roll my eyes. "All right, you win. I was a complete dick."

"That's more like it," mutters Dex.

"Yeah, yeah." I look down at the grass and back up at the eyes on me. "The game this weekend, against Texas"—I shake my head—"I won't lie; we have our work cut out for us. So far this season, a lot of the wins have come easy. This team won't be like that. I promise you," I tell them the truth.

This team was my dream school. They have a quarterback who's a junior this year. One of the best I've seen. He's part of why I didn't go to Texas. I knew I wouldn't get any playing time. Of course, there were other reasons. But that did play a small part in my decision.

"Anyway, get your ugly asses on out of here," I joke. "See you tomorrow, bright and early."

I've got to get my shit together for the game in a few days. Coach chose me to be his starting quarterback, and I can't let him down. Not after he trusted me to do this job and I promised him I could handle it.

I told him I'd help him lead this team to a championship, and that's what I'm going to do.

I just need to figure out how to get my mind off of Ally.

twenty-six

ALLY

The last few weeks, I've kept myself so busy that I don't even have a split second to stop and think about Cole. Or any of my problems.

I miss him—so fucking much.

But on a positive note, I don't have to constantly keep dodging his questions or lie to him. Which is a relief.

Between working at Lenny's, classes, and homework, I haven't been much of a friend to Sloane. But when she asked to go out tonight to dinner, I was all for it. I have grown to really love her these past few months of knowing her. I trust her, which is a hard thing for me to do.

"We just can't go to King's Pub again," I tell her. "That's his competition, and Lenny will kick my ass."

Her forehead wrinkles, and she makes an odd face. "We're not going to King's Pub. We're going to a steak house, and they have pasta too. But I don't get it. Lenny's is, like, a mom-and-pop restaurant. King's Pub is just that—a pub. Why would they be in competition?"

"Because weekend nights, they steal all the business. And now, they're doing shit like milkshakes and trying to mimic Lenny's burger. He's pissed." I laugh. "I told him I'd go over there and put a bag of flaming dog shit on the doorstep." Shaking my head, I recall his face when he heard my ridiculous offer. "He definitely contemplated it, but he said no."

"I swear, you like Lenny more than me sometimes." She pouts. "It's like he's your old-man bestie."

"I do not." I giggle. "I love you both. But just in different ways. He's sort of like the grandfather I never had."

Her face looks remorseful. "Ally, I'm sorry. I didn't even consider that. I'm a bitch."

"Oh my good God, it's fine. I know it's weird that I have an old-man friend." I smile. "Coming to Georgia, I've met so many great people. You, Carla, and my old-man bestie, Lenny. It's been really nice, having people. I finally am experiencing what it's like to have a village."

"And Cole …" she says curiously.

"Yeah, and Cole. But I had him before I came here, and I know he'll always have my back. It's just … I don't know, Sloane. I hate that he always wants to rescue me. You know?"

Before Cole, I never needed anybody to protect me. I got through life all on my own. Even as a toddler, I didn't die from malnutrition. Yet I made it even though I have no idea how. And then there's Cole, constantly trying to save me like I'm some damsel in distress.

I wish he'd see me for how strong I am. I went through hell my last day in Charlotte's Falls. I thought I was going to die that day. Yet here I am, alive.

"It could be worse. He could *not* want to rescue you. He could be a guy who didn't give a shit. You know?"

She speaks the truth. That would be much worse, and I'm aware of that. But how can I explain what the hell my deal is when I barely understand it myself sometimes.

I'm a fucking confusing, weird, temperamental creature.

Putting my lips in a straight line, I roll my eyes. "Oh fuck, girl. Why you gotta go and make me feel like a gigantic bag of dicks?"

She smiles. "Because, sometimes, it's easier to see things from the outside instead of from the inside. And I know I don't know your whole story, or his, or yours together, but I know he loves you. And I can tell you love him too."

Her words hit me like a ton of bricks. But I attempt to laugh it off. That beats diving into the real nitty-gritty shit.

"All right, Dr. Phil," I tease her. "I want carbs. Let's roll."

Xo

158

COLE

"Thanks for the meal, Cap. It was A-fucking-one," chirps Knox as we sit around the large table at the steak house with most of the entire team.

"Eh ... my steak was a bit overcooked. But it's all good," Weston grumbles.

"Dude"—I look at Weston—"your steak was fucking bleeding. In what universe is that overdone?"

It was barely cooked to even be considered rare. It was nasty. Don't get me wrong; I'm all about having a pink center, but if there's blood pouring out, fuck, that shit's just nasty.

"Whatever. You're clearly not a steak connoisseur." He rolls his eyes.

Ignoring him, I turn toward Knox. "Hey, why did you thank me? Who the fuck said I'm paying?" I frown.

I have money that Jenn and Matt gave me. They have more money than God himself, so I know they wouldn't care. But I still hate using it. Nothing in life is ever free. Eventually, they'll want some sort of reimbursement.

"We won that game last night that you've been running us ragged over." Knox hits me in the side. "That means, you buy us dinner."

"Fine, I'll buy your fucking dinner, you cheap fucks."

That game was tough as hell, and I worked them like dogs the practices before. Mostly because I wanted to win, but partly because my mood was sour after my fight with Ally.

Winning against a team like Texas did brighten my mood—for a little while anyway. They are highly ranked, yet we beat them. It wasn't all me either. Our team has the potential to go all the way.

Throwing some cash on top of the check, I stand up, stuffing my phone into my pocket. "Let's roll."

ALLY

Shutting the car door, I follow Sloane toward a restaurant I have yet to go to. The way my stomach is growling though, they could feed me cow balls, and I'd probably still eat it.

"I've heard this place has the best pasta." She sighs. "I loooove pasta."

"I think I'll have a salad, no dressing," I say, keeping my face straight.

"What?" She whips her head toward me. "A damn salad? In a place that is known for delicious steaks and pasta?"

"I'm just playing. If I ever order a salad, check my temperature. And if I ever order it without dressing, go ahead and check me into a mental institute. Because I've gone and lost my damn mind."

She laughs. Just as she reaches for the door, it flies open. Revealing Cole, Knox, and Weston as they walk outside.

"Hey, gorgeous." Knox winks as he looks at Sloane. "Long time no see."

Nervously playing with her hair, she gives him a small smile. "Yeah, uh, how have you been? Still undefeated, I see."

"Oh yeah, baby. That's how it'll stay too. We're going right to the top." He grins, showing his perfect teeth.

I glance at Cole, taking in his black hat pulled low on his head and his black T-shirt. As he stuffs his hand in his pocket, he fishes his keys out.

"Let's go, boys," he says coolly, not so much as sparing me a glance. "We've got early practice tomorrow."

Knox holds his hand up to his ear like he's in the fifth grade. "Call me," he says, winking at Sloane.

She blushes and turns toward me. "Ready to get our table?"

"Yeah," I say, looking in Cole's direction as he walks into the parking lot, not even looking back. "Yeah, I'm ready."

Pushing the restaurant door open, Sloane heads to the hostess station and gives the pretty brunette standing behind the counter her name. Shortly after, we follow her to our table.

As I plop my ass down in the booth across from Sloane, she gives me a look of sympathy.

"What?" I say, leaning forward on my elbows. "Get on with it. Say whatcha need to say."

"So … he was frosty …"

"Cole?"

"No, Weston." She rolls her eyes. "Yes, Cole!"

"Yeah, well, I told you we didn't exactly leave on a good note the other night."

I told her everything I said, everything he said. I told her how I'd never seen him look at me that way, with that kind of anger and hate. Because I hadn't. Even when I had pissed him off before, he always looked at me with love. The love was gone.

"I sort of figured you were blowing it out of proportion."

My mouth hangs open. "Why in the hell would you think that?"

She shrugs. "Because that boy loves you more than he loves anything else. The sun rises and sets on your left asscheek in his eyes. So, yeah, I didn't think he could possibly be that mad at you."

"And now?" I ask her.

"And now, I see that you weren't exaggerating. It's clear he's hurt. And I know you are too."

I sit back against the wooden booth. "I just can't see how I could ever be with him and deal with all the ruckus that is his life now." I sigh.

Truth is, the closer he gets to me, the more I push away. Because there's too much shit buried underneath. If I let him in, he'll find out everything.

She gives me a sad smile. "Ally, he loves you; he wants you. You are the one who keeps finding excuses to run. You are the one pushing him away."

I know that she's right. I have so many secrets I'm not ready to open up about. And I know me sabotaging us is just me avoiding him finding out what I've worked so hard to keep hidden. In my mind, if I keep the truth buried, I'll never have to feel the effects of it. If it stays in the past, I can try to move on and forget it.

"That boy let you use his truck—his sexy, very expensive truck," she points out. "If that's not love, I don't know what is. Y'all need to figure your shit out."

I shake my head and attempt to smile. I remember how much she oohed and aahed when I told her that he had done that.

What it boils down to is, I'm a coward. When you're with someone, you have to be honest. And I'm not willing to be honest with Cole right now.

"I know," is all I say. I don't have any answers that I feel comfortable sharing out loud.

Changing the subject, I turn to make sure all the football players are gone. "So, are you and Knox off or on right now? Or do you even know?"

"Off … I think." She sighs. "I don't freaking know."

"I don't get you guys. At all," I admit. "You talk, then you don't talk, then you do talk, then you go back to not talking." I pause, resting my hand on my cheek. "By the way, I'm aware that those who live in glass houses should not throw stones, so I should probably keep my mouth shut. But I'm just curious, I guess. About the two of you."

Her fingers mindlessly toy with the napkin on the table. She seems so sad.

Dropping the napkin and her hands down in front of her, she shrugs her slender shoulders. "I don't know. I just … we just … seem to not be able to get on the same page."

The waitress comes and takes our order. We each get chicken Alfredo because I need carbs after that interaction with Cole. Badly. And then I need to polish this dinner off with cheesecake. Food is always the answer.

"What did you mean by that? That you can't get on the same page?" I ask her.

"Well, when I want to give it a go with him, he backs off. Yet when I put my hands up and I have had enough, he comes back around. And the most pathetic thing is, I let him." She looks at me. "He's so damn wishy-washy." She laughs once. "About like you with poor Cole."

Well, shit. I guess she has a point.

"Have you guys … banged?" I mutter quietly.

I feel like if they had, she would have told me. Then again, she's much more proper than I am, so maybe she'd keep that tidbit bottled up inside. Either way, I'm asking.

"What?" she says nonchalantly, having no freaking idea what I mean.

Sometimes, I wonder how innocent this girl really is. She told me she wasn't a virgin and that she had sex with her ex-boyfriend, but she seems purer than I am. Which, let's be real, wouldn't take much. After all, I had sex in a restaurant break room and would do it all over again.

"You know, hanky-panky, birds and the bees, rode the donkey, bump and grind, bounce on the pogo stick, butter the muffin, ro—"

"Ally!" she hush-yells. "What is wrong with you?" she says, holding her hand up to her face to shield it, like she's embarrassed, but I can see she's trying not to laugh.

"Sorry," I say, sipping my drink. "I was curious."

"It's fine," she clips back.

"Well, did you though?" I try to keep a straight face.

She pretends to act mad but soon fails and laughs uncontrollably. "You are literally the worst!" She howls with laughter, wiping her eyes.

I shrug. "Give a bitch a break. I've never had a friend who was a girl before. I'm used to Cole constantly bringing up his dick and balls, not having to ease into conversations gently."

"Well, as a matter of fact, we have not. We've never even kissed." She looks embarrassed, her cheeks growing crimson red. "It's like he doesn't find me attractive."

The waitress sets our plates down, and it smells absolutely amazeballs, causing my mouth to water.

Picking up my fork, I point it at her. "Trust me, he thinks you're attractive. Who wouldn't?" I raise my eyebrows at her. "Buuuut … maybe he's got a tiny penis, and he's nervous for you to find out."

"To find out about his small penis?" she says, scrunching her face up.

Twirling my fork into my pasta, I glance at her. "I mean, what could be more embarrassing than a tiny wiener for a man? Especially a baller."

She covers her mouth to hide her laughter. "Have you looked at him? There's no way in hell his dick is small." Her cheeks grow even redder, if that is possible. "Besides, I sort of know it isn't tiny."

Whoa, Sloane said dick.

"Wait, how do you know?"

"Well, remember that time that we went to their house and you and Cole went for a walk, which ended up with you two fighting—shocker—which ended up with you running home, but I stayed and watched a movie?"

I nod slowly, my eyes likely as big as the dinner plate. As I wait for more juicy details, I take a bite of pasta. "Yes."

"Well, we watched the movie in his bed, and he dozed off. He was tired after the game."

"And you … what? Like, took his dick out to see how big it was?" I ask, confused. *Now, that would be fucking weird.*

"What? No! Oh my God, what is wrong with you? No!"

"Sorry." I shrug. "How do you know he's got a big dong then?"

"Did you just say don—" Putting her hand on her forehead, she rolls her eyes. "You know what? Never mind. As I was saying, we were watching a movie, he dozed off, and when he did, he pulled me against him."

Never blinking, I bob my head up and down in understanding. "He popped a chub."

"I mean, I was going to say he got excited in his sleep, but yes, he … popped a … chub." She grimaces. "That's a nasty way to put it. You are such a guy sometimes."

"Eh, I'm gross. What can I say?" I wipe my mouth with my napkin. "So, anyway, he got a boner, and it was large?"

Her eyes widen. "Yes. Very."

Raising one eyebrow, I pull my mouth to the side. "So, he isn't hiding a small peen … interesting. We must get to the bottom of this."

She acts irritated and then laughs. "The only other thing is …"

"What?" I ask curiously.

"Maybe I scared him away … at open mic night." She covers her face up with her hands.

"Why would you have scared him away?" I play dumb.

I get it though—shit was hard to watch. I thought about running into the wall to injure myself and make a scene to get everyone's attention off her. Or flashing my tits. Anything to make everyone stop watching Sloane slaughter a perfectly good song.

She gives me a pointed look. "Ally, I sucked. I'm aware of this."

"You didn't suck." When I find her eyes narrowed at me, I shrug. "All right, fine. So, maybe singing isn't in your future. Big deal. You got up there, and you did it anyway. I'm damn proud of you."

"Thanks," she sighs. "At least I can dance."

"Hell yeah, you can." *Thank fuck for that.*

"Cole's eyes didn't leave you when you were on the stage. Neither did anyone else's in the room. Your voice is amazing, Ally." She smiles. "But the way he watches you, it's beautiful. You are all he sees."

Nervously playing with my hair, I blow out a breath. "I know."

From the first moment we met, I've known I'm the only girl he sees. Like two stars, bound for nowhere, we collided, and instead of burning out, we became one.

The secrets I'm keeping buried are eating me alive. I can't have him close until I'm ready to tell him. But the truth is, I'm beginning to wonder why I'm fighting so hard to keep things hidden from a man who would die for me.

I sat in the passenger seat of the social worker's car. Gazing out the window at the endless trees we passed. Never really thinking about where I was going because honestly, I didn't really care.

This was the day I'd be moving in with a new family. I should have been scared or nervous or something. Some feeling, no matter how miniscule it might be. Yet there I sat, feeling nothing besides numbness.

"This couple just took in another twelve-year-old. It's a boy, but maybe you two will be friends."

She tried to make small talk. I found it annoying. I was exhausted from getting no sleep since my birthday five days before. All I wanted was for her to shut her piehole.

I didn't care about a twelve-year-old boy. I didn't care about how many kids those assholes took in. I just wanted to be eighteen and on my own.

"Here we are," she muttered under her breath, pulling into the dirt driveway in front of a white double-wide trailer.

Turning toward me, she offered me a small smile. "Home sweet home, Ally."

I refused to smile back. I simply turned my attention back to the window.

"I'm sure you're still grieving your mother, sweetie, but—"

"I am not grieving my mother," I cut her off. "Save your breath."

She sighed. "All right. Well, let's go in and check it out. I'm sure they are anxious to meet you."

As we opened the car doors and made our way to the doorstep, it swung open, showing me a lady who had messy black hair, her eyes cold and ruthless. Beside her stood a man who had a bald head, except for some at the sides, making him look like Bozo the Clown. I instantly found him creepy, to put it mildly.

The vibe I was getting from this couple was not good; it was dark. The social worker was nice. She had taken me to stay at other houses before when my mom wasn't doing well. I knew I could tell her that I was uncomfortable, that they weren't good people, and she would take me somewhere else. I seriously considered doing that.

Until I saw him.

He was sitting on a run-down swing set at the edge of the lawn. He was scrawny yet so handsome.

My heart beat irrationally for an unfamiliar boy whom I knew nothing about. And when he saw us, he began to walk our way.

And when his eyes met mine, I felt something I had never felt. I felt like I was home.

It was like I knew him. Even though I knew that was impossible. I knew I'd never seen him before in my life. Yet, somehow, I felt like we were connected.

He owned the same broken eyes that I did. And his mouth looked as though it had no idea how to form a smile. The same as mine.

When he reached me, his eyes bored into mine, never faltering. Before finally, the most beautiful sight came to my eyes. That boy—that sad, tattered-clothes-wearing boy—he smiled. And though it looked like the most foreign thing for him, it was the most beautiful thing I'd ever seen.

And for once in my life, I knew I was exactly where I was meant to be.

"The angel," he said quietly, nodding his head. "You're finally here."

I shook my head and frowned. "No ... Ally. My name is Ally."

When he came over to me, his eyes stared into mine, calming my nerves. "Ally, my angel."

twenty-seven

COLE

Another game, another win, leaving us undefeated in the season. That's great and all, but I looked up in the seats where Ally and Sloane usually sit, and once again, they weren't there. For her to stop coming to my games, she must be really fucking mad. Not that I can blame her, but honestly, I'm pissed too. She told me she hated me more than that bitch mother of hers. Told me she wished we'd never met. That shit was hard to hear even if I know those were words of anger and that she didn't mean it.

Seeing her the other night at the steak house sucked. I kept it together, never even glanced her way. But fuck me, it was hard.

Walking out of the locker room, I prepare myself for the vultures that will undoubtedly be circling for interviews. I'm not ever excited to celebrate by talking to the press. I'd rather stick my dick in ice water than talk to those nosy bastards.

They want me to fuck up and say something so that they can spin it into a story. They try to find one tiny imperfection, one minuscule insecurity, and pick at it until it's a full-blown thing. Not to mention, they crowd my space.

It's hard for me to accept the fact that when you play for a D1 school, just like when you sign to play pro ball, you owe the world everything they want to know. Kiss privacy good-bye. Suddenly, it's their God-given right to know your shit. And college is only the beginning. Once I make it into the NFL, this will seem like nothing. But I suppose that's a small price to pay in the grand scheme of things.

"Heads-up, brother, I had to give—" Knox starts to say from behind me but stops when he hears my phone ringing.

Pulling it out, I frown at the unknown number. "Hello?"

"Um, hi. Is this Cole?" a vaguely familiar, sweet Southern voice says softly.

"Depends. Who's asking?" I toss back. I don't give my number out to anybody. So, I don't have the slightest clue who this could be.

"It's Sloane, Ally's friend and roommate. I got your number from Knox." She's quiet for a moment. "This is probably a mistake, and Ally will likely never trust me again, but I need you to come over here and … check on her." She pauses, and I can hear the uneasiness in her voice. "Something … something just isn't right. She hasn't even left the room today. I don't know, Cole. She's a mess. I'm really worried."

I don't have to hear any more. "I'll be there in five," I say quickly, almost ending the call but stopping myself. "Sloane? You still there?"

"Yes." She seems panicked.

"Whatever you do, just don't let her leave," I say before ending the call. Stuffing my phone back into my pocket, I head toward the parking lot.

"Cole Storms! Hey, can I get a—Cole? Excuse me, we'd like an interview! Storms!" one reporter yells relentlessly.

"Excuse me, I'd like to ask a few questions," another one says, stepping in front of me.

"Not today." I try to keep my tone somewhat calm.

"It'll only take a few minutes." She smiles, pulling out a pad of paper with no doubt a shit-ton of questions she's concocted for me.

"Not. Happening," I say sharply before stepping around her.

She attempts to catch me again, and I've fucking had enough. All I care about right now is getting to my girl. Fuck these people standing between her and me.

"Fuck off. The answer is no." *I'm going to pay for that, I'm sure.*

Jogging to the parking lot, I hop into my truck. Once she purrs to life, I step on the gas. I'm glad Sloane knew she could call me, but I also know Ally is likely going to be fucking livid that she did. But she'll have to get over it. She can't push away everyone who loves her. Not anymore.

XO

Reaching forward, I lightly pound on the door a few times. "Ally? Open up."

Silence greets me.

"Ally? Sloane? Open the fucking door, or I'll kick it—"

The door opens, and Sloane stands in the doorway.

With her eyes wide, her face pales. "I can't get her to talk to me. I don't know what's wrong. I came home, and she was just ... like this," she whispers, shrugging her small shoulders. "She was supposed to be at work today."

Looking past her, I see Ally's body curled up on her side as she visibly shakes. Her dark brown hair is a mess all around her pillow.

Moving around Sloane, I make my way to her bed. Lying down, I pull her against me. Which only makes her cry harder. Her petite body trembles against mine.

"Shh ..." I whisper against her hair. "I'm right here, baby. I've got you now."

I hear the door shut, telling me Sloane has left us alone. She's a good friend to Ally. I'm thankful as fuck that she was around to call me.

I have no idea what is going on with her. In all the years I've known her, I've never seen her this wrecked, and that says a lot because we've had some really deep conversations about some even deeper, fucked up shit. But she was never this bad off.

For the next hour, that's all I do—I just hold her. I don't speak; I don't move. I just hold on to her so that she knows I'm here. So she knows I'm never letting go.

When she finally calms down enough so that her breathing has slowed down, she pushes herself up to sit. Standing up, she walks over to her desk. She pulls out a piece of paper, folded into a square.

Holding her arm out, she hands it to me. "Read it," she says, moving her eyes to the floor.

"Ally—"

"Please, read it."

Slowly, I take the note. Unfolding it, I prepare myself for whatever the fuck could be written there. For whatever I'm about to see.

To my Storm,

I'm sorry that you've returned home, only to find me no longer here. I'm so sorry that not only am I gone, but I also didn't get a chance to even tell you good-bye. Please know that I did not leave because I wanted to. I hope you know that I'd never leave you if it was my choice. Today was a very bad day, and I only wish I could be in your arms right now. Only then would I know I was safe.

All my time on this earth, you have been my only family and the only person who has ever loved me. We have had each other's backs since the day we met, and with you around, I always know I am protected. Protected from my fear of being alone, protected from the nightmares of the past, and protected from the monsters that roam this earth.

I've also realized that the only home I've ever known is you, Cole. I've finally figured out that a home doesn't always mean walls, a door, and a place to sleep at night. I know for me, it isn't. To me, it is your familiar arms, your steady heartbeat against mine, your calming touch, and most importantly, your ability to love me. Growing up, I never knew what it was like to be loved, and the feeling felt so foreign to me. Yet somehow, I knew that's exactly what it was with you. So, thank you for showing me that I'm not unlovable after all because it turns out, the greatest human being on this earth has loved me with so much grace and patience. God knows I don't always make it easy.

The birthdays that you made special, the times you held me when I needed to feel close to someone, and the storms we chased together, basking in them just to escape our shitty world for a while—those times were the best days of my life. You were the best days of my life. And my fondest memories are the ones I have of you and me.

One day, I hope to see you and explain it all. And to tell you what happened on this horrible day, a day where they are forcing me to pack my things and leave you. But for now, that isn't a burden that I want you to carry. You don't deserve to cart around such a heavy load after all you've been through on your own.

Promise me something, Cole. Promise me you'll always stay optimistic. Promise me you'll continue to see the good in the world, even when you have every reason not to. Promise me you'll think of me often, but don't let the memories of us dictate your future. Because, Cole, your future is so damn bright. So much brighter than this shithole town has so far granted you. Promise me you'll chase your dreams but never let them make your life any less than wonderful. If you find yourself too overwhelmed with the pressure of the game or your needs are not being fulfilled, please take a step back. Just find happiness, and the rest will follow.

I hope one day to see you. I hope one day to feel your lips on mine and your arms wrapped around my body. I hope one day to laugh so hard that I almost pee my pants again from one of your stupid-ass jokes. I hope to watch you play football from the stands, wearing your name and jersey number on my back and screaming way too loud. And I hope one day to sing for you again. I hope for all of those things so damn much.

But if that doesn't happen, if we never find each other again, if life doesn't grant us that gift, I know you'll be all right. And that's what will get me through. Because even though we're as thick as thieves, I also believe in you on your own, without me. I always will. And I promise I will never stop being your biggest fan. And no matter where I am, know that I am rooting for you always.

Thank you for being my favorite person in the entire world.

Forever and always. In the good and in the grit.

Love,

Ally

xo

I stare at the letter for a few minutes. Processing that she did try to say good-bye, that she wanted to. She just couldn't.

"Thank you for sharing this with me," I tell her. Folding the piece of paper up, I grip it in my hand. Like I'm scared it will magically disappear, taking her with it. "I should have known that you didn't want to leave without a good-bye."

She sighs. "I wanted to leave you that letter, but when I left, it was abruptly. I tried to slide it under your pillow, but *they* came in before I could. I ended up having to bring it with me, so you never got to see it," she tells me before moving her body between my legs. "I wanted you to see it *so* badly, Cole. I needed you to know that I wasn't like everybody else in our lives. I didn't *choose* to leave."

"Thank you. But I don't understand. What's going on today?" Reaching up, I tuck a strand of hair behind her ear as she stands between my legs, looking down at me.

"I think that the weight of the fight we had finally caught up to me," she answers honestly. "You are the only person I've ever had in my corner, and I pushed you away to keep my secrets safe. Secrets that ate away at my soul for too damn long. I ... cracked." She shakes her head sadly. "No, actually, I broke."

Holding the letter up, I lean into her. "Can you tell me more ... about everything?"

Taking a deep breath, she blows it out shakily. "It was a few days before you got back from football camp," she says, mindlessly digging her nails into her own palm. "I was in my room, and the younger kids were all outside. Marion had gone to the store or ... something, and ... Dave ... he, uh ..." she stutters. "He was home."

As much as the words pain her to say, I need to hear them. I need to know.

Moving my hand to hers, I squeeze it. "I'm right here, baby. It's all right."

She visibly swallows, wiping her eyes with her sleeve. "He was drunk. And … and he came into my room. He started going off about how ungrateful I was. How I was trash, nothing, worthless." She wipes a tear that escaped her eye and shakes her head, looking down at the floor. "He got in my face, pushed me down. So, I … told him off. I shouldn't have. But I couldn't help it. I really couldn't help it."

"He hurt you?" I ask her, praying to God she says no. Right now, the things running through my head that could have happened are making me feel like I'm going to faint.

She nods once. "Yes. But not in the way you might be thinking." Her cheeks redden, and I hate the fact that she feels ashamed for something that monster did to her. "Once I told him off, he got *really* mad. He grabbed me, throwing me against the wall." A cry escapes her throat. "He … he pressed his hand to my throat. Pressing harder and harder." Her lip trembles. "I swore … I swore I was going to die. I could feel the life leaving my body with every second."

I bite my lip so hard that I taste blood, and I feel my heart shatter inside of my chest.

"I've been through a lot of fucked up shit, Cole. But … I don't know … that day really sucked."

I pull her to me, and she sits on my lap. I kiss her head. "I am so, *so* sorry, baby. I should have been there. I was at fucking football camp."

"This wasn't your fault. Don't ever think that any of it was your fault." She licks her dry lips. Her voice sounds so sad and so vulnerable as she opens up about everything. "I knew I was going to black out soon, but I gathered up every single ounce of energy I had, and I kneed him in the balls. Thinking, you know, if I did that, I would have a split second to run. To get away. But I was wrong. So wrong."

"What happened next?"

"When I tried to run, he … he grabbed my hair." Tears run down her cheeks. "He beat the hell out of me, Cole. I don't think he would have stopped if … Marion hadn't come home. My ribs, my nose … I was in so much pain."

"She stopped it?" I ask, surprised.

She shakes her head and wipes her cheeks with her sleeve. A bitter, sad laugh escapes her. "Not because she wanted to. She said if he killed me, they'd go to jail. So, instead, they said if I ever told a soul, if I ever breathed a word of it to you, not only would they ruin your future, but they'd also kill me."

Her cries are the most heartbreaking sound. I'd give anything in the world to take her pain away.

She was beaten. By a fucking man. And I wasn't even there. I'm supposed to protect her, and I fucking failed. I failed so badly. And now, she'll pay for my letdown for the rest of her life. How can she ever come back from this?

God gave me an angel, and I couldn't even protect her.

"Cole"—her lip trembles—"it was …" She can't get the words out through her emotion. "It was aw-awful. I-I have these dreams. Well, nightmares. They feel like I'm back in that room. Like he's right here, still trying to kill me."

I cradle her in my arms. She seems so much smaller right now than she usually does. So defeated and drained.

Rocking her, I hold her as tightly as I can. "Shh. I'm so sorry, Ally. I'm so fucking sorry. I shouldn't have left. I failed you, but I will never let anything happen to you ever again. I promise you."

How can she trust my words? My words are completely invalidated because I *did* leave and she *did* get hurt. All for what? A fucking football camp? None of that matters. Not when it comes to her. She should have mattered more than the game did.

Sitting up, she tries to look at me, but soon, she averts her eyes to the ground. Her makeup is streaked across her beautiful face, and her body looks completely crushed. She looks broken. The toll of everything life has put her through finally showing on her face. She's the strongest woman I have ever met in my life, but all the life and joy has been taken from her eyes. Leaving behind someone that I wish so badly I could fix.

Her words from a few months ago filter through my brain. *"You can't fix me this time."*

I get it now. I fucking get it so much.

Slowly, I reach down and cup her cheek. "Ally, is that why you have a hard time looking me in the eyes now?"

She's quiet for a minute before finally answering, "Yes. But not for the reason you think." She stops, licking her dry lips. "I wanted to keep this hidden from you. Partly because I was too proud to say the words out loud. And also because I didn't want to weigh you down with these secrets. You've had too much put on you for one lifetime already."

"I am so sorry you were all alone, baby." I hold her closer. "I am so fucking sorry."

Her small frame cripples slightly as she tries to force the next words out. "Did you ever try to find me? Or … or at … at least ask where I went?" Her voice breaks.

"Of course I tried to find you, Ally. I promise you that I did. Marion and Dave wouldn't tell me anything. They wouldn't say a fucking word. But I tried anyway." Now, it's my own tears that are running out of my eyes as I imagine her all alone after experiencing something like that. Watching, waiting for me to show up.

I'm in between wanting to throw up and wanting to fucking murder a man with my own bare hands. I want to watch the life drain from his cocksucking body. And the part that makes me realize I'm likely not a good person is, I could do it without thinking twice. And I know I'd sleep fine at night.

But I need to be strong right now—for her. This isn't about me or my anger or vengeance. I need to just take care of my girl.

"I'm s-sorry I didn't tell you sooner. I was-wasn't ready." She stops and takes a breath. "I knew if I looked into your eyes, I'd want to tell you every-everything, and I was to-too scared to do that. Scared for you and for me."

"I'm so fucking sorry, Ally."

"After covering me head to toe in a hat, scarf, sweater, and pants to hide my wounds, they forced me on a bus and sent me to live at Sisters Safe Place." Glancing up at me, she shakes her head. "And yes, that place is as horrible as the tales about it."

The Sisters Safe Place is a church group that houses troubled teenage girls. We've heard stories of them drugging the girls to allow pastors to come in and rape them, working the girls to near death, and damn near starving them.

"Did they ... hu—"

Holding her small hand up, she stops me. "No. Nobody hurt me there. But I saw it happen to others. I escaped just in time."

"Why didn't you reach out to me?" I ask her as softly as I can. Though inside, I'm furious that she didn't contact me for help. "You changed your number. You deleted all social media. Fuck, Ally, I tried to find you. I could have helped you."

She shrugs slowly, her eyes puffy and red. "I felt like I couldn't reach out. Apparently, a lot of people were calling, wanting to adopt you." She looks down. "Dave and Marion didn't want to risk you opening your mouth up to your fancy new parents about what he had done to me." She cringes. "I guess it was easier to send me far, far away."

"Fuck everybody. I was almost eighteen anyway."

"Yes," she says. "But people were offering money. They were ... basically taking the highest offer."

Her words burn my soul. The realization that Matt and Jenn possibly paid for me makes me sick to my stomach.

"That's illegal," I state the obvious.

"Yeah, it is. But Marion and Dave are crooked as fuck—you know this. The only reason they ever took in foster kids to begin with was for the state to pay them. So, obviously, when people came knocking after hearing you were talented, they weren't going to go by the book."

"Motherfuckers," I growl.

"It gets worse," she sighs.

How the fuck could this shit get any worse? How do people like this even exist?
"Go on," I tell her.

"I put up a fight, Cole. I promise I did. I wanted them to at least tell you I had no choice. And for them to grant me saying good-bye to you. The last thing I ever wanted was to leave you alone. We had been each other's one constant thing for years. I never would have left you." She rubs a hand over her forehead, and her shoulders slouch. "But if I didn't leave, they threatened to have you blacklisted from any and all college football teams. They said they could spin a good enough story to have no college ever want you." Licking her lips, she looks at me. "If no college team wanted you, I knew no NFL team would want you, Cole."

"Ally—"

"Damn it, Cole! You know it's true too," she yells.

"Of course it is! But fuck football, Ally. Fuck everything when it comes to you and me. I'm so glad you opened up to me, and I am so sorry that I left you. But it makes me so fucking angry that you didn't realize that what we had trumped football. Hands down," I tell her honestly. "You've been my life since we were twelve years old. How did you not realize that?"

Ignoring me, she opens her mouth to speak, "The minute I turned eighteen, I left Sisters Safe Place, and I stayed in a homeless shelter. All alone. With nobody. I just …" Her hand forms a fist, and more tears fall down her cheeks. "I just couldn't get past this anger. From what he did. It lingered and festered and grew. So, I decided I wanted a fresh start. I saw an ad for Brooks University on the computer one day. A day when it would have been so easy for me to give up on life completely. It looked so warm and inviting, and then I discovered they had a music program here." She smiles. "I just had to come. I knew it in my heart."

"And then I was here," I state the obvious.

She nods. "Yep. And one look at you, and I just wanted to jump back into the closest thing to a home that I had ever known." Her eyebrows pull together. "But not only did I hold an anger inside of me that I couldn't control, but I was also terrified to get close to you. I didn't know if Dave and Marion were lurking in the shadows, afraid that I'd get close to you and spill my secrets. Or if I told you, I worried you'd go off the deep end and ruin your entire life." She shakes her head. "I was so scared. But I knew I couldn't keep this from you forever."

"Baby, you don't have to worry about them anymore. You hear me?"

Looking at me, she attempts to nod.

"They want to threaten to take football? Well then, fuck football," I tell her honestly. Because if I had to choose between this girl and football, I'd choose her. Every. Single. Time.

"I would never want to make you choose." She sighs. "But life is so crazy … I mean, I just can't believe we both ended up here," she whispers, pressing her forehead to mine.

"I came here after reading the success rates of being drafted from here," I answer her truthfully. "But when I was choosing a college, the first question I asked each and every one of the teams who approached me was, 'Do you have a music program there?' Because even though I knew the chances were next to zero, I was holding on to a tiny bit of hope that just maybe, you would end up where I went." My body calms slightly at the memory of seeing her at the movie theater. I shake my head. "But I never thought you actually would. Quite a sign from the universe, us both being here, huh?"

"It was," she says softly. "It really was."

Looking at her, realizing where she's been, I think back to the day I came home to find her gone.

I couldn't accept thinking she'd just upped and left. Even if that was what Dave and Marion had led me to believe.

I searched for her, going to the bus station and everywhere I could think that might lead me to her. Now hearing her say they bundled her up to hide her wounds, I realize why I was unable to find out anything at the bus station.

"The number you are trying to reach is not available." I listened to the annoying-as-fuck automated message playing in my ear after trying to call Ally's phone for what was likely the thirtieth time.

As I pulled my piece-of-shit truck into the bus station, I took the picture of her out of my wallet and went up to the counter.

"Have you seen this girl?" I yelled as I smashed the photo of her to the glass. "Hey! Have you seen this girl?!" I asked again, watching the older man behind the counter ignore me.

Finally, he eyed it over. "I see hundreds of people a day, but I'd remember a face like that. Sorry, son. I haven't seen her."

"What about the others? There must be somebody else," I said as I lean toward the small opening in the glass. "Please, I'm desperate. I'm really fucking desperate."

"I'm sorry. I wish I could help." He nodded to the other tellers. "Maybe they can help."

After asking five different people, I came up with nothing.

Nobody had seen her. If she had come through here, how the fuck would they have all missed her?

With each passing moment, I could feel her slipping farther from my reach. Hard to tell where she was. Or who she was with. My heart was racing, and my stomach ached at the thought that she was gone.

I was almost to my truck when I heard the old man's voice behind me. "She must be some girl for you to go through all this trouble."

Wiping my eyes like the little bitch that I was, I slowly turned to face him. "Yeah, she is. She's ... my guardian angel."

His eyes gave me a knowing look. "Found my angel sixty-six years ago. And up until two years back, when the Lord took her from me, she never left my side." He shook his head and glanced down. "My advice to you, young man: don't give up. Love always finds a way. Even when it seems impossible."

He patted me on the shoulder and walked away.

I hoped like hell he was right. But right then, it seemed impossible as hell.

I prayed to God that she was safe. I prayed nobody hurt her and that she wasn't in any sort of trouble.

My angel had come into my life abruptly. Sadly, it seemed like she had left it abruptly too.

The world had never granted me much. Just a string of people who either hadn't wanted me or had left me.

Why did I think she was the exception?

I guessed it turned out, she wasn't.

I shake my head at the flashback to that dreaded day. The day that was likely the worst day of my entire life. The day I realized I was on my own yet again.

The important thing is, she's here now. And she needs me more than ever.

twenty-eight

ALLY

Cole's body has been as rigid as stone since I told him all of my secrets and unleashed the past. It hurt, letting it out. A part of me had felt so ashamed since it'd happened. Like somehow, I could have prevented it if I had just kept my mouth shut. But in reality, I know deep down that it wasn't my fault. And now that it's out there, I feel much lighter.

I knew he was so angry as he heard what had happened. But instead of focusing on that anger, he held me and listened, and he was exactly who I needed him to be in that moment. And it hit me—he doesn't suffocate me constantly because of the fact that I'm his pet and he thinks he owns me. He does it because he wants to keep me safe. This whole time, he's just wanted to keep me safe.

Leaning against each other on the bed, like we have been doing for the past forty-five minutes, feels comfortable. And even though I know there are monsters out there, with him in this room, this close to me, I feel completely safe.

"You know"—his deep voice pulls me from my emotionally exhausted stupor—"I can't just let him get away with this. I'm going to fucking kill him, Ally."

I shake my head. Reaching over, I cup his cheek, angling his head toward mine. "No. You will not hurt him. Do you hear me?" This is what I was afraid of. I knew he'd want to head straight back to Ohio and find Dave. "I will not have you risking your future for a guy like Dave."

"I'm not risking it for him. I'm risking it for you. Because we belong to each other, Ally, and I love you. So, yeah, I'm going to risk my future in football, and I'm okay with it. Because at the end of the day, I failed to protect you. But I can do it now. I can take Dave out of this world. And I won't think twice when doing it," he says bluntly.

I know he isn't bluffing. I know he loves me and would do anything for me.

"Cole," I whisper.

"Yeah?" he says, sounding completely defeated.

"I'm really sorry for how everything played out. I'm sorry you were alone," I tell him, praying for his forgiveness.

"Baby, there was nothing you could have done. I am so sorry that I blamed you. I'm a fucking idiot."

"You aren't. You couldn't have known," I whisper.

I don't speak again for a while, and neither does he. He's quiet—too quiet—and I can tell that he mentally wants to be here for me right now but is having a hard time because he can't see past his anger. I get it. Anger can be blinding. Take it from me; that was the only feeling I was able to feel for quite some time.

Putting his forearms on his legs, he leans his face toward the floor. "I don't know what to say, Ally. I can't … fuck, I am just so mad at myself, and I can't think about Dave and Marion without imagining murdering the pair of them." Looking back up, his blue-green eyes are now so dark that they almost look black. "I would do that for you after what he did. I'd take him off of this earth. That way, you'd never have to worry again. I want to do that for you."

Sitting down on his lap, I throw my arms around his neck. "Nothing is ever worth you becoming a murderer." Leaning in, I kiss his cheek. "That would make you no better than him … but I agree. I want him to pay."

"He will," he says sharply. "Ally?"

"What?"

"I need to go to Ohio. They can't just be walking free," he says. The color is still drained from his face. "He could be hurting someone else."

My stomach turns. I've thought about that for months. "Please, just wait. A little bit longer. At least until football is over. I have a plan, I promise."

He thinks about it for a moment before looking up at me. "The season is more than halfway over. The second I play my last game, I'm going to Ohio." Burying his head into my neck, he pulls me even closer. "I need to make this right, Ally. I left you vulnerable, and this terrible thing happened to you. I need to make it up to you." His voice strains. "Or else I'll never fucking forgive myself."

"Hey," I say softly, pulling my head back and looking into his eyes. Gently, I cup the sides of his face. "I understand. I held resentment for a long time, but I *don't* blame you, Cole. I'm the one who pushed you to go to that camp. Hell, I'm the one who sent the letter in, pretending to be you, so you would get accepted."

It's all true. I knew how badly he wanted to go to it. But it was expensive, and the money we made—him helping out in the tattoo shop and me waitressing—well, it wasn't going to cover the cost. So, I sent in a letter, expressing how much "I" wanted to attend this camp. Then, I signed his name. A few weeks later, he got the phone call.

He isn't to blame for what that monster did to me. And I'm well aware of that. I wish he could have found a way to me, but really, how could he have?

Bringing my mouth to his, I press my chest against his and attack his lips viciously. Needing him to be closer than ever.

He pulls back. "We don't have to ... do that. I'm sure that's the last th—"

Pulling my shirt over my head, I throw it on the floor. "Make me forget." Attacking his lips with mine again, I cry, "Make me forget it all. Please, Cole."

I'm sure it isn't healthy that I want to mask the memories of the attack with sex. I'm aware of how fucked up that probably makes me look. But right now, I need Cole to make me feel whole again. He's the only one who can do it.

Shaking his head softly, he looks away. "I don't want to make it all worse. I love you way too much for that."

Reaching down, I pull his shirt over his head. Exposing his tattoo with my handwriting on his chest. It's so incredibly sexy to me that he did that.

"I've lost too much over other people's cruel actions." I put my forehead to his. "I need you, Cole. Fix me. Make me yours."

His eyes watch mine for a moment before he finally brings his lips to mine. Kissing me, devouring me, *owning* me, just like I need him to. "You're already mine, Ally."

And I know he means the words he's saying. He always says I belong to him, but I know he belongs to me too. Mind, body, and soul.

"All yours. Forever yours."

He pushes me off of his lap, just long enough to pull his pants down, followed by my own.

He pulls me back onto his lap, and I straddle him as he pushes my panties to the side. His lips kissing me the entire time, completely consuming me as he brings me down onto his length.

Tears flow from my eyes as we make love. Finally unleashing this secret, a secret that weighed on me so heavily, I feel a sense of freedom. Though I know I will never feel completely free again.

His fingers dig into my back as he brings us closer. But it will never be close enough. I wish we could blend into one, sharing the same skin. I need this more than I need air, water, or food. He could replace all of those things. Even if I haven't acted like it these past few months. I tried to keep him far enough away, so I could hide the past. I tried not to taint him with my secrets, but it was no use. We share a soul. I couldn't keep it from him any longer. And now that it's out, I feel like we're closer than we've ever been.

"I love you," I cry as I move up and down on him. "So fucking much."

"I love you more." He kisses my lips like he's starved for me. "Always and forever. You and me."

"Yes," I whisper back. Well on my way to oblivion.

And when he comes with my name on his lips, I feel whole, if only for a moment.

He can't fix me. I know that. Nothing can besides time. But he is my person. And if anyone is going to walk next to me through the darkness of hell and make it less painful, it's him. This beautiful, selfless, damaged boy that I have grown to love so damn much.

I know all of his secrets, and now, he knows all of mine. I know how much pain he holds inside of him. I want to help him through his, just like he has done for me.

It truly is us against the world.

twenty-nine

ALLY

After hours of using each other's bodies to escape reality, we lie there, wrapped up in one another. I know he has questions for me that he's dying to ask. But because Cole is so invested in being there for me, he's not making this day about him. I don't want him doing that anymore. We are in this together. And as much as I need his emotional support right now, he needs mine too.

Turning to my side, I prop myself up on my elbow and face him. "Cole ... what I said earlier, about ... people offering money for you?"

"Were Jenn and Matt part of the equation?" he asks softly, putting his hands behind his head. "Did they illegally offer money for me too?"

Sadly, I nod.

"Fucking awesome," he mumbles. "Have you known the whole time?"

My heart sinks. *What if he leaves me for not telling him? What if he's mad? He should be mad.*

Sitting up, I pull the sheet with me to cover my bare chest. "Yes. And I am so sorry for that. But at dinner, when you first walked away from the table, I put them on the spot about it. Told them I knew."

His eyes dart to mine. "How'd they react to that?"

"They didn't deny it. But they said they would explain everything really soon. And that they promise, as bad as it looks, it isn't what it seems."

"And?" His eyes narrow. "What's that supposed to mean?"

"You're probably going to think I'm crazy, but ... I don't know ... I believe them. I think they did what they did for a reason. I think they aren't like Dave and Marion. I think they might be all right people," I tell him honestly.

Moving his hand to his face, he drags it down and lets out a long breath, blowing his cheeks out. "So, now what?"

Lying down on his chest, I press a kiss to his skin. "Now? Well … now, I think you talk to them."

He doesn't get angry. He doesn't run away. He doesn't accuse me of keeping secrets about Matt and Jenn. He does none of that. Instead, he just holds me. Because that's the kind of love he has in his heart.

And I don't think words will ever express how much I love this man.

He was there for me at a time when I felt like I wasn't wanted by anybody. I pray my gut feeling is right and that Jenn and Matt are good people. But if they aren't, if they really are using Cole for his talent, I'll be here for him. The way he was for me that day. The day that I asked him to help me find my own dad.

"Cole?"

"Yeah, Al?" he asked softly, lacing up his cleats.

"Could you, um … help me find out who my dad is?" My cheeks burned. I shouldn't have cared to find out who my dad was. But there was some part of me that thought maybe he was looking for me. Maybe my mother never allowed him to know me.

I was embarrassed to bring this up, but I knew he wouldn't laugh at me. He never laughed at me.

He stopped mid-lace and looked up. "I, uh … I guess." After he saw my cheeks redden deeper, he grabbed my hand. "Hey, if that's what you want, that's what we'll do. Okay?"

I had a name written on a photo I'd found in my mother's trailer. Maybe it wasn't him, but I was ninety percent sure it was because I'd heard her talking to her friend once. They'd needed money for drugs, and she was going to call him and ask for money to take me to the doctor. She was going to tell him I had some rare disease.

I kept thinking, What if she never allowed him to see me? What if he tried?

"Before we do though, I need you to promise me that if it doesn't go well, you won't get down on yourself."

I shook my head. "No, I won't. I'll be fine. I'm just … curious."

He gave me a sympathetic look. "Ally, I need you to promise me. Because right now, it's easy to feel that way. But if he ends up being a complete waste of space, I don't want you to blame yourself. So, I need you to be sure."

"I promise. I just feel like if I never find out, it will haunt me. You know, the what-ifs?"

He nodded. "I understand."

"Do you want to look up your mom?"

"No," he answered sharply. "I don't."

The way he loved me was unlike anything I'd ever known even existed. I shouldn't have pushed to know my father when I had a guy like Cole in my life, showing me love every day. I didn't know why I cared so much about the man who was basically a sperm donor.

Over the next few weeks, we used the computer at the library along with Cole's boss's social media to track my father down. And after finding his phone number, I decided to call him.

As I dialed the number, I sat at the desk at the tattoo shop as Cole cleaned. Everybody had gone home for the night, making it a quiet place to make a call like this.

My palms were sweating, and my stomach turned as it rang once and then twice, and by the third time, I felt like I could puke.

"Hello?" a deep voice rasped.

"H-hi ... is this Wesley?"

"Maybe," he said back sharply. "Who's speaking?"

"Um ... well, my name is Ally. I'm Holly's daughter."

The line was quiet for a few moments, making my anxiety only grow.

"Are you there?" My voice shook slightly.

"How'd you get my number?" he said, not sharply, but not softly either.

"I ... well ... I researched you a little."

"Look, I'm not sure what you're looking for, but I have no money to give."

"I don't need money." I frowned. "I just thought ..."

I glanced at Cole, who was as pale as a ghost, his hands on the top of his head. He had been so worried about me doing this. Scared to death I'd get hurt.

I gulped, daring to get the words out. "I just thought you might want to ... you know, meet me?"

"Sorry, kid. When I was with your mother, I was so high that I didn't know where I was. That woman turned my life upside down. I heard about what happened, and I'm sorry you lost your mother, but I'm not the guy your hopes and dreams are made of." He sighed through the phone. "I'm sure you're great, but I don't ever want to find out. I'm not meant to be a dad. I wouldn't be any good at it. Trust me." And with that, he ended the call.

And even though I had promised Cole I'd be all right, I crumbled onto the floor.

But as always, he was there to pick me up. He spared me the I told you so. He showed no judgment. Instead, he just held me and rocked me until I calmed down.

This was the day I stopped looking for comfort in other places. To take what I had and absorb it. Because what I had was pretty freaking awesome.

thirty

COLE

It's hard to get amped up for today's game when all I can think about is what Ally told me yesterday. I'm here physically, but that's it. Mentally, I don't know where the fuck I am.

Not only was Ally hurt badly, but she was also forced to go away, to be on her own.

And then there's the other side of it. The side where Matt and Jenn are possibly crooked people. I always told myself they were using me, but a bigger part of me felt like they actually thought of me as family.

I remember the day my dad died. I mean it when I say that I didn't really care. For some reason, the chance of losing Matt and Jenn feels worse.

The day my father died is as clear as day in my brain. The worst part of it wasn't when he died; it was the events leading up to it that occurred earlier that day.

"Son, if you're going to play on this team, you need appropriate gear."

The other kids snickered and laughed as their eyes took in the sneakers I was wearing, which were worn with holes, and sweatpants that were too small and tattered at the bottom.

As I stared at the other boys in their new cleats and gear, I knew I didn't belong. I would though. One day. I'd make damn sure that one day, all of these assholes knew my name. Heck, maybe their kids would have posters of me on their walls.

"I'll get some," I told Coach White. Knowing I had no money to buy anything. And even if I did, how would I get to a store to do it? Still, I lied to get the conversation over with.

I was past embarrassment. I'd lived this life too long to care. But listening to someone who had no idea what it was like at my house, with my dad, was annoying.

All I wanted to do was play football. Who cared if I didn't have cleats or name-brand clothing? It didn't take away from my talent. Not to sound cocky, but I was more talented than all these jerks combined.

"Go back to the trailer park, where you belong, trash," a kid sneered once the coach was gone.

"Yeah," another kid named Luke said, poking me in the chest. "Go back to the crack shack you were raised in."

I ignored them. I was used to it by now. And I did live in a crack shack, so I guessed he was right.

"He's so dumb that even his own mom didn't want him." The meanest kid of them all, Andrew, chuckled. Watching me, waiting for me to react.

I snapped, "What did you say to me?" I shoved him backward. "I'll kill you, motherfucker. I'll fucking kill you," I yelled and punched him in his nose. Causing the coaches to run over.

I could take a lot. Being called the poor kid, being told my dad was a junkie, being called dirty—it didn't matter. But for some reason, when they talked about my mom leaving, I lost it. Though I had no idea why.

Coach White grabbed my arm and hauled me to his truck. "I'm taking your ass home. Now," he growled.

I didn't say anything, just followed him to a white truck.

"Where do you live?" his angry voice asked.

My cheeks reddened. He was going to see where I lived. Worse than that, Daddy would find out I got into trouble, and he wouldn't be happy that someone had to bring me home. He never liked anyone interrupting him when he was home.

"Coach White, can I walk? Please," I begged him.

Pulling his hat down further on his head, he eyed me over. I was hopeful he'd let me go.

"No."

"I don't want to be any trouble to you. I'll walk."

"Boy, sit your ass in this truck. I need to know where you live. I'd like to talk to your folks about getting you some cleats and practice gear."

He had no idea what he was talking about. He had his nice truck. He had a cool hat and expensive sunglasses. Heck, he had probably even eaten dinner last night. Maybe even dessert after. Lucky bastard.

Sitting back in the seat as we drove, I gave him the address. "Please don't ask my daddy that. Please. I'll … I'll get some new shoes. I'll figure it out. Just please don't ask him to buy me anything."

His head whipped toward me, his brow furrowing. "Does he hurt you, Cole?" When I didn't answer, he asked again, "Cole, does he hurt you? You can talk to me about it. You can trust me."

I sighed. "Are you going to tell my daddy that I punched Andrew?"

"Why? Are you hoping I won't?"

I nodded my head, watching the trees as we passed them. His truck was nice. I liked trucks. One day, I knew I'd have one. One day when I made it to the NFL.

"All right," he muttered. "All right."

At least I knew he wouldn't tell my dad—that was one good thing. But I knew my dad still wouldn't be happy when a stranger pulled into his yard. He was going to beat me. I knew it. I thought of the scar on the bottom of my back, and I felt an ache in it even though it didn't actually hurt. Not anymore anyway.

Nobody at school wore clothes that were dirty or too small, like the ones I did. Nobody else had a hard time paying attention at school because they were so hungry. The teachers thought I just didn't care, but I did. I really did care what they were saying. I wanted to go to college one day. I just couldn't stop thinking about food, and it made it so hard to pay attention to what they were teaching me.

"You can drop me off in front of the road to the trailer park. I can walk up."

He didn't answer. He just rested his hand on the steering wheel and kept driving until he pulled right into my road. That gnawing pain in my belly grew, and I couldn't tell if it was because I was hungry or because I was scared of my dad. I was guessing it was both.

I knew my dad was going to be so mad. Last time he got really mad, I almost died. I didn't want to die. I just wanted to play football.

"Please, Coach White. Please don't drive up to my house," I begged him. "I really don't want you to."

"Cole"—he blew out a breath—"something isn't right with your home life. I know it's not. I've watched you this season, and I know that you need help."

I suddenly wished I had told him a different trailer number back when he asked for my address. I could have told him the one no one lived in, the abandoned one at the end of the park that I sometimes hid in. At least then I could have just said Daddy wasn't home.

"Coach, I know you're trying to help, but … but you'll make him mad. Really mad."

Slowing the truck as we got to trailer number eighteen, he sighed. "And then he would hurt you?"

"No," I lied.

"Son, I've seen the bruises on your body. I've watched you as you look for food the other kids leave behind. I want to help you. This isn't how your childhood is supposed to be. You might not know that yet, but it isn't."

My head hung down. I could have jumped out and run, but I knew he'd likely still talk to my dad, and it would be the same result. Me getting my ass beat. Or worse, he could decide to make me a human dartboard again.

I climbed out of the truck and heard Coach White's footsteps following close behind me. I couldn't take him inside my trailer. That would be so embarrassing. With the old food, clothes, needles, and cigarettes everywhere, what would he think?

I knocked on the door. "Dad?"

I was greeted by silence.

Normally, I would go right inside. But if Daddy was in the middle of putting that stuff in his arm, I didn't want Coach White to see him.

Leaning over the side of the rail, I peeked in through the window.

I saw him. He was lying on the couch, asleep.

"He's asleep," I told Coach White. "We'd better leave him be. He'll be mad if we wake him."

Coach knocked again loudly before leaning over and looking in the window himself.

He looked in at my dad for a few moments before finally, his head pulled back, and he frowned. "Go sit in my truck, Cole."

"But I thought—"

"Go on." He patted my back. "Go on, son. I'll be right over, and we can go for burgers while your daddy naps."

A burger did sound really good. All I'd had that day was a cold cheese sandwich with a carton of milk for lunch. Cold lunch was for kids whose parents were so far behind on paying their lunch bill that they got the cheapest thing the kitchen could make. I wasn't complaining though; food was food.

I walked back to his truck and climbed in. My heart lurched into my throat when I saw him push the door open and go inside. My dad didn't take to strangers well. This wasn't going to end well for Coach ... or me.

A few minutes later, he came out and pulled his cell phone from his pocket. He paced as he talked on the phone to whoever it was. I just hoped to hell he didn't wake up my dad. I knew Coach wanted to help, but he didn't know how mad my dad got sometimes.

Once he hung up the phone, he walked back over to the truck and opened the door.

"Cole?" His voice sounded nervous as he ran his hand on the back of his neck.

"Yeah, Coach?"

"Your daddy ... he's, uh ... he isn't well. I called the ambulance. All right?"

"Because of the drugs? The ones he puts in his veins with needles?" I asked, not surprised. He was always passing out after he did that stuff.

I didn't know who would want to put something that made them feel so awful inside their own body. I often wondered what he would be like if he didn't use that stuff. I wondered if maybe, just maybe, he would like me more.

"Yeah." He looked at me and took his sunglasses off. "I think ... I think this time, he might have overdone it, son." Reaching over, he rubbed my shoulder. "I'm so, so sorry."

"He'll wake up," I told him. "He always does." Glancing out the window, I watched the trees sway in the wind.

"I don't know if he will," he said. "Is ... is there anyone I can call?"

"It's just him. I don't have anybody else." My stomach growled, reminding me the sandwich was long gone. But I was used to this. Normally, I wouldn't even eat until the next day at school. Unless one of the neighbors saw me passing by and offered something. I loved it when that happened.

A few minutes later, an ambulance screeched in. Followed by a cop car. Causing everyone to pop their nosy heads out of their trailers. I'd had to call an ambulance for Daddy before. They had given him medicine, and he had come back to life. They'd do the same thing. And by the next day, he'd be back to himself. His mean, angry self.

I started to open the door. It was clear we weren't going to get burgers.

"Stay in here, buddy," Coach's voice told me. "Just stay in here. I'm going to go check with the paramedics. I need you to stay here, okay?"

I nodded. Maybe he wanted to take me to dinner after all.

I watched him walk up to the officer standing on the stairs. Pulling his hat off, he clutched it in his hand before shaking his head. He glanced at me in the truck before walking over.

Getting back in the truck, he closed his eyes briefly. "Cole, your dad … he's … I'm sorry to tell you this, son, but he's gone."

"Gone," I mimicked.

I'd hoped for that man to be gone for a long, long time. I doubted today was the day it finally happened. He'd go on to live another day and hurt more people.

"He … died. I'm sorry." He reached over and clutched my shoulder, causing me to jump. Noticing my reaction, he pulled his hand back slowly. "Do you want to stay? Or go and say your good-byes or …"

"No," I said before turning my attention back to the window. "I don't want to go back in there."

A big part of me still thought he was probably going to be saved, and then I'd be stuck, living with him. Back in that hell. I despised that old, dirty trailer so much. Even though I was just a kid, a kid who shouldn't think these types of thoughts, I wished I could light it on fire and watch it burn. Some days, I even wished for this to happen with him inside of it.

I knew that was awful to say. He was my dad. But he made me feel so worthless. He hated me so much, and I didn't even know what I had done wrong. I did okay in school. I got mostly Bs. I passed my tests. They said I was talented at football. I didn't know what I had done that made him hate me so much.

I still prayed each day for my angel. My hope was wearing thin—and fast. But I knew my angel was out there somewhere, waiting for me.

"Are you sure he's dead?" I asked him one last time.

His jaw was tense as he nodded his head once. "Yes, he is. I'm sorry."

The thing is, I didn't feel sadness. I wasn't angry or upset. I wasn't in shock either, and I didn't cry. Not even a little.

The day my father died, I felt a different type of feeling. I felt … relieved. And I understand how completely messed up that really is.

thirty-one

ALLY

"They are going to lose this game," Sloane mutters to me.

"And it'll be Cole's fault," I say the sentence I know she's thinking.

"Well ... I wasn't going to say that. But ..."

I can't defend him because he is sucking ass out there. But I know why he's struggling so much. Not only did I unload my secrets, but I also unloaded Jenn and Matt's too. I damaged him before this game. If they lose, it'll be as much my fault as his.

Normally, he dominates the field. He demands attention. He's six foot two and as graceful as a damn tiny dancer. He's light on his feet, and he always seems to know exactly what's going to happen next. It's truly an honor to watch him play to his full potential.

Unfortunately, tonight isn't that.

"Storms is fucking terrible tonight," a guy with gelled hair says in front of me. "They ought to shit-can his ass. Embarrassment to the team."

"And you ought to shit-can your hairstyle, *asshole*. It isn't exactly hiding your receding hairline," I mumble much louder than I anticipated.

"What the fuck did you say, bitch?" He stands up, not looking intimidating at all.

"Pfft ... please. You're a balding, middle-aged man who likely never played sports and who likely didn't get off your mom's tit till you were fifteen years old. Please sit down and shut your mouth. Or better yet, shove some more of that popcorn in it."

Reluctantly, he huffs and puffs before sitting back down. Never saying another word besides a few inaudible grumbles.

"Remind me not to piss you off," Sloane says quietly, leaning into me. "You go for the jugular."

"Fuck with my family, and I'll piss in your Cheerios." I shrug. "Cole is family, and so are you."

She smiles and pats my shoulder. "Thanks, Al."

Cole's body is out there, running around. Physically, he's there. Mentally, he's not even in the same state. It's heartbreaking to watch. Each throw that he doesn't catch, sack he doesn't avoid, and incomplete pass he launches into the air only seems to make losing feel inevitable.

Normally, if he messes up, he turns his game up to one hundred and ten percent, just to prove himself. But not this game. This game, he just seems more defeated with each mistake he makes.

Looking at the clock winding down, I can't wait for it to be over. All I want to do is run to him and make sure that he's all right. He's saved me more times than I can count. It's my turn to save him. Or at least try.

XO

COLE

Pulling my helmet off, I walk into the locker room. Unable to even look my teammates in the eye, not wanting to see the disappointment I'm sure is written all over their faces.

They really fucking wanted this win.

I'm not one who gets inside my own head. I don't make mistakes, yet I just blew the game for my team because I made one mistake after another. We'd set out to be undefeated this season, and now, we can kiss that good-bye. All. Because. Of. Me.

The press is the absolute last thing I want to deal with right now. I'd rather go to Ally, find a long dirt road to drive down in my truck, and let off some steam before going and seeing Matt and Jenn.

That would make me feel much better.

But Coach says we need to let a few people interview us and that it isn't an option. So, I'll suck it up and do it.

After all, I did just lose this game for him, so the least I can do is a lousy interview.

"Cole Storms, your team was expected to win tonight. What do you think happened?" the first vulture asks, shoving a microphone in my face.

"You know what? No game is a guarantee. All we can do is our best. My team did their job. Unfortunately, I had an off night. It happens to all of us."

"Are you worried you won't make it to the championship? That's been your goal this season along with being undefeated, hasn't it? Now that that's gone, do you still think you've got a shot?"

"I'm not worried at all," I say calmly. "It wasn't our night. Wasn't *my* night. It won't happen again. We'll be there. I'll make sure of it."

"You sound so sure for a guy who just lost a game against a team who has lost half their games," the asshole says. His bald head shining in the stadium lights, basically blinding me.

I choose that moment to give the reporters my most charming smile. "All right, that's all from me. Have yourselves a good night."

The questions continue to fire at me, but I hoist my duffel bag over my shoulder and walk away. I have bigger fish to fry tonight than football.

It's called finding Ally and forgetting the hell that has been this day.

thirty-two

COLE

"Hey," I hear Ally's voice come from the darkness before I see her beautiful face. "Tough loss. I'm sorry, baby," she says and wraps her arms around me.

Before I can answer, some of my teammates join us near my truck.

"We're going out. Going to go get drunk and soften the blow of what just happened. You coming with?" Weston says to me.

"Nah, not tonight, man. Have fun."

"So, you lose the game for us, and then your pussy ass is too much of a bitch to even respect us enough to come out?" Dex's voice speaks with fury.

"Dex," Knox warns. "Cut the shit."

"No, fuck that. Ricky would have gone out with us. He wouldn't have ditched us for some piece of as—"

Ally's hand lets go of mine, and before I even have time to process it, she's in Dex's face.

"Get off his dick, douche bag. He's your fucking team captain. Treat him like it." She might be small, but she can be a savage.

"A shit team captain at that." He smirks.

Ally is on her tippy-toes and in his face. Her dark hair whips around as she furiously shakes her head at him, coming to my rescue. "Bitch, it took you till your senior year to even get off the fucking bench," Ally spews more words. "Just because you are a mediocre football player with, I'm sure, a teeny pencil dick, leave him the hell alone."

He looks baffled, and I'm enjoying watching this tiny girl put this meathead in his place. "I can see why he likes you. A psychotic bitch like you is probably wild in the shee—"

I have him by the throat, pressed against the wall before he even saw me coming.

"Finish that sentence," I growl, "and you can forget about football because you won't even be able to walk. I'll break your legs, motherfucker. And your fucking hands."

He gasps for air, and I press down harder.

"Storm!" Coach's voice booms. "What the fuck is going on?"

When I release him, he falls down, grabbing his neck. "He disrespected me and my girl."

Coach's eyes slowly shift from mine to his. "That true?"

"He's the team captain. He should fucking play and act like it," he manages to say between coughs.

"Dex, you weren't out there, setting the world on fire yourself, son. So, if I were you … I'd shut the hell up!" His voice rises with every word he says. "Now, I'm going to say this once: all of you, get the hell out of my sight. You all sucked tonight. Each and every one of you!"

And with that, he storms off. Luckily, the others do too—besides Knox and Weston, who both laugh and look at Ally.

"Shit, Ally. You had even me shaking in my Nikes." Knox shakes his head.

"For real, I think Sexy Dexy almost shit his *pantalones*." Weston puts a hand on his stomach and laughs.

I smile proudly at my girl. Who at one hundred ten pounds, soaking wet, just put a two-hundred-forty-pound dude in his place with ease.

Just another reason why I fucking love this girl. Because when it comes to me, she'll go to war, just to stand by my side.

ALLY

Once everyone's gone, Cole backs me up against his truck.

"You can say it. I sucked donkey dick tonight."

"I saw no such thing." I widen my eyes. "Wait, there were donkeys there?"

"Har-har, so funny," he sighs. "I feel like a useless fuck, losing that game for the guys."

Running my hand through his hair, I kiss his cheek. "You had an off night; it happens to everyone."

"Even Tom Brady?" he says, trying to act surprised.

He knows I've always had a thing for Brady.

"Fuck yes." I nod. "Most games, that fine motherfucker doesn't even show up until the fourth quarter."

"But at least he shows up," he says, looking at the ground. I can tell it's eating away at him, losing that game. "Dex was right to say what he did about me. Not about you."

"Fuck Dex," I say bluntly. "He's a toolbag who needs to stay in his own damn lane." I look at him and sigh. "I feel like tonight's loss is my fault. If I had just kept it together until the end of football season, I wouldn't have burdened you with all of this shit."

He vigorously shakes his head and tilts my chin up. "I would have been pissed if you'd kept that from me any longer. I needed to know. There will never be a right time for information like that."

When I look unconvinced, he presses his minty lips to mine. "Trust me when I say, any pain you're carrying, well, I want to carry it with you. If I could, I'd take the whole load on my back so that you didn't have to feel it." He looks discouraged. "Unfortunately, life doesn't work like that."

My eyes water as I wrap my arms around his huge frame. "I know you would."

thirty-three

ALLY

"You sure you don't need me to come in?" I ask Lenny on the phone. Praying he'll say he needs me to work.

After telling Cole everything and the tough loss his team had, things were finally starting to settle down. Until today.

Birthdays aren't my favorite. In fact, they sort of put me in a weird funk. Every. Single. Year.

"Kid, it's slower than a herd of turtles walking through peanut butter," his Southern accent says, unimpressed. "Stay the heck home. We're thinking of closing early anyway."

"All right," I sigh. "Guess I'll see you in a few days."

"Yes, you will. Go study or learn something. Damn kids these days just want to party."

"Yeah, yeah. Whatever you say, old man," I joke back before ending the call.

I glance at the clock. It's only three in the afternoon. I've finished my classes and schoolwork for the day. Sloane has a late class tonight, and Cole had an away game yesterday and isn't due back for another few hours.

Lying back on my bed, I close my eyes. *Just get through this day. It'll be over before you know it.*

A knock at the door sends me shooting straight up.

"Allycat, open up," Cole's deep voice yells. I don't even have time to answer when he drawls, "I know what day it is, you knucklehead. I know you're in there, hiding."

Rolling my eyes, I walk over and pull the door open. "I was hoping you wouldn't look at the calendar." Putting a hand on my hip, I give him a cutting look. "I thought you wouldn't be back until later."

He gives me a charming look before kissing my cheek. "Why, it's November 2, sweetheart. You know I wouldn't forget your birthday," he says, holding his arm behind his back. "And I lied about the time. I didn't want your ass trying to escape before I got home."

"I hate this day," I point out. "I wish we could just skip it."

Pulling out a pack of Hostess CupCakes from behind his back, he opens them, and then he pulls a candle out of his pocket and sticks it in the middle of one. "Traditions are traditions, Al."

Birthdays were never a thing when I was growing up. It also didn't help that I spent my twelfth birthday dealing with the aftermath of finding my mother's overdosed body that morning.

I'd already hated birthdays because she never remembered mine. And if I'd tried to tell her, she'd usually flip her shit and call me ungrateful.

So, yeah, birthdays have never been my favorite thing. Once I found her dead, that was just the icing on the cake for why I fucking hate birthdays.

He pulls a lighter out of his other pocket and lights the candle. "Make a wish and blow it out."

Closing my eyes, I make a wish. A wish that means more to me than anything else. *I wish for Cole's dreams to come true.*

He's done this every year since I was thirteen. Our foster parents never acknowledged our birthdays either, and we obviously didn't have much money for presents or cakes. But he knew I loved cupcakes, so a pack of cupcakes was what I got. He made sure of it each year.

Looking at him, I blow the candle out.

Holding it up to my mouth, he nods at it. "Take a bite."

I do as I was told. No doubt, my face is covered in the creamy filling. Taking it from him, I glance down before smiling. He looks away for a split second, just long enough for me to smash it against his face.

I can't stop myself from laughing as he wipes his arm over his cake-covered face.

"Oh, you're going to pay for that!" he says before pulling me against him, wiggling his eyebrows. "Or you can lick it off of me. I think you got some down here," he says, patting his crotch.

I roll my eyes. "You are such a perv." Leaning up, I kiss his frosting-covered face. "But thank you for always doing this. It means a lot to me." I smile. "Even if I still fight it every year."

"Every. Single. God. Damn. Year." He shakes his head with his hands on my hips. His eyes are more green today than blue as they dance between mine. "Well, besides the one we were apart." His expression looks pained.

"But you did this with all the other ones," I point out. "Because that's who you are."

He's the guy who knows that, deep down, I'd be sadder if we didn't acknowledge my birthday at all, so he does something small yet special like this. He's also the guy who could try to throw a surprise party or tell Sloane it's my birthday, but he knows I would hate that. So, instead, he does something that is comfortable for me.

Like I said … that's who he is.

And who he is, is way too good for who I am. But I hope he never figures that out.

xo

COLE

I know Ally's birthday is a hard day for her. It's a painful memory of her mother's death. And honestly, I don't think she's sad because her mom is gone—because her mom was a rotten bitch to Ally—but that day still clutches the trauma of it all. What probably holds more significance is how shitty birthdays were when we were kids. I think it's hard to love a day the way the rest of the world does when, growing up, you watched the other kids' parents make the day they had been born so special while our parents couldn't even lay off the drugs long enough to realize what day it was.

Can't go wrong with Hostess CupCakes though when it comes to Al. She doesn't want extravagant or expensive. She just wants the familiarity of the same thing. And the comfort of knowing that somebody cares and that someone remembers her.

Something else Ally also hates? Change. So, I knew this was the one thing that was familiar, that she likely wouldn't stab my dick for doing. If I had tried to throw her a party, that shit would have landed me in the hospital—no doubt about it.

"Where are we going?" she says from the passenger seat.

Her bare feet up on the dashboard is a sight I could surely get used to.

"You'll see, sweetheart." I wink. "Just sit back and let your sexy ass enjoy the ride."

"Better not be a fucking surprise party," she mumbles under her breath. "I'll murder you."

"Ally, you know better than that. I like my nuts, and I'd like to keep them intact. Don't need to piss you off and have you go cutting them off or some shit."

"Good thinking," she deadpans.

She turns her body toward me, and her forehead creases. "Hey, um … I hate to bring this up, but have you thought about talking to Matt and Jenn yet?"

"Not yet," I lie.

The truth is, I've thought about it a disconcerting amount of times. For some reason, I'm as nervous as a little bitch. I didn't live with them long, yet they treated me good in that time. I guess part of me isn't ready for it to end. But I'm afraid telling Ally that will make her feel like she is no longer my number one. Which isn't it at all. She'll always be my number one. But this whole *having family in the stands, cheering for me,* thing, well, it feels better than I imagined it would.

"Okay," she answers quietly. "Just wanted to check in on it. Sorry to pry."

Reaching across the console, I take her hand in mine. "Don't be sorry." I sigh. "All right, I have thought about it. I just don't know how to go about it."

"Can't avoid them forever, Storm."

I nod. "I know. Since it's only four hours away, I think we should drive down to their house sometime this weekend. Get it over with, you know? I have practice Sunday morning at five thirty, but we could head down after that. Don't have to be back until six at night on Monday, so we could get a motel." I wiggle my brows and wink. "Unless you have to work?"

She looks thoughtful. "I work Sunday breakfast shift, but I could see if Carla could cover it, and then I'll cover for her next weekend."

"Sounds good, sweet cheeks. Can't go down there and face the awkwardness without you."

She giggles. "You just know I'll protect your ass if they get mouthy."

"Pretty much." We get closer to our destination, and I grin at her. "We're almost to the surprise party, where fifty people are going to jump up when you walk in."

"Fuck off. You know bet—" She stops mid-sentence as she looks up at the huge sign as we turn into the parking lot. "Wait …" Her lips tremble. "Here?"

"You've always wanted to go to a Shinedown concert. So, here we are. Happy birthday, Al."

Her eyes grow misty as they dance between the large stadium and me. "Cole, I don't … I don't … wow, I can't believe you got me tickets." She shakes her head. "I've never been to a concert before."

"Neither have I, so I guess today's the day we break our concert cherry, huh?"

"You're too good to me." She reaches over the console, throwing her arms around my neck. "Way too good."

"Not true." I press a kiss to her lips. The sweet taste of Juicy Fruit lingers on her pouty lips. "But you can pay me back later. Let's go find our seats."

Xo

ALLY

"How did you get seats this close?" I ask him, gazing up at the stage a few rows in front of me.

He looks uneasy before he answers, "Matt and Jenn are always pushing their credit card on me. I told them I'd use it for certain things, important things, but I'd pay them back every cent once I made it into the NFL." He frowns. "Well, maybe sooner if it all blows up with them Sunday night."

"I don't think it will," I tell him. "I really think it will all be okay. I'm telling you, they aren't bad."

"I hope you're right," he mutters just as the music begins.

The curtain slowly lifts, showing Shinedown behind it. "Black Cadillac" comes booming out of every speaker, and I'm so thankful that nobody around us is actually sitting.

Dancing against Cole, singing and laughing like we don't have a million problems going on inside of our heads, is exactly what I need.

When the song switches to "I'll Follow You," Cole murmurs into my ear, "This will be our wedding song."

Craning my neck around, I grin up at him and mouth, *It's perfect.*

And it is. It really is.

thirty-four

ALLY

The ride to Florida on Sunday has my stomach in knots. We decided tonight would be for us and us alone. We got a fancy motel not far from Matt and Jenn's house, and we will go there Monday morning for breakfast before making the drive home.

I take in the giant bathtub, which is actually a full-sized hot tub.

"Cole, this is nuts."

Setting his bag down, he shrugs. "Guess Jenn and Matt wanted to do something nice. They probably know we're going to drop the bomb that I know tomorrow, and they're trying to butter my ass up."

Swaying my hips as I walk over to him, I glide my hand up his shirt, feeling his deliciously hard abdomen.

Shit, he is absolute perfection.

"Either way, there's a lot of area in this suite." Backing up, I walk toward the bathroom, where a huge glass shower awaits.

Pulling my shirt over my head, I drop it on the floor, followed by my pants. Only in my bra and thong, I spin around and face the man I love. Whose chest is now rising and falling much harder.

Reaching around, I unclip my bra, letting it drop to the floor before slowly gliding my thong down. "Think I'll take a shower. I'm dirty."

Turning around, I don't even make it two steps before his arms are wrapped around me, dragging me to him as he walks us into the shower.

Tugging his jeans down as quickly as I can, I basically tear his clothes off like a rabid animal.

Fisting my hair, he puts his mouth to my ear, and his facial hair tickles my neck, making me squirm. "You trying to tease me, angel?"

"Oh no, I wouldn't dream of it." I giggle against him. "It isn't teasing if at the end of it, we both get what we want."

"Yeah? And what do we want?"

Acting shy, I bite my lip. "What do you want?"

Leaning down, he takes my nipple into his mouth and licks.

"What do I want?" He smirks. "What I want is to taste you and to watch as you come undone on my tongue. What I want is to fuck that pretty mouth of yours so hard that you almost have to tell me to stop. And then when you've had enough and when I'm almost over the edge, I want to fuck you against that glass shower." His eyes intensify. "That's what I want."

Backing up into the shower, I pull him with me. His body is enough to make a bitch quiver on the spot.

The water sprays down over us as our lips, tongues, and even teeth clash.

He hoists me up, and a devilish grin plays on his lips. "So fucking beautiful. And so fucking mine," he says before he sits down on the shower floor and brings me right down onto his face.

I cry out. The need I've had for this release all day has been taunting me. "Yesss," I hiss.

His tongue moves with as much grace as he does on the damn football field. Each stroke serves a purpose. Each touch making me cry out in pure desperation for more.

The only words that could express how I'm feeling are *pure ecstasy*. My entire body trembles as I look down at him invading me this way.

It isn't long before that feeling takes over. But I don't want it to. Not yet anyway.

"Let go," he demands. "Let go right now. All over my tongue."

My body does what it was told before my brain even has a moment to think about it. And I grip his short hair and pull lightly. Moaning as I call out his name.

Climbing off of him, I waste no time in pulling him onto his feet before I drop onto my own knees.

Stroking his length with my hand, I lean forward and take him into my mouth.

"Jesus fucking Christ, Ally," he growls.

Moving my mouth up and down on him, I work him over with my tongue. Making sure every spot gets sucked, licked, or touched.

Reaching down, he takes a fistful of my hair and angles my head up slightly to look at him. I watch his throat move as he swallows, his chest heaving as he breathes.

Knowing he's close, I take him into my hand and pump him until, soon, he's spilling himself on my hand and in the shower.

Once he's finished, he sinks down against the shower wall, pulling me onto his lap. I straddle him as the water pours down over our bodies as if it's washing away this night.

"Two out of three things you wanted, we just accomplished in one," I tell him.

"And the night is still young." Running his hands up my back, he grins. "And I also want to fuck you against the window, overlooking the city—with the lights off, of course. And on that shag rug in front of the fireplace." Moving his hands down to my ass, he chuckles. "Hold on tight, baby. It's going to be a long and wild ride."

We might have just had intense orgasms, but here I sit, ready for the next.

xo

COLE

Here we lie, completely tangled up in each other, her heart beating next to mine. The last thing I want to do is ruin the mood, but I know I can always talk to her.

"I've been having some flashbacks," I say, causing her to crane her neck to look up at me.

"About your dad?" she says softly.

"Yeah," I breathe out. "One of when he died and another of … when he … well, when I got the scar."

"Maybe … it's your brain just reminding you of things you've blocked out? Things you've tried to outrun?" she suggests.

I have always tried to just stuff my feelings down and focus on the present. No sense in dwelling on the past when there isn't a damn thing I can change.

"Maybe," I mutter. "Maybe I'm fucked up."

"Well then, babe, we're both fucked up," she says, snuggling closer against my chest. "But that's what makes us who we are. We connect through pain."

I grimace at my next words. I've always been vocal about my feelings for Ally. But other shit? Hell no.

"Sometimes, I feel like I just don't … fit. At the fancy college, with this team … I don't know … I'm an imposter, it seems."

She mindlessly traces over her name on my chest. "You fit more than you think, Cole. You don't have any idea what anybody else has had to walk through. I'm sure a lot of people could relate to you and me than you think."

I nod. "Very true. This is why I keep you around—you straighten my ass out."

She sits up, and her hair falls to the side. "I do it because I love you. And don't ever forget: you fit with me—perfectly. Rough edges and all."

Rough edges and all.

thirty-five

COLE

Reaching her hand over, Ally runs it up my arm. "You okay, babe?"

"I'm good." I nod. "I've got you with me, so it'll all be fine."

"You freaking know it," she deadpans. "I'll knock them out if I need to." She hits her fist against her tiny palm.

I laugh. "No doubt, angel. No doubt."

I know she would in a heartbeat, if shit got out of hand. She'd do just about anything for me.

"But for real, what is the plan here?" She seems concerned. "Are we going in there, guns blazing? Or are we going to first eat some of the dope-ass food you say Jenn cooks? You know I love a good home-cooked meal. Lord knows we haven't had many of those to enjoy."

"I don't really know. I feel like I won't form a plan until I'm actually there. Should we have a signal?" I wink.

Her face lights up, and some of the worry leaves it as a laugh bubbles out of her. "*Ca-caw*, like a crow, could be bad news bears. And the words *gummy bears* could be, *Let's take it nice and easy.*"

"Gummy bears?"

She nods. "I mean, yeah. That seems like the nicer approach, the more likable one. And I mean, come on, who doesn't love gummy bears?"

"You've got a point, ghost rider. You've got a point."

She nods, looking forward out the front window. "Let's just take it as it comes. Whatever happens, I'm here."

Thank fuck for that.

"It's probably no secret we didn't come here to bond over lasagna," I say, glancing between Matt and Jenn. "I want answers. And I want them now."

Even though I must admit, this lasagna is fucking delicious. Which is why I waited until we were almost done with dinner to drop my bomb that I know what's going on.

Ally basically moaned with every bite she took of the fucking stuff, so I couldn't *not* let her finish her food. Growing up, we never had home-cooked meals like this. I didn't want to cut her experience short. Nobody loves their food as much as Ally.

Jenn looks at Ally. "You told him?"

Ally nods. "Damn straight I did. I should have told him much sooner. As in right when I found out."

Jenn nods slowly. "It's okay. I know we put you in a hard spot."

Matt takes his wife's hand into his and looks at her.

Giving him a small nod, she smiles sadly. "Go on. He deserves to know."

Fucking right I do.

He pushes his chair back, and it scrapes against the expensive tiles. He stands and disappears down the hallway briefly before returning with a picture. Once he sits back down, he slides it across to me.

I feel Ally's hand tighten on mine, reminding me she's here. In this moment, everything seems like I'm in a damn tunnel. One I am stuck inside of and want to get out of.

Looking down at the picture, I feel my heart pounding in my chest so loud that I wonder if everyone else can hear it.

A boy, likely age eight or nine, stares back at me. The boy looks vaguely familiar, but what is really familiar is the run-down trailer that sits behind him.

"I don't understand," I say out loud, not to anyone in particular, more to myself. "I don't get it."

The room is eerily quiet for a beat before Matt finally clears his throat.

"I lived in that trailer for the first ten years of my life," Matt says, looking down at the table. "With the same monster you grew up with."

I jerk my head up at his confession. His head lifts, and his eyes meet mine.

"Wh-what?" I ask, feeling Ally's grip tighten and her thumb moving up and down along my hand.

"Cole, there's no easy way to tell you this." He looks at Ally and Jenn before his eyes land back on me. "Your dad ... was my dad. I'm your ... brother."

The only word I can think of right now for how I'm feeling in this moment is *numb*.

I have no idea how to feel or what to think. So, I just sit here. Completely emotionless and unable to form a thought, much less a sentence.

"Cole?" Ally's sweet voice pulls me from my trance. "Baby?"

Turning toward her, I'm greeted by worried eyes. "Huh?"

"I asked if you were all right." Her eyes dance between mine, no doubt searching for something, anything, to let her know I'm okay. "Are you?"

"I, uh ..." I drag my free hand over my face before pushing the picture away. "I don't ... I don't know what the fuck I am right now."

"Cole," Jenn speaks now. "We are so sorry we didn't tell you sooner. We just didn't want to compromise anything."

"Compromise what?!" I stand abruptly, causing my chair to topple over backward. Finally able to feel something as the reality of what I just heard hits me. "What the fuck are you even saying? Because nothing is adding up. You apparently paid to adopt me, but now, Matt is my fucking brother? Are you serious?"

"Just listen, would you? Damn it, Cole, hear us out," Matt says through gritted teeth. A handful of his own hair in his hand as he tries to explain this shitshow to me.

And as I look at Matt, I see something that I never noticed before. *He has my dad's eyes.* Actually, he looks a lot like my dad. I don't know how I missed it before.

"Okay, he will listen," Ally says, leveling them with a look only she can give. "But you will not—and I repeat, not—swear or raise your voice at him again, or we will leave this house so damn fast that your head will spin. You two are the ones who created this situation, not Cole. Understood?"

They both look at each other and nod.

"Yeah, fair enough," Matt mumbles.

"Why offer money for me if I was your family? Why not just say so? The payment seems unnecessary," I say, looking at Matt.

Matt's forehead creases. "First off, I didn't even know I had a little brother until a few years ago. My mother, she slipped up about it, and I had to find you."

"How did I not know about you?" I ask him.

"Because our dad was a very dark part of my mother's life. Mine too. Our time there was hell on earth. Both of us fell victim to his disgusting ways, the physical and emotional abuse. When I was ten, we left. She changed my last name and never spoke of the man again. To anyone. And our dad, well, he hated me, so it's not surprising that he never spoke of me either."

He pauses, nervously fidgeting with the napkin in front of him.

"Our dad had me when he was young. I'm thirty-eight; you're eighteen. By the time you came along, he had probably done so many drugs that he didn't even remember he had another son. Besides, he'd spent most of his time pretending I didn't exist when I did live there." I can hear the pain behind Matt's voice. "That man, our father, was a piece of shit. I hated him with every cell in my being."

"How'd you know where to find me?" I question him.

"That wasn't hard to do. My wife is a private investigator." He jerks his thumb toward Jenn. "She found out everything we needed to know within an hour."

"I thought you were a schoolteacher?" I ask Jenn.

She sadly shakes her head. "No, I'm not. But we had to spin a perfect story for Dave and Marion. A private investigator wouldn't have exactly worked."

"So, why offer money for him then? It doesn't make sense," Ally states the obvious. "I mean, you are *brothers*, for Christ's sake."

"Because Dave and Marion had been under investigation for a while, without even realizing it. Once we found that out, we knew we could be a final piece to locking them up," Jenn says, her eyes moving between Ally and mine before locking on Ally. "You being thrown out to live in Sisters Safe Place was just another red flag."

"How so?" Ally continues to ask what I want to, and I'm so thankful she's here right now. Dealing with this bullshit with me.

"Because you were their responsibility and they failed you along with many other children they'd once fostered. We'd been watching over the two of you after finding out about Cole. We knew you wouldn't leave Cole, not unless you were forced out." She reaches across the table, patting Ally's hand. "We are going to take them down."

"How can you be so sure?" I question her.

"Because I have connections. I was able to show proof that they were doing shady things. I turned my evidence over a while back. The investigators are just closing some loose ends, and they'll be getting arrested."

My eyes find Ally's. Jail will never be enough for that scumbag. I want his blood on my hands.

She nods once, her eyes filled with fear before she looks at Jenn. "What if I have something else on them?" She flicks a tear that escapes from her eye. "Something ... really bad."

"Well then, I'll pass that along as well. These two are crappy people. They need to go down."

"I agree," Ally whispers before looking at me. "And this way, Dave can be punished without you getting involved."

I don't say anything. Instead, I just hold her hand and let her believe I'll stay out of it. As much as I want to respect her wishes, I also still really want to kill that piece of shit.

Nobody hurts my angel.

thirty-six

ALLY

Jenn gives me one final hug good-bye before we leave to head back to Georgia. I told them my truth about Dave, and the rest is in their hands. I know I'll have to make a statement, but other than that, she promised she'd take care of it. Apparently, she's a hotshot private investigator, and Dave and Marion aren't going to know what hit them by the time she gets done with them.

When Matt approaches Cole, he simply tucks his hands into his pockets and dips his chin down. He isn't ready for hugs, handshakes, or anything of the sort. And I don't blame him. He needs to do everything on his own time. He just found out that the man he'd thought was just an adoptive father is actually his brother. It's a lot to wrap my head around, never mind his.

Releasing me, Jenn moves to Cole. "Y'all let us know when you make it back, please." She wraps her arms around him. "I know you need space, and I know you have boundaries, but damn it, we've grown to love you in the short time we've had together. You are a part of this family"—she moves her eyes to mine—"both of you."

"Thank you." I smile. "Cole will text you when we make it back." When she watches me, I widen my eyes and laugh. "I promise."

Hand in hand, Cole and I walk to his truck.

I don't know what the next few days, weeks or months will hold. But I know I'll be here, by his side, through it all.

They say love makes you do crazy things. Well, I'd have to disagree. Cole's love, though it might make me act insane at times, has calmed my soul. Bringing me to a place of self-acceptance and security.

I only hope that I can bring that to him too.

XO

COLE

The drive home is going good for the sole reason that Ally's next to me. Chatting endlessly about things like football, singing, college life, and everything in between. She's trying to keep my mind from wandering off to the fact that I have a damn brother. It's hard for me to wrap my brain around my old man treating another person the way he treated me. In a way, it's comforting. It wasn't *just* me. It wasn't *my* fault.

"You sure you're ready to share your story with the judge when it comes time? I know that's going to be so hard."

She's quiet for a moment before answering, "For a long time, I thought letting it out would make it worse. Make me feel dirtier than I already felt. But I'm beginning to realize that somewhere out there, there's a girl who is scared to share her story. She probably feels alone and helpless. Maybe people like me, who choose to share their story, can help them."

I take her hand in mine and press it to my lips. "Baby, you're so damn brave. I'm so proud of you."

"Thanks." She smiles. "Thank you for making everything better in life. You don't know how good you are, Cole Storms."

I think back to the first time I met Matt. How the hell did I not know that he resembled our dad? They say I look like my mother. But him? He's a more rugged, cleaner-cut version of my father. Minus the drugs and booze, of course.

"What's going on in here?" Ally says softly, pulling her hand from mine and touching the side of my head. "I'm right here if you need me."

"Do you think Matt and I look alike?"

She frowns. "Honestly, aside from the eyes, not really."

"I'd never tell him this, but he looks like my dad did. Or *our* dad, I should say. I can't believe I didn't notice it before."

"Your brain probably tried to hide it from you. Your father is a painful memory for you. The mind has an amazing way of doing that."

"Maybe. Ally?"

"Yeah?" she says, watching me closely.

"Thanks for always being here. You're the most loyal person I know."

"Through the grit, baby."

I grin at her. "And the good."

"And the good," she mimics me softly. "And I promise, we will have a lot of good. We just need to sort all of this shit out first. Deal?"

"Deal."

She's right. In order to get through our problems, first, we need to face them. Head-fucking-on.

I'm so damn proud of her for sharing her past with Matt and Jenn. I know that wasn't easy, yet she did it. That's another reason to add to why she's the strongest person that I know. I'll never understand how I was so damn lucky to have her delivered to me the way that she was.

I love the way that she loves me. Hard and fierce. She sees the ugly, and she knows my insecurities. Yet she holds on, clinging to me when I need her most. When I hurt, she feels it—ten times harder. She's my ride or die. If I robbed a bank, she wouldn't just be driving the getaway car. Hell no, she'd be right next to me the entire way. If I killed someone, she wouldn't just help me hide it. She'd dig the fucking hole. A kind of love like that doesn't come around often. And when it does, I've learned to hang the hell on.

Hang the hell on and never, ever let go.

thirty-seven

ALLY

"So, things seem to be going good?" Sloane pauses. "Between you and Cole?"

She must be picking up on my *I am happy as fuck* vibes. I'm as giddy as a damn grandma in a nursing home who's hitting on the male nurses. I just can't help myself.

"Yeah … they really are." I smile. "I guess I just needed to let go of some stuff before we could get to a good place."

"I think y'all are sure good for each other," she gushes. "He'd move mountains for you, that boy."

"I know." I smile. "I know he would."

Her phone rings just as I back Cole's truck out of its parking spot and drive toward the mall. I don't miss the uneasy expression on her face when I glance over.

After a few rings, she slides her thumb across the screen and answers it. "Hello, Mom." Her voice is slightly shaky. "I'm good. I'm headed to the mall with Ally."

Her mom talks for a minute while I watch as Sloane's free hand clenches into a fist, her nails digging into her skin.

"It isn't a big deal. It's just Ally." She listens to her mom's voice again before her head finally droops. "Yes, I know. All right, bye. Love you too."

"Is everything all right?" I ask her.

When I first met her, she tried to make it seem like her life was completely normal. Yet the more time goes on, the more I can sense that it isn't.

She forces a smile, and that makes me sad. I hate that she feels like she has to smile just for my benefit. "Yeah, my mom, she can be … difficult."

I can tell part of her wants to open up and part of her doesn't. I decide maybe it'll help her out if I open up about myself too.

"My mom was too." I've never told her what happened to my mother. She just knows she's dead. "She sucked as a mom. What does your mom do that drives you nuts?"

"Well, she just doesn't let me have much say in my future. My parents want it to be a certain way, and they think I should just go with it." She sighs. "I really don't want to go with it. I want to make my own life. And choose my own happiness."

"Then, do it," I challenge her. "Say fuck everyone else. Those who want what's best for you will stand by you."

Clasping her hands together on her lap, she shakes her head. "It's not that easy. My family is very powerful. And extremely intimidating. Telling them no is hard."

Cole's at an away game this weekend. I was sort of bummed he was going and that I had to work tomorrow morning, so I couldn't. But maybe it's a good thing. It gives me some time with Sloane.

One thing I suck at is opening up. And Sloane is someone who takes a little bit of time to get comfortable with sharing. But I feel like we're at the point of our friendship where we start to trust each other.

Things about Cole or Cole and me will stay between us. Because first and foremost, I will always protect his secrets. But as far as my life is concerned, I'll tell her whatever she needs to hear.

"How about this?" Sloane says thoughtfully. "How about I ask you something and you ask me something? We could use it to get to know each other."

"All right," I agree reluctantly. "Shoot."

"What is your biggest regret?"

"Being cold to Cole when we reunited at Brooks. Hands down," I answer quickly. "He was hurting, and that's why he lashed out. I should have pulled the stick out of my ass and been the person he needed me to be. The person he always believed me to be."

"Why is that?"

"Because I'm not the only one with scars. His cut just as deep as mine. I needed to be there for him, like he always was for me, and I failed."

I did fail him. I was so caught up in my own problems and my own pain that I forgot about his. When you love someone, you can't do that. I see that now. Why I was so set on facing my problems alone, I don't know. When you have a soul mate, the beauty is that you can face your problems together, hand in hand. I took that for granted. I took *him* for granted.

"My turn." I wag a finger at her. "Are you a virgin?"

"Wow, Ally. Out of all the things you could have asked me"—she shakes her head—"you chose *that*?"

"The game is young, my friend," I say with an evil laugh.

"All right. Well, no, I'm not. I have been with two guys." She stops talking. "Not at the same time. Separately. Not like in the same night, but—"

Holding my free hand up to stop her, I laugh. "I wasn't thinking you were just out there, having threesomes, Sloane." I shrug. "Although no judgment if you ever decide to. YOLO, girl. Live yo' life."

"Ew, no. I would never."

"All righty then. Well, tell me about these two lucky fellows then," I say.

Tucking her long blonde hair behind her ear, she sighs. "Well, one was my first boyfriend. We dated from the time I was thirteen until I was seventeen. His name was Austin, and he had no damn clue what he was doing." She shakes her head. "Talk about awful."

I can't contain my laughter. "And the other?"

"The other was a one-night stand at a party. I wanted to be a little rebellious. He was the captain of the football team and was hot. So hot."

"Dayum, girl. Look at you, playa-playa." I adjust my seatbelt and giggle.

"My turn," she chimes. "What's the worst thing that's ever happened to you?"

My stomach drops out of my ass. There are a lot of things that have happened to me that I could name. But I trust her enough to share my story with her. Besides, after she had to call Cole because she was so worried, I owe her the truth.

Taking a deep breath, I blow it out slowly. "My birthday was last week. I don't celebrate it because on my twelfth birthday, I found my mom dead. It was an overdose."

That isn't the worst thing to happen to me. What happened with Dave was, but I'm not ready to talk about that with Sloane yet. Telling Cole was a huge step. Maybe one day, I'll be ready to tell Sloane too. I'd like to think so anyway.

"Ally, I ..." she stumbles over her words. "I'm so sorry."

"I'm not telling you for sympathy or anything like that. I just ... want you to know that I trust you." A small, sad laugh escapes my mouth. "That's a huge deal for me."

Slowly nodding her head, she wipes her eyes with her sleeve. "Thank you for sharing that with me." She reaches across the console and pats the top of my hand. "If you ever want to share more about it, I'll always be here. I just don't want to be pushy."

"Thanks." I lick my suddenly dry lips. "Now, your turn. What's your deepest, darkest secret?"

I wait for her answer as the cab of the truck grows eerily quiet for a few moments. Maybe we've taken this game too far, or maybe I've made her feel uncomfortable. I'm new to this *having a girlfriend* thing, but I'm guessing shit like this isn't the norm of what bitches like to discuss with each other.

"My parents are criminals," she croaks. And I can tell she had to all but force the words out. "My life isn't all cupcakes and rainbows." She turns toward me and grimaces. "Even if that's how I try to be perceived."

I'm completely shocked. Not one part of me saw that coming. I always sensed something was up. I just didn't think it was *that*.

Glancing at her, I nod to let her know I understand.

"Do you want to talk about it?" I ask softly.

Looking down, she clasps her hands together and gently shakes her head. "Not yet."

"Okay." I grin. "Favorite type of candy?"

Her eyes find mine, and she smiles. Understanding fills her eyes. I don't need to dissect each and every shitty detail in her life for her to share with me. A true friendship is being there when you're needed, and I plan to do that for her. But I'm not going to push for details on something that she isn't ready to open up about. Just like she didn't push for details from me.

I might not have known her since I was twelve, but I can already tell that one of the best things in life that has happened to me is when I was chosen to share a dorm with Sloane.

"Favorite type of candy ... hmm." She thinks about it. "Candy corn."

I widen my eyes and look at her in shock. "You sick fucker."

Sloane was put in my path for a reason. I just know it. Life has never gifted me that many wonderful people, but it has given me Cole, Sloane, Lenny, and Carla. And for that, I'm so damn thankful.

thirty-eight

ALLY
SIX WEEKS LATER

"They are totally going to do it!" Jenn squeals, jumping up and down. "They are going to win the championship!"

I smile, looking down at the only player on that field that my eyes care to see.

As the clock runs out, all of the players throw themselves on Cole before Knox and Weston pick him up and put him into the air.

Champions.

Cole, a freshman, led his team to a football championship and won. He'd wanted an undefeated season, yet that one game was his setback. After that loss, he came back ten times harder. Just like I had known he would. Training harder, working out harder, and practicing harder. And he did it. He really freaking did it!

Unable to stop herself, Jenn flings her arms around me. Embracing me in a full hug. "I'm so proud of him. So proud," she cries, wiping tears from her cheeks as she releases me.

I smile, continuing to watch him. "Me too."

As soon as his team puts him down, his head turns to find me.

What a wonderful feeling, knowing that even after a huge moment like this one, I'm the first person he thinks of. I'm the first one he looks for to see if I'm watching.

I'm watching, baby. I'll always be watching.

Once he spots me, he takes off in a fast jog, making his way up the bleachers.

I waste no time in pushing through the other spectators to get to him. Not giving a damn how ridiculous I might look.

Once we get to each other, I leap into his arms, throwing my entire body around him. He holds me like I weigh nothing, lifting me up higher.

"I'm so proud of you," I say, cupping his cheeks before pressing my lips to his. "So damn proud."

"I couldn't have done it without you, angel," he murmurs against my skin. "My good-luck charm."

"You could have, and you would have," I argue. "But I'm so happy to be a part of it. I never doubted you, not for a second."

Watching him play football and command a game he was destined for is such a turn-on. And honestly, I can't wait to get him alone.

"Cole!" Jenn says from behind us. "Congratulations!"

"Thanks, Jenn." He smiles before setting me down.

She throws her arms around him, her small body squeezing him. "Thank you for giving us a second chance. I'm so happy that we get to be in your lives."

Matt clears his throat behind her. "Good job, bud."

Once Jenn releases him, Matt holds his hand out, but Cole does something that shocks us all. He pulls Matt in for a hug, and though Matt might be a grown-ass man who works out daily, I swear his eyes turn misty.

Cole has been a little standoffish with him. It's been hard for him to get used to the fact that they are brothers.

But Jenn and Matt have been so emotionally supportive of both of us. And not to mention, they are the reason why Dave and Marion are now behind bars.

Their hearing is coming up next month, and I'll have to testify. But I meant what I told Cole—if I can show one other person that it isn't their fault that this happened to them, if I can be brave for them, then that is exactly what I'm going to do. I hope it gives me some closure as well. Though I know there is no finish line, where I'll magically forget the past. But I'm going to take it day by day and lean on those who have my back. I finally have a circle of people around me who care about me. It was a foreign feeling. Aside from Cole's love, I had never felt that before. But when I opened my heart up and accepted it, I was so glad to have it.

I think love can be defined differently in each and every relationship. My version of love might not be the same as someone else's. But to me, love means feeling everything the other person feels. It's about absorbing their pain, feeling it on top of your own and yet not wanting it any other way.

My heart only beats peacefully when it beats along with Cole Storms's. He's far from the perfect person. But he's my perfect person. And that's all anybody needs. We don't need a hundred people surrounding us with love. Sometimes, we just need one.

In his eyes, I'm the one he was waiting for. His angel who came down and took away his pain. But what he doesn't know is, he's my angel, my saving grace, my medicine to numb the pain of life's cruel ways.

They say to love, one must love themselves first, but I disagree.

What if you find someone who shows you how to love yourself? What if they show you how they see you through their eyes? Without Cole, I wasn't even a fraction of the person that I am when I'm with him. His soul feeds mine, awakens it, and brings it to life.

Our future will have its hurdles. With him being in the limelight in the NFL and me doing whatever the hell I decide to do, there will be tough times. But I know that as long as we have each other, we'll be all right.

Throwing his arm around me, he kisses my hair. "A few more years, and maybe this will be a Super Bowl win, huh?"

I nod softly. "If that's what you want, handsome, then, yes, I'm positive it will be."

He's a force, a weapon, a *storm*. If a Super Bowl win is what he wants, a Super Bowl win is what he'll get because once he has the hunger for something, there is absolutely no stopping him.

Add that to the other millions of reasons why I love him so much.

thirty-nine

ALLY
JUNIOR YEAR
DRAFT DAY

"I feel like I should be the nervous one." Cole smirks. "You're over there, about to shit a brick."

"Shut up! Am not! I'm just … nervous," I fire back.

I'm not nervous that he won't get picked—I know he will. I'm nervous for what team will pick him. I'm in Georgia for another year, and while I know our relationship could withstand long distance, shit, I'd miss the hell out of him.

Kansas City has been hot on his tail. Kansas City is a long way away from Georgia. Over fourteen hours by car. That would suck.

"Promise me something?" I say, putting my hands on his rock-hard abs and looking up into his eyes that are clearly blue today.

"What's that, beautiful?" he says, tipping his chin up.

"Don't forget me when you're famous, deal?"

"Oh, cut the shit." He rolls his eyes. "Never going to happen. Even if I do get drafted on the opposite side of the country, you'll still be my pain in the ass all the way over here in Georgia."

My bottom lip involuntarily pokes out as tears well up in my eyes. I bury my head into his chest, embarrassed as hell that he'll see I'm crying on a day that's so important to him.

"Ally, what's going on?" His deep voice vibrates against my ear. Pulling me back, he dips his head down to make his eyes meet mine. "Hey, talk to me."

"I'm fine." I wipe my eyes. "I'm so proud of you. This day is monumental." My lip trembles. "A life changer."

Sitting down on the couch behind him, he pulls me into his lap. "That can all be true, and I know you're proud. But I want to know why you're crying. I don't give a fuck how important this day is."

"I just … I'm going to miss you so much if you go far away." The tears run down my cheeks in a steady stream. "I know; I know. I'm being a whiny, selfish bitch."

"Hey, look at me." His eyes gaze into mine. "Let's cross that bridge if and when it gets here. Okay?"

I nod. "Okay."

"All right, lovebirds, quit the fondling. I'm coming out here to eat my dinner, and I'm too old for this shit," Lenny grumbles before sitting down across from us. "Go eat, Ally. You're scrawny as hell."

"Am not," I say before standing up. "But I will go eat. But because I want to and not because you told me to," I tease him, sticking my tongue out.

I hate the fact that I'm having these feelings on such a huge day. But since this morning, I have been a ball of nerves. Feeling like I could burst into tears at any second.

We knew this day was coming. It was inevitable. And now, I need to put my big-girl panties on and toughen the hell up.

The problem is, I don't know how to stop this deep ache in my chest.

COLE

Sitting back, I watch Ally as she nervously makes her way to the kitchen, where Jenn and Matt are serving up everyone's plates, and I frown.

"She'll be all right," Lenny says, reading my mind as I continue to watch Ally. He chuckles. "She's a stubborn, mouthy thorn in my side at times, but she's strong," he says, wearing a knowing look on his face.

He pretends she's a pain in his ass, but he loves her like a daughter. She's become his family. And he, hers.

I nod. "I know she'll be all right. She's Ally." I blow out a breath. "This is stupid. Why the fuck am I leaving her? I could stay and get a degree, figure the NFL out next year."

Taking a bite of his salad, he wipes his mouth and gives me a pointed look. "That isn't the plan."

"I *know* that. But fuck, how am I supposed to leave behind the one person who has always been there?" Waving my hand toward the kitchen area, I shake my head. "Especially when she's already upset and I haven't even left yet. Fuck, I haven't even been drafted yet, and she's crying."

"Because"—his eyes grow serious—"it doesn't matter where you are, you're still together. This is something you are doing to give both of you a better life. This is your dream, Cole. And she wouldn't want you to pass up a dream to stay back. It'd make you resent her."

I grimace. "I could never resent Ally. No fucking way."

"You say that now, but things change. Say you stay in college and you injure yourself next year. All those dreams of the NFL? Poof, gone." Pushing himself up, he pats me on the shoulder. "I will be right here, looking after her, while you're away. I'm not going anywhere," he says softly before walking away.

I know he will look after her. Hell, he's become family to both of us. But nobody can look after her the way I can. Besides, it's not just that. I don't want to be without her either. I can't imagine not waking up next to her in the morning.

My phone rings loudly in my pocket, and I instantly feel sick when I pull it out and see an out-of-state number.

"Cole!" Ally yells from the kitchen. "It's okay! Wherever it is, it will be okay. I'm sorry I was being a little bitch." Stomping her feet, she points her finger. "Answer your damn phone!" When I continue to stare at her, she yells, "*Now!*"

Sliding my thumb across the screen, I put it to my ear. "Hello?"

"Cole Storms?"

"Yes."

"Just the man I want to talk to." I hear a deep chuckle on the other line. "This is Brett Veach, the general manager for the Kansas City Chiefs. I want to start off by saying you've been chosen as the number one draft pick, so congratulations on that."

I knew Kansas City was interested in me, but I had no idea I would be number one.

"Number one? Fuck—I mean, sorry—"

He laughs. "No apology needed, son. How'd you like to come on board and play with us?"

"I'd … I'd … can you hold on a minute?" I ask him without thinking.

"Uh … sure." He sounds surprised.

231

Walking over to Ally, I crane my neck to look at her. "Kansas City."

"Cole, that's amazing." Her face lights up. She might be nervous to lose me, but I know she's happy as hell for me too.

"Ally …"

"No." She shakes her head vigorously. "You need to go. This is one of the teams you were wishing for. We will figure it all out. We will *always* figure it out." Pressing her lips to mine, she wipes her eyes. "I'm so proud of you, Cole. You made it. You really made it."

"No, *we* made it," I correct her. "Are you sure?"

"I'm sure, baby. I'm sure." Nodding her head to my phone, she smiles. "Go on. He won't wait forever."

"Sir?" I say, pressing the phone back to my ear. "My answer is yes."

"Good, good. Jesus, son. Had me sweatin' for a minute there." He laughs. "That must be some girl if you were willing to put it all on the line for her."

I watch Ally, my eyes never leaving hers. "She is."

"Well, welcome to the NFL, Mr. Storms. We're happy to have you. We will be talking to you real soon."

"Yes, sir." The words leave my mouth, and even though this should be the best damn day of my life, the only thing I'm thinking about is how I don't know how I'm supposed to go out there, living my life when she isn't by my side.

She's stubborn as hell, quick to anger, intimidating as hell, and sometimes a downright pain in my ass. But, Jesus, I love her.

XO

Collapsing onto my bed, I wait for Ally to come out of the bathroom.

We moved into an apartment just off-campus last year. And while I miss the guys sometimes, I'm a helluva lot happier, living with Ally and having a place to ourselves. Especially on nights like tonight when we need to talk about the fact that I'm the newest team member of the Chiefs.

Now that I have had time to reflect, I can't believe that I actually made it. A goal that always seemed so many years away has now been achieved.

Stepping into the room, Ally wears a Chiefs jersey and nothing else. Her dark hair spills over her shoulders. As she makes her way over to me, my eyes drink her in like water.

"So, I guess that's why you stopped at the mall on the way home and wouldn't let me come in with you, huh?" I laugh. "And here I thought, you went to Victoria's Secret for some lingerie." I shake my head, pulling her on top of me. "This though? This is better. Much better."

She straddles me, looking damn fine. "Congratulations, Mr. Storms." Pressing a kiss to my chest, she smiles. "And chosen as the number one draft pick? Very impressive. And very … sexy."

"Yeah?" I narrow my eyes. "How sexy?"

Kissing her way down my abdomen, she stops when she gets to the waistband of my briefs. "So sexy," she purrs before pulling them down and setting my excruciatingly hard cock free.

We should talk. We should hash everything out. But that can all wait. Life can wait. All I want right now is to live in this moment with her.

I watch as she slowly licks her plump lips before fully immersing herself into sucking my dick. When she licks up one side of it and down another, I can't help my hips from jerking against her mouth.

"Fuck," I hiss. "So … good."

"Mmhmm," she hums against me, and I almost lose my mind.

When she flicks her tongue at the base of me, my eyes roll back into my head.

So. Fucking. Good.

Taking a fistful of her hair, I have to think of anything besides getting off.

"Angel, unless you want me to come all inside that pretty mouth, you'd better stop fucking my dick with it. Now," I growl.

She gives me a smirk and continues on, intensifying her suction, but I don't give her a choice.

Pulling her on top of me, I slam her down onto my dick, causing her to cry out.

"Love that jersey on you, sweet cheeks. But I need to see your bare tits. All right?"

Like a good girl, she instantly pulls it off and tosses it to the floor. Exposing her full, creamy chest to me.

She moves up and down on me, her tits bouncing as she does, looking like the angel that she is. Her dark hair all around her, her cheeks red from being so turned on, her eyes burning with a need only I can give her.

I wouldn't need much more in this life to die a happy man.

Sex can be just that—sex. But when two bodies share one soul and two people love each other this much, sex can be everything.

I feel her love. I see her heart right before my eyes.

Reaching up, I gently cup her throat. "All mine. Forever mine."

"Forever," she grits out, getting closer. "Cole," she cries out, biting her lip.

I nod. "Now, baby. Right now."

And I see her come apart before me.

"I love you," she says, breathless. "So much."

And I know that she does. And that right there is an amazing fucking feeling.

COLE
THREE MONTHS LATER

I've been here in Kansas City for two weeks now.

I used to think that once I got here, to the NFL, I'd want to hold my middle fingers up to everyone who had abandoned me. I thought I'd want to tell them all off as I sat at the top. It turns out, I don't want to do that anymore. Because that would mean I was holding on to anger, and honestly, life's too fucking good for that shit.

Except for the fact that I haven't heard from Ally recently.

I frown as I get Ally's voice mail after trying to call her for the fifth time today and hearing nothing back. I called her before practice, and I was sure I'd hear from her by the time I got done, yet nothing.

We always text or talk off and on throughout the day whenever we have a second. Stupid GIFs during the day, some phone sex at night, anything to get us the fuck through being apart.

Leaning against my truck, I leave yet another message. "Baby, it's me. Look, why the fuck aren't you answering? I'm about to call Lenny or Sloane. Shit, maybe even Carla. Pick up. I'm getting worried. Love you."

"Who you leaving those sweet messages for, big boy?" I hear her smooth voice from behind me.

Walking toward me, she tries to play it cool for a moment before she starts running. She leaps into my arms and straddles my waist with her legs.

"Wh-what the fuck is going on?" I smile, confused. "How—what are you doing here?"

She kisses my cheek and shrugs. "Turns out, I can get the same degree at a few colleges around here. And after I did some soul-searching, I figured out singing as a career isn't even what I want. I just want to help people, Cole. I want to volunteer at shelters. I want to help teenagers who have no one. I don't give a damn about being on a stage in front of thousands of people. A music teacher? Maybe. But not a singer or songwriter. That's why I want to stick with a degree in music because I can totally see myself teaching it. And besides, I already have so many of my credits."

I'm not surprised that she's decided on a different career path. I could tell during the past year, she was starting to second-guess it. She already had a few people approach her to sign with them after seeing her at open mic nights, yet she turned them all down.

What I am blown away by is the fact that she's here, with me, right now.

Setting her down, I look down at her, holding her by her sides.

"You sure, baby? I mean, I'd love to have you here, but a big part of you not moving here at least for the summer before your senior year was that you wanted to work for Lenny the last few months he owns the restaurant. And Sloane—you felt bad about leaving her since she wasn't going home for the summer."

"I'm sure." She nods. "I'll miss the crap out of Sloane and Lenny too. But Lenny had been considering selling that joint for a while, and he did." She sighs. "I would have loved to buy it. I would have turned it into a place to feed those in need. With his permission, of course."

I keep my face straight. "That's what you wanted to do with it? You always told me you never wanted him to sell it, but you never said what your plans might be if you bought it."

"I guess it doesn't matter that much now anyway. I'm moving here, and it's already sold."

"True," I say before scratching my chin. "But wait a second. What if … your fiancé bought it?"

Scrunching her nose up, she looks puzzled. "I don't have a fiancé. My asshole boyfriend won't give me a ring, remember?"

"Ah, yes. This is true. Let's fix that, shall we?"

Opening my truck door, I reach in the center console before pulling out a box.

When I get down on one knee, she covers her mouth with her hands as tears well up in her eyes. "Oh my fucking gosh, Cole."

I chuckle. Even during the most romantic moment, that damn potty mouth comes out.

"I prayed for an angel in my darkest times. Times when it would have been so easy to give up, I closed my eyes and somehow felt your touch. I just knew you were out there. I only had to be patient, and I knew that, one day, you'd find me. And you did."

I recall the first time I saw her. Everything about her told me she was who I'd been waiting for my entire life.

"Ally, I've loved you since I was twelve years old. And even before then, I knew you were a part of me. I could live a million different lives, and I'm willing to bet money that I'd find my way to you in each and every one of them."

Taking her hands in mine, I gaze up into my future. "You know me better than I know myself. When I hurt, you hurt. When I'm happy, you're happy. We live to keep each other alive, Ally. And we also live in each other's sorrows. If that isn't the realest, rawest form of love, I don't know what is. Because I promise you, baby, I'd take a hundred hard days with you over a thousand perfect days with anybody else.

"I've always said you belong to me and that you're mine. But I hope you know that I belong to you too. Every single part of me does. And that's how I want it to be for the rest of our lives—and all of the other lives we're granted."

Wiping my own eyes with my sleeve, I open the box. "A ring and a piece of paper don't mean jack shit to me. Because you and I? We're already a family. But I want to call you my wife. I want to see you walk to me in a white dress. I want us to share the same last name. So, my question to you is, will you please make me the happiest son of a bitch in the world, Ally Lee James? Will you marry me?"

Tears stream down her beautiful skin. "Yes! Yes times a million!" After I slide the ring onto her finger, she hauls me up onto my feet before barreling into me. "I love you, Cole. I love you so much."

Ten minutes later, we're in my truck and on the way to my temporary apartment. Ally's gazing down at her ring. I'm so happy in this moment right now. All of my dreams have come true. And the look on her face, it's priceless.

"So, what is this about Lenny's place? What were you saying before you gave me this gorgeous rock?" She grins, staring down at it.

"You always said you hated the thought of him selling it to some 'douchey schmuck.'" I laugh at her choice of words. "You knew how much that place meant to him, and it meant a lot to you too."

"And?" Her eyes stay trained on mine.

"And a few months ago, he mentioned he was ready to sell it, but he thought he'd never find anyone he felt comfortable with to take it over. So, I offered him money."

"But how will I take it over? We're here."

"Because Carla wants to manage it the months we're here. And in the off-season, we'll go back."

"To Georgia?" she asks softly.

I nod. "To Georgia. Lenny is there. Sloane is there—for now. So, it makes sense."

When she doesn't say anything, I start to panic. "If you don't want this, we can—"

She throws her arms around me and begins crying harder. "I don't know what I ever did to deserve someone like you." She sniffles. "You don't know what you mean to me."

She doesn't know it, but saving her saves me. I'd walk a thousand miles, fight a hundred battles, just to put that smile on her face.

Nobody should ever have to go through what she has, but I plan to spend my life making sure she never feels any of those things again. For as long as I'm living, she won't ever feel alone or unwanted. I'll make it my mission to brighten all of her days. Because that's exactly what she does to mine.

Lenny and Carla have become family to her, and I wanted to do this for her. She deserves it.

Now, she's switching schools to make my life in the NFL easier. She's leaving behind friends and her job. All for me. But I know it'll make her happy too. Being apart isn't meant for us. Could we do it? Sure. But why should we have to? We spent the first twelve years of our lives separated and were ripped apart all those years ago. I don't ever want to be apart from her. Next to my side is where she belongs. It's where she's always belonged.

Looking at Ally, I know she's all I will ever need. In the good and in the grit, she'll be here. Always.

forty-one

COLE
FOUR YEARS LATER

"You nervous or what?" I joke with my teammate Link, punching him in the shoulder.

"Fucking right I am. This is the Super Bowl," he says, gazing around the locker room.

I grin. "I remember my first time too, big guy."

"Fuck off," he grunts, but it's all in good humor. "This is, like, what … your fourth?"

"Yep, this time, I get to face off with one of my best friends though. Can't let that fucker win. He'd never let me live that shit down."

"Knox Carter?"

I nod.

"Fuck, he's as fast as lightning. Gonna be hard to shut that fucker down."

"Not helping," I growl.

Once he's gone, I reach in my duffel. Oftentimes, during away games, Ally finds a way to sneak a new note into my bag. She knows her words are the calm I need before a game. I find a fresh, crisp, folded-up paper. Unlike the one I still carry everywhere with me to this day. That one is worn and tattered and basically falling apart.

Sitting on the bench, I think of how fucking blessed I am. From a kid in dirty clothes and shoes two sizes too small … all the way to Super Bowl champion and co-owner of a chain of facilities that feeds those in need.

Lenny's Place now has twelve different locations across the United States. Ally had a dream, and she made it happen. And I'm so damn proud to be a small part of it.

On the side, she teaches music lessons and has even started a program that gives less fortunate kids access to it. She is very attentive to each and every one of them. She says she never wants them to feel alone or like they're not enough.

We got married about two weeks after I proposed. On a beach in Hawaii, a place both of us had always wanted to go. We kept the ceremony small— only Matt, Jenn, Lenny, Sloane, Weston, and Knox in attendance. I've been trying to impregnate my wife since that night, but she just hasn't been ready. She's so afraid that she won't be a good mom because her mom wasn't. I don't want to pressure her, but fuck, what I wouldn't give to have a little mini Ally running around.

One day, she'll be ready. I'm a patient man. I'll wait forever if she made me.

Unfolding the letter, I see Ally's handwriting.

To my Storm.

Another year, another Super Bowl. You the man, am I right?

Don't be nervous. We all know you'll go out there and kick ass. (But, really, you have to win. I sort of made bets with some loudmouths at the original Lenny's Place when I went back to Brooks last month, and I can't stand the thought of listening to them gloat if you lose.)

I can't wait to cheer you on and to also watch your ass on the field— it's a damn fine ass.

I only hope I can watch the game and gorge myself on as much junk food as possible. My worry is, I'll end up getting sick.

Remember how I have been feeling under the weather lately?

Well, after you left yesterday, I went to the doctor to confirm my suspicions. It turns out ... I'm pregnant!

Yep ... you read that right. You're going to be a daddy. Which I know has been your dream for a while now. I'm still nervous, but I'm also very excited. I might not know what the hell I'm doing, but I know you'll be there, and something tells me you'll be the best dad there ever was.

Go out there and kick some ass. Baby S and I will be cheering you on every step of the way.

Love you. In the good and in the grit. (This is definitely the good.)

Love,

Ally

xo

I grin down at the paper. *I'm going to be a father.* No, anyone can be a father. To me, a father is basically a sperm donor. I'm going to be a *dad*. And even though I don't know jack shit about babies, I'll be the best damn dad in the world.

After I tuck the paper into a safe place in my bag, I lace my cleats up. All I want to do is get this game over with, so I can hug my girl. The mother of my unborn child.

XO

Red confetti rains down on us in the stadium as the clock runs out. Super Bowl champions once again.

"I'll let you have this one, big fella. Next year's mine," Knox says from behind me.

I throw my arm around him, and he pulls my forehead against his.

"Good job, brother. Good fucking job," he says.

"You too. You guys weren't easy to beat."

It sucks when I have to go head-to-head with my best friends' teams. But it happens. And next year, if we play against each other again and he wins, I'll be happy for him.

Slapping his back, I nod. "I gotta go find Ally. Good game, man."

He grins. "I figured as much. Give her my best."

I debate on telling him the news. All I want to do is shout it from the rooftops. But Ally and I haven't even discussed it in person. It's not just my news to share.

Gazing around the stadium, I spot Ally, Jenn, Matt, and Lenny coming down the stairs. Once she sees me, she breaks out in a sprint until she reaches me. The others stay back, letting us have our moment.

Hoisting her into the air, I spin us around.

"Well, hello, Daddy."

"Hey, pretty Mama." I'm aware we sound corny as fuck. But truthfully, I couldn't care less. "Ally, we're going to have a baby."

"We sure are." I feel her tears against my skin. "Are you happy?"

"I'm so fucking happy, Al. So fucking happy." My voice cracks at the end. "We'll do this right, baby. She'll never feel alone. I'm going to make sure of it."

"She?" She laughs. "Easy, killer. We don't know what it is yet."

"I'll be happy as hell either way. But when I read your letter, the first thing I saw was you pushing a little girl on a swing, and she looked like you," I tell her honestly. "And her name was Charlotte."

"Charlotte," she says softly. "Charlotte's Falls does hold some painful memories. But … also some really good ones."

"That it does," I agree. "If there wasn't pain, would we appreciate the good moments as much? Would times like this feel as significant if it was all rainbows, all the time?"

Somehow, I don't think so. I think pain is there for a reason. We need it to exist.

"Very true. But … if it ends up being a boy, he'll probably be pretty weirded out that you called him Charlotte when he was in the womb."

"I'm so confident that it's a girl … I'll even paint the nursery. *Her* nursery."

"So cocky." She giggles, her forehead pressing against mine. "I'm so proud of you. I'm so proud to be your wife. Your determination never ceases to amaze me. It is a gift to watch you play, and I can't wait for our baby to watch you too."

I set her down on her feet before putting my palms on her stomach. "I can't wait for your belly to grow big. Or to watch you waddle around the house like a duck." Reaching up, I wipe my eyes. "I'm even excited for you to crave weird shit, like pickles on top of ice cream. Or gummy bears and mashed potatoes."

She cringes. "Gummy bears and mashed potatoes? That's gross." She pauses. "My body is going to change, you know … a lot."

I shrug. "All I know is, I want it all when it comes to you. And no matter how much your body changes, you'll still be just as beautiful to me."

I always wanted to be as close to Ally as humanly possible. Yet it never seemed close enough. But this baby? It's a piece of her and a piece of me, all wrapped into one. Something we created together.

"I hope she or he has your selflessness." She smiles. "And your hunger to achieve anything you set your mind to."

"I hope she has your dark hair and your baby-blue eyes. But mostly, I hope she has your feistiness."

She laughs. "Careful what you wish for. You'll have to live with us, you know?"

Sometimes, she's so feisty that she's intimidating. But she takes no shit from anyone, and I wouldn't have her any other way. That's what makes her Ally. That's what makes her mine.

When I first saw her, back when I was twelve, it felt like I'd found my beginning. Like I could finally breathe without pain. But now? Well, now, I know that when it comes to Ally, she's my beginning, my middle, and my end. She's where my life began and where it will end.

She's my forever and always.

epilogue

ALLY
EIGHT MONTHS LATER

"Charlotte Ellis Storms." I smile down at my beautiful daughter before glancing up at Lenny. "I'm sad I never got the chance to meet Ellis, but from what I've heard about your wife, she was truly an angel."

"She was." Lenny nods, wiping his eyes. "We all need an angel in our life sometimes."

Cole pulls his eyes off of our daughter and glances up at me. "We do."

My husband was right about us bringing a baby girl into the world. A dark-haired, blue-eyed, sweet-angel baby. And if I thought I loved Cole before, I think that love tripled when I saw him snuggle her against his chest as he whispered to always love and protect her. He told her she was the luckiest baby in the world to have me as her mom.

Truth is, she's lucky to have him as her fierce guardian.

I have no idea how someone like Cole could exist. But I'm so damn thankful to call him mine. And I feel like the luckiest person in the world to belong to him. I spent a good portion of my life wondering where the heck I belonged, and now, I know I wouldn't want to belong anywhere else than right here, next to him.

I told you our story wasn't pretty. But I wouldn't trade this story for anyone else's. Because … it's ours. And our story, flawed and gritty as it might be, is so much more than I could have ever imagined.

It's perfectly imperfect. And perfectly us.

OTHER BOOKS BY HANNAH GRAY

NE UNIVERSITY SERIES

Chasing Sunshine
Seeing Red
Losing Memphis

BROOKS UNIVERSITY SERIES

Love, Ally
Forget Me, Sloane

playlist

This playlist can also be found on Spotify.

"Chasing After You" by Ryan Hurd and Maren Morris

"Broken" by Seether, featuring Amy Lee

"forget me too" by Machine Gun Kelly, featuring Halsey

"All We Know" by The Chainsmokers, featuring Phoebe Ryan

"Monsters" by All Time Low, featuring Blackbear

"Sorry Not Sorry" by Demi Lovato

"Nightmare" by Halsey

"Never Forget You" by Zara Larsson, featuring MNEK

"Astronaut in the Ocean" by Masked Wolf

"At My Best" by Machine Gun Kelly, featuring Hailee Steinfeld

"No Matter What" by Papa Roach

"I'll Follow You" by Shinedown

"If I Ever Lose My Faith in You" by Disturbed

acknowledgments

I have so much gratitude for so many people when it comes to my writing career. Behind each story told is a team of people cheering me on. And I am so thankful for each and every one of them.

My daughters—Charlotte, Carter, and Ava. I love you all beyond words. One of you is curious, kind, and quirky. The other is hilarious, sassy, and sensitive. And my third, my sweet little baby A, I'm still trying to figure out who you will be. But I know one thing: your personality will be one of a kind. Just like your sisters. You three are my reasons for pushing myself as hard as I do.

My husband. Thank you for being the glue that holds us all together. Your long hours of working on the boat, only to come home and jump into full Daddy mode, doesn't go unnoticed. Because of you, I am able to balance being a mother and a writer. I love you so much.

Mom, I love you so, so, so much. I know without a shadow of a doubt that if it wasn't for your constant love and support, I would have never even dared to write. You put so much of your heart and soul into each relationship you have. Whether it be your kids, grandkids, friends, family members, or customers who come into your shop, you give it everything you can. Because of you, I know what unconditional love is. I learned that forgiveness feels better than anger. And what I wish more than anything is that you could see yourself through my eyes.

Dad, my whole life, I've watched you give your all to your businesses. You work harder than anyone I know, and I am so proud of you for that. Thank you for showing me that hard work pays off and that I can be anything I want to be. Working Wednesdays with you, doing yard care, is so special to me. I so enjoy our time together. I love you so much.

My best friends—Tatum, Kayla, and Tara. You all are my biggest cheerleaders, and I appreciate your constant love and support so much. Whether you're giving me options on covers, beta-reading my work, or just giving me that pat on the back that I need, it does not go unnoticed, and I am so thankful for all of you.

My mother- and father-in-law. You two are more than I deserve. Thank you for loving me like your own. Kim, thanks for always lending an ear when I need to talk. And, Fenton, thank you for being the best father-in-law to me and Bampie to my girls. I love you guys. Thanks for letting me be a part of your family.

Hank, my squishy face, three-legged bullmastiff. I love you so much. You are a big, furry body to cry on when I'm overwhelmed. Your sweet brown eyes look at mine, and it's like you know when I'm struggling. You are the best friend a girl could have.

Jovana Shirley at Unforeseen Editing. We did it again! Four books down, so many more to go! I feel so lucky that I found you for my debut novel a year ago. Thank you for not only editing my manuscripts, but for also helping me to learn how to be better. Working with you is also a joy, and I can't wait to continue into the future.

Autumn Gantz at Wordsmith Publicity. Woohoo! Our second series together has begun! I say this every single book, and I'm unapologetically saying it again: you are an absolute godsend! You are stuck with me forever now because I never want to author without you!

My readers, I am so grateful for all of you. I hope you enjoyed Ally and Cole's story. What I love most about them is that they are raw and real. And despite their hardships, their love was truly built to conquer all. Thank you for taking the time to read *Love, Ally*.

about the author

Hannah Gray spends her days in vacationland, living in a small, quaint town on the coast of Maine. She is an avid reader of contemporary romance and is always in competition with herself to read more books every year.

During the day, she loves on her three perfect-to-her daughters and tries to be the best mom she can be. But once she tucks them in at night—okay, scratch that. Once they fall asleep next to her in her bed—because their bedrooms apparently have monsters in them—she dives into her own fantasy world, staying awake well into the late-night hours, typing away stories about her characters. As much as she loves being a wife and mom—and she certainly does love it—reading and writing are her outlet, giving her a place to travel far away while still physically being with her family.

She married her better half in 2013, and he's been putting up with her craziness every day since. As her anchor, he's her one constant in this insane, forever-changing world.

OTHER BOOKS BY HANNAH GRAY

NE UNIVERSITY SERIES

Chasing Sunshine
Seeing Red
Losing Memphis

BROOKS UNIVERSITY SERIES

Love, Ally
Forget Me, Sloane
Hate You, Henley

Printed in Great Britain
by Amazon

86492725R00147